DEATH OF A DOLL . . .

Weil deposited a folder on top of the teetering pile marked "For Immediate Action," then leaned back again. Back eyed the stack of paper—and the circular file mounted in the wall not half a meter from it, leading to the incinerator—and thought about having an accident. Just a careless nudge with an elbow . . .

"Aren't you even going to open it?" Weil asked, sounding disappointed. "It's not every day I'm going to hand-deliver a case."

"You tell me about it, since you want to so badly."

"All right. We've got a body, which is cut up pretty bad. We've got the murder weapon, which is a knife. We've got thirteen eyewitnesses who can describe the killer, but we don't really need them since the murder was committed in front of a television camera. We've got the tape."

"You're talking about a case which has to have been solved ten minutes after the first report, untouched by human hands. Give it to the computer, idiot." But she looked up. She didn't like the smell of it. "Why give it to me?"

"Because of the other thing we know. The scene of the crime. The murder was committed at the barbie colony."

"Oh, sweet Jesus."

—From John Varley's
The Barbie Murders

ISAAC ASIMOV'S DETECTIVES

EDITED BY
GARDNER DOZOIS
AND
SHEILA WILLIAMS

ACE BOOKS, NEW YORK

This book is an Ace original edition,
and has never been previously published.

ISAAC ASIMOV'S DETECTIVES

An Ace Book / published by arrangement with
Dell Magazines

PRINTING HISTORY
Ace edition / August 1998

All rights reserved.
Copyright © 1998 by Dell Magazines, Inc., a division of Crosstown Publications.
Cover art by Andy Lackow.
This book may not be reproduced in whole or in part,
by mimeograph or any other means, without permission.
For information address:
The Berkley Publishing Group,
a member of Penguin Putnam Inc.,
200 Madison Avenue, New York, NY 10016.

The Penguin Putnam Inc. World Wide Web site address is
http://www.penguinputnam.com

Check out the Ace Science Fiction/Fantasy
newsletter, and much more, at Club PPI!

ISBN: 0-441-00545-4

ACE®
Ace Books are published by The Berkley Publishing Group,
a member of Penguin Putnam Inc.,
200 Madison Avenue, New York, NY 10016.
ACE and the "A" design are trademarks
belonging to Charter Communications, Inc.

PRINTED IN THE UNITED STATES OF AMERICA

10 9 8 7 6 5 4 3 2 1

For
Kathleen Halligan
—our inspiration!

ACKNOWLEDGMENTS

The Editors would like to thank the following people for their help and support: Susan Casper; David Bruce; Torsten Scheihagen; Adrienne Mastromonaco; Kathleen Halligan, who set up this deal; Robert H. Seiden, who cleared the permissions; and thanks especially to our own editor on this project, Susan Allison.

CONTENTS

THE BARBIE MURDERS

John Varley

"The Barbie Murders" was purchased by George Scithers, and appeared in the January/February 1978 issue of Asimov's, *with a cover by Paul Alexander and an interior illustration by Jack Gaughan. Some of Varley's earliest stories appeared in Asimov's, two of them in our very first issue (one of them his classic story "Air Raid"), and although the magazine has seen less of him in recent years as his career as a novelist predominated, we still hope to coax more stories out of him in the future. John Varley appeared on the SF scene in 1975, and by the end of 1976—in what was a meteoric rise to prominence even for a field known for meteoric rises—he was already being recognized as one of the hottest new writers of the seventies. His books include the novels* Ophiuchi Hotline, Titan, Wizard, *and* Demon, *and the collections* The Persistence of Vision, The Barbie Murders, Picnic on Nearside, *and* Blue Champagne. *His most recent book was the major novel,* Steel Beach. *He has won two Nebulas and two Hugos for his short fiction.*

In the vivid and wildly inventive high-tech thriller that follows, one of SF's best murder mysteries, he postulates a case where the detective, before he can

*determine Who Done It, first has to figure which of
the suspects is which . . .*

The body came to the morgue at 2246 hours. No one paid
much attention to it. It was a Saturday night, and the bodies
were piling up like logs in a millpond. A harried attendant
working her way down the row of stainless steel tables picked
up the sheaf of papers that came with the body, peeling back
the sheet over the face. She took a card from her pocket and
scrawled on it, copying from the reports filed by the investigating officer and the hospital staff:

*Ingraham, Leah Petrie. Female. Age: 35. Length: 2.1 me-
ters. Mass: 59 kilograms. Dead on arrival, Crisium Emergency Terminal. Cause of death: homicide. Next of kin:
unknown.*

She wrapped the wire attached to the card around the left
big toe, slid the dead weight from the table and onto the
wheeled carrier, took it to cubicle 659a, and rolled out the
long tray.

The door slammed shut, and the attendant placed the paperwork in the out tray, never noticing that, in his report, the
investigating officer had not specified the sex of the corpse.

Lieutenant Anna-Louise Bach had moved into her new office
three days ago and already the paper on her desk was threatening to avalanche onto the floor.

To call it an office was almost a perversion of the term. It
had a file cabinet for pending cases; she could open it only
at severe risk to life and limb. The drawers had a tendency
to spring out at her, pinning her in her chair in the corner. To
reach ''A'' she had to stand on her chair; ''Z'' required her
either to sit on her desk or to straddle the bottom drawer with
one foot in the legwell and the other against the wall.

But the office had a door. True, it could only be opened if

no one was occupying the single chair in front of the desk.

Bach was in no mood to gripe. She loved the place. It was ten times better than the squadroom, where she had spent ten years elbow-to-elbow with the other sergeants and corporals.

Jorge Weil stuck his head in the door.

"Hi. We're taking bids on a new case. What am I offered?"

"Put me down for half a Mark," Bach said, without looking up from the report she was writing. "Can't you see I'm busy?"

"Not as busy as you're going to be." Weil came in without an invitation and settled himself in the chair. Bach looked up, opened her mouth, then said nothing. She had the authority to order him to get his big feet out of her "cases completed" tray, but not the experience in exercising it. And she and Jorge had worked together for three years. Why should a stripe of gold paint on her shoulder change their relationship? She supposed the informality was Weil's way of saying he wouldn't let her promotion bother him as long as she didn't get snotty about it.

Weil deposited a folder on top of the teetering pile marked "For Immediate Action," then leaned back again. Bach eyed the stack of paper—and the circular file mounted in the wall not half a meter from it, leading to the incinerator—and thought about having an accident. Just a careless nudge with an elbow . . .

"Aren't you even going to open it?" Weil asked, sounding disappointed. "It's not every day I'm going to hand-deliver a case."

"You tell me about it, since you want to so badly."

"All right. We've got a body, which is cut up pretty bad. We've got the murder weapon, which is a knife. We've got thirteen eyewitnesses who can describe the killer, but we don't

really need them since the murder was committed in front of
a television camera. We've got the tape.''

"You're talking about a case which has to have been solved
ten minutes after the first report, untouched by human hands.
Give it to the computer, idiot.'' But she looked up. She didn't
like the smell of it. "Why give it to me?"

"Because of the other thing we know. The scene of the
crime. The murder was committed at the barbie colony.''

"Oh, sweet Jesus.''

The Temple of the Standardized Church in Luna was in the
center of the Standardist Commune, Anytown, North Crisium.
The best way to reach it, they found, was a local tube line
which paralleled the Cross-Crisium Express Tube.

She and Weil checked out a blue-and-white police capsule
with a priority sorting code and surrendered themselves to the
New Dresden municipal transport system—the pill sorter, as
the New Dresdenites called it. They were whisked through
the precinct chute to the main nexus, where thousands of capsules were stacked awaiting a routing order to clear the computer. On the big conveyer which should have taken them to
a holding cubby, they were snatched by a grapple—the cops
called it the long arm of the law—and moved ahead to the
multiple maws of the Cross-Crisium while people in other
capsules glared at them. The capsule was inserted, and Bach
and Weil were pressed hard into the backs of their seats.

In seconds they emerged from the tube and out onto the
plain of Crisium, speeding along through the vacuum, mag-
netically suspended a few millimeters above the induction rail.
Bach glanced up at the Earth, then stared out the window at
the featureless landscape rushing by. She brooded.

It had taken a look at the map to convince her that the
barbie colony was indeed in the New Dresden jurisdiction—
a case of blatant gerrymandering if ever there was one. Any-

town was fifty kilometers from what she thought of as the boundaries of New Dresden, but was joined to the city by a dotted line that represented a strip of land one meter wide.

A roar built up as they entered a tunnel and air was injected into the tube ahead of them. The car shook briefly as the shock wave built up, then they popped through pressure doors into the tube station of Anytown. The capsule doors hissed and they climbed out onto the platform.

The tube station at Anytown was primarily a loading dock and warehouse. It was a large space with plastic crates stacked against all the walls, and about fifty people working to load them into freight capsules.

Bach and Weil stood on the platform for a moment, uncertain where to go. The murder had happened at a spot not twenty meters in front of them, right here in the tube station.

"This place gives me the creeps," Weil volunteered.

"Me, too."

Every one of the fifty people Bach could see was identical to every other. All appeared to be female, though only faces, feet, and hands were visible, everything else concealed by loose white pajamas belted at the waist. They were all blonde; all had hair cut off at the shoulder and parted in the middle, blue eyes, high foreheads, short noses, and small mouths.

The work slowly stopped as the barbies became aware of them. They eyed Bach and Weil suspiciously. Bach picked one at random and approached her.

"Who's in charge here?" she asked.

"We are," the barbie said. Bach took it to mean the woman herself, recalling something about barbies never using the singular pronoun.

"We're supposed to meet someone at the temple," she said. "How do we get there?"

"Through that doorway," the woman said. "It leads to

Main Street. Follow the street to the temple. But you really should cover yourselves.''

''Huh? What do you mean?'' Bach was not aware of anything wrong with the way she and Weil were dressed. True, neither of them wore as much as the barbies did. Bach wore her usual blue nylon briefs in addition to a regulation uniform cap, arm and thigh bands, and cloth-soled slippers. Her weapon, communicator, and handcuffs were fastened to a leather equipment belt.

''Cover yourself,'' the barbie said, with a pained look. ''You're flaunting your differentness. And you, with all that hair . . .'' There were giggles and a few shouts from the other barbies.

''Police business,'' Weil snapped.

''Uh, yes,'' Bach said, feeling annoyed that the barbie had put her on the defensive. After all, this was New Dresden, it was a public thoroughfare—even though by tradition and usage a Standardist enclave—and they were entitled to dress as they wished.

Main Street was a narrow, mean little place. Bach had expected a promenade like those in the shopping districts of New Dresden; what she found was indistinguishable from a residential corridor. They drew curious stares and quite a few frowns from the identical people they met.

There was a modest plaza at the end of the street. It had a low roof of bare metal, a few trees, and a blocky stone building in the center of a radiating network of walks.

A barbie who looked just like all the others met them at the entrance. Bach asked if she was the one Weil had spoken to on the phone, and she said she was. Bach wanted to know if they could go inside to talk. The barbie said the temple was off limits to outsiders and suggested they sit on a bench outside the building.

When they were settled, Bach started her questioning.

"First, I need to know your name, and your title. I assume that you are . . . what was it?" She consulted her notes, taken hastily from a display she had called up on the computer terminal in her office. "I don't seem to have found a title for you."

"We have none," the barbie said. "If you must think of a title, consider us as the keeper of records."

"All right. And your name?"

"We have no name."

Bach sighed. "Yes, I understand that you forsake names when you come here. But you had one before. You were given one at birth. I'm going to have to have it for my investigation."

The woman looked pained. "No, you don't understand. It is true that this body had a name at one time. But it has been wiped from this one's mind. It would cause this one a great deal of pain to be reminded of it." She stumbled verbally every time she said "this one." Evidently even a polite circumlocution of the personal pronoun was distressing.

"I'll try to get it from another angle, then." This was already getting hard to deal with, Bach saw, and knew it could only get tougher. "You say you are the keeper of records."

"We are. We keep records because the law says we must. Each citizen must be recorded, or so we have been told."

"For a very good reason," Bach said. "We're going to need access to those records. For the investigation. You understand? I assume an officer has already been through them, or the deceased couldn't have been identified as Leah P. Ingraham."

"That's true. But it won't be necessary for you to go through the records again. We are here to confess. We murdered L. P. Ingraham, serial number 11005. We are surrendering peacefully. You may take us to your prison." She held out her hands, wrists close together, ready to be shackled.

Weil was startled, reached tentatively for his handcuffs, then looked to Bach for guidance.

"Let me get this straight. You're saying you're the one who did it? You, personally."

"That's correct. We did it. We have never defied temporal authority, and we are willing to pay the penalty."

"Once more." Bach reached out and grasped the barbie's wrist, forced the hand open, palm up. "*This* is the person, this is the body that committed the murder? This hand, this one right here, held the knife and killed Ingraham? This hand, as opposed to 'your' thousands of other hands?"

The barbie frowned.

"Put that way, no. *This* hand did not grasp the murder weapon. But *our* hand did. What's the difference?"

"Quite a bit, in the eyes of the law." Bach sighed, and let go of the woman's hand. Woman? She wondered if the term applied. She realized she needed to know more about Standardists. But it was convenient to think of them as such, since their faces were feminine.

"Let's try again. I'll need you—and the eyewitnesses to the crime—to study the tape of the murder. *I* can't tell the difference between the murderer, the victim, or any of the bystanders. But surely you must be able to. I assume that . . . well, like the old saying went, 'all chinamen look alike.' That was to Caucasian races, of course. Orientals had no trouble telling each other apart. So I thought that you . . . that you people would . . ." She trailed off at the look of blank incomprehension on the barbie's face.

"We don't know what you're talking about."

Bach's shoulders slumped.

"You mean you can't . . . not even if you saw her again..?"

The woman shrugged. "We all look the same to this one."

• • •

Anna-Louise Bach sprawled out on her flotation bed later that night, surrounded by scraps of paper. Untidy as it was, her thought processes were helped by actually scribbling facts on paper rather than filing them in her datalink. And she did her best work late at night, at home, in bed, after taking a bath or making love. Tonight she had done both and found she needed every bit of the invigorating clarity it gave her.

Standardists.

They were an off-beat religious sect founded ninety years earlier by someone whose name had not survived. That was not surprising, since Standardists gave up their names when they joined the order, made every effort consistent with the laws of the land to obliterate the name and person as if he or she had never existed. The epithet "barbie" had quickly been attached to them by the press. The origin of the word was a popular children's toy of the twentieth and early twenty-first centuries, a plastic, sexless, mass-produced "girl" doll with an elaborate wardrobe.

The barbies had done surprisingly well for a group which did not reproduce, which relied entirely on new members from the outside world to replenish their numbers. They had grown for twenty years, then reached a population stability where deaths equalled new members—which they called "components." They had suffered moderately from religious intolerance, moving from country to country until the majority had come to Luna sixty years ago.

They drew new components from the walking wounded of society, the people who had not done well in a world which preached conformity, passivity, and tolerance of your billions of neighbors, yet rewarded only those who were individualistic and aggressive enough to stand apart from the herd. The barbies had opted out of a system where one had to be at once a face in the crowd and a proud individual with hopes and dreams and desires. They were the inheritors of a long tra-

dition of ascetic withdrawal, surrendering their names, their
bodies, and their temporal aspirations to a life that was ordered and easy to understand.

Bach realized she might be doing some of them a disserv-
ice—there could be those among them who were attracted
simply by the religious ideas of the sect, though Bach felt
there was little in the teachings that made sense.

She skimmed through the dogma, taking notes. The Standardists preached the commonality of humanity, denigrated
free will, and elevated the group and the consensus to demi-
god status. Nothing too unusual in the theory; it was the practice of it that made people queasy.

There was a creation theory and a godhead, who was not
worshipped but contemplated. Creation happened when the
Goddess—a prototypical earth-mother who had no name—
gave birth to the universe. She put people in it, all alike,
stamped from the same universal mold.

Sin entered the picture. One of the people began to wonder.
This person had a name, given to him or her *after* the original
sin as part of the punishment, but Bach could not find it written down anywhere. She decided that it was a dirty word
which Standardists never told an outsider.

This person asked Goddess what it was all for. What had
been wrong with the void, that Goddess had seen fit to fill it
with people who didn't seem to have a reason for existing?

That was too much. For reasons unexplained—and impolite
to even ask about—Goddess had punished humans by intro-
ducing differentness into the world. Warts, big noses, kinky
hair, white skin, tall people and fat people and deformed people, blue eyes, body hair, freckles, testicles, and labia. A bil-
lion faces and fingerprints, each soul trapped in a body distinct
from all others, with the heavy burden of trying to establish
an identity in a perpetual shouting match.

But the faith held that peace was achieved in striving to regain that lost Eden. When all humans were again the same person, Goddess would welcome them back. Life was a testing, a trial.

Bach certainly agreed with that. She gathered her notes and shuffled them together, then picked up the book she had brought back from Anytown. The barbie had given it to her when Bach asked for a picture of the murdered woman.

It was a blueprint for a human being.

The title was *The Book of Specifications. The Specs*, for short. Each barbie carried one, tied to her waist with a tape measure. It gave tolerances in engineering terms, defining what a barbie could look like. It was profusely illustrated with drawings of parts of the body in minute detail, giving measurements in millimeters.

She closed the book and sat up, propping her head on a pillow. She reached for her viewpad and propped it on her knees, punched the retrieval code for the murder tape. For the twentieth time that night, she watched a figure spring forward from a crowd of identical figures in the tube station, slash at Leah Ingraham, and melt back into the crowd as her victim lay bleeding and eviscerated on the floor.

She slowed it down, concentrating on the killer, trying to spot something different about her. Anything at all would do. The knife struck. Blood spurted. Barbies milled about in consternation. A few belatedly ran after the killer, not reacting fast enough. People seldom reacted quickly enough. But the killer had blood on her hand. Make a note to ask about that.

Bach viewed the film once more, saw nothing useful, and decided to call it a night.

The room was long and tall, brightly lit from strips high above. Bach followed the attendant down the rows of square locker doors which lined one wall. The air was cool and humid, the floor wet from a recent hosing.

The man consulted the card in his hand and pulled the metal handle on locker 659a, making a noise that echoed through the bare room. He slid the drawer out and lifted the sheet from the corpse.

It was not the first mutilated corpse Bach had seen, but it was the first nude barbie. She immediately noted the lack of nipples on the two hills of flesh that pretended to be breasts, and the smooth, unmarked skin in the crotch. The attendant was frowning, consulting the card on the corpse's foot.

"Some mistake here," he muttered. "Geez, the headaches. What do you do with a thing like that?" He scratched his head, then scribbled through the large letter "F" on the card, replacing it with a neat "N". He looked at Bach and grinned sheepishly. "What do you do?" he repeated.

Bach didn't much care what he did. She studied L. P. Ingraham's remains, hoping that something on the body would show her why a barbie had decided she must die.

There was little difficulty seeing *how* she had died. The knife had entered the abdomen, going deep, and the wound extended upward from there in a slash that ended beneath the breastbone. Part of the bone was cut through. The knife had been sharp, but it would have taken a powerful arm to slice through that much meat.

The attendant watched curiously as Bach pulled the dead woman's legs apart and studied what she saw there. She found the tiny slit of the urethra set far back around the curve, just anterior to the anus.

Bach opened her copy of *The Specs*, took out a tape measure, and started to work.

"Mr. Atlas, I got your name from the Morphology Guild's files as a practitioner who's had a lot of dealings with the Standardist Church."

The man frowned, then shrugged. "So? You may not approve of them, but they're legal. And my records are in order. I don't do any work on anybody until you people have checked for a criminal record." He sat on the edge of the desk in the spacious consulting room, facing Bach. Mr. Rock Atlas—surely a *nom de métier*—had shoulders carved from granite, teeth like flashing pearls, and the face of a young god. He was a walking, flexing advertisement for his profession. Bach crossed her legs nervously. She had always had a taste for beef.

"I'm not investigating you, Mr. Atlas. This is a murder case, and I'd appreciate your cooperation."

"Call me Rock," he said, with a winning smile.

"Must I? Very well. I came to ask you what you would do, how long the work would take, if I asked to be converted to a barbie."

His face fell. "Oh, no, what a tragedy! I can't allow it. My dear, it would be a crime." He reached over to her and touched her chin lightly, turning her head. "No, Lieutenant, for you I'd build up the hollows in the cheeks just the slightest bit—maybe tighten up the muscles behind them—then drift the orbital bones out a little bit farther from the nose to set your eyes wider. More attention-getting, you understand. That touch of mystery. Then of course there's your nose."

She pushed his hand away and shook her head. "No, I'm not coming to you for the operation. I just want to know. How much work would it entail, and how close can you come to the specs of the church?" Then she frowned and looked at him suspiciously. "What's wrong with my nose?"

"Well, my dear, I didn't mean to imply there was anything *wrong*; in fact, it has a certain overbearing power that must be useful to you once in a while, in the circles you move in. Even the lean to the left could be justified, aesthetically—"

"Never mind," she said, angry at herself for having fallen

into his sales pitch. "Just answer my question."

He studied her carefully, asked her to stand up and turn around. She was about to object that she had not necessarily meant herself personally as the surgical candidate, just a woman in general, when he seemed to lose interest in her.

"It wouldn't be much of a job," he said. "Your height is just slightly over the parameters; I could take that out of your thighs and lower legs, maybe shave some vertebrae. Take out some fat here and put it back there. Take off those nipples and dig out your uterus and ovaries, sew up your crotch. With a man, chop off the penis. I'd have to break up your skull a little and shift the bones around, then build up the face from there. Say two days work, one overnight and one outpatient."

"And when you were through, what would be left to identify me?"

"Say that again?"

Bach briefly explained her situation, and Atlas pondered it.

"You've got a problem. I take off the fingerprints and footprints. I don't leave any external scars, not even microscopic ones. No moles, freckles, warts or birthmarks; they all have to go. A blood test would work, and so would a retinal print. An x-ray of the skull. A voiceprint would be questionable. I even that out as much as possible. I can't think of anything else."

"Nothing that could be seen from a purely visual exam?"

"That's the whole point of the operation, isn't it?"

"I know. I was just hoping you might know something even the barbies were not aware of. Thank you, anyway."

He got up, took her hand, and kissed it. "No trouble. And if you ever decide to get that nose taken care of . . ."

She met Jorge Weil at the temple gate in the middle of Anytown. He had spent his morning there, going through the records, and she could see the work didn't agree with him. He took her back to the small office where the records were kept in battered file cabinets. There was a barbie waiting for them there. She spoke without preamble.

"We decided at equalization last night to help you as much as possible."

"Oh, yeah? Thanks. I wondered if you would, considering what happened fifty years ago."

Weil looked puzzled. "What was that?"

Bach waited for the barbie to speak, but she evidently wasn't going to.

"All right. I found it last night. The Standardists were involved in murder once before, not long after they came to Luna. You notice you never see one of them in New Dresden?"

Weil shrugged. "So what? They keep to themselves."

"They were *ordered* to keep to themselves. At first, they could move freely like any other citizens. Then one of them killed somebody—not a Standardist this time. It was known the murderer was a barbie; there were witnesses. The police started looking for the killer. You guess what happened."

"They ran into the problems we're having." Weil grimaced. "It doesn't look so good, does it?"

"It's hard to be optimistic," Bach conceded. "The killer was never found. The barbies offered to surrender one of their number at random, thinking the law would be satisfied with that. But of course it wouldn't do. There was a public outcry, and a lot of pressure to force them to adopt some kind of distinguishing characteristic, like a number tattooed on their foreheads. I don't think that would have worked, either. It could have been covered.

"The fact is that the barbies were seen as a menace to society. They could kill at will and blend back into their community like grains of sand on a beach. We would be powerless to punish a guilty party. There was no provision in the law for dealing with them.''

''So what happened?''

''The case is marked closed, but there's no arrest, no conviction, and no suspect. A deal was made whereby the Standardists could practice their religion as long as they never mixed with other citizens. They had to stay in Anytown. Am I right?'' She looked at the barbie.

''Yes. We've adhered to the agreement.''

''I don't doubt it. Most people are barely aware you exist out here. But now we've got this. One barbie kills another barbie, and under a television camera . . .'' Bach stopped, and looked thoughtful. ''Say, it occurs to me . . . wait a minute. *Wait a minute*.'' She didn't like the look of it.

''I wonder. This murder took place in the tube station. It's the only place in Anytown that's scanned by the municipal security system. And fifty years is a long time between murders, even in a town as small as . . . how many people did you say live here, Jorge?''

''About seven thousand. I feel I know them all intimately.'' Weil had spent the day sorting barbies. According to measurements made from the tape, the killer was at the top end of permissible height.

''How about it?'' Bach said to the barbie. ''Is there anything I ought to know?''

The woman bit her lip, looked uncertain.

''Come on, you said you were going to help me.''

''Very well. There have been three other killings in the last month. You would not have heard of this one except it took place with outsiders present. Purchasing agents were there on the loading platform. They made the initial report. There was nothing we could do to hush it up.''

''But why would you want to?''

''Isn't it obvious? We exist with the possibility of persecution always with us. We don't wish to appear a threat to others. We wish to appear peaceful—which we *are*—and prefer to handle the problems of the group within the group itself. By divine consensus.''

Bach knew she would get nowhere pursuing that line of reasoning. She decided to take the conversation back to the previous murders.

"Tell me what you know. Who was killed, and do you have any idea why? Or should I be talking to someone else?" Something occurred to her then, and she wondered why she hadn't asked it before. "You *are* the person I was speaking to yesterday, aren't you? Let me re-phrase that. You're the body . . . that is, this body before me . . ."

"We know what you're talking about," the barbie said. "Uh, yes, you are correct. We are . . . *I* am the one you spoke to." She had to choke the word out, blushing furiously. We have been . . . *I* have been selected as the component to deal with you, since it was perceived at equalization that this matter must be dealt with. This one was chosen as . . . *I* was chosen as punishment.''

"You don't have to say 'I' if you don't want to."

"Oh, thank you."

"Punishment for what?"

"For . . . for individualistic tendencies. We spoke up too personally at equalization, in favor of cooperation with you. As a political necessity. The conservatives wish to stick to our sacred principles no matter what the cost. We are divided; this makes for bad feelings within the organism, for sickness. This one spoke out, and was punished by having her own way, by being appointed . . . *individually* . . . to deal with you." The woman could not meet Bach's eyes. Her face burned with shame.

"This one has been instructed to reveal her serial number

to you. In the future, when you come here you are to ask for 23900.''

Bach made a note of it.

"All right. What can you tell me about a possible motive? Do you think all the killings were done by the same . . . component?''

"We do not know. We are no more equipped to select an . . . individual from the group than you are. But there is great consternation. We are fearful.''

"I would think so. Do you have reason to believe that the victims were . . . does this make sense? . . . *known* to the killer? Or were they random killings?'' Bach hoped not. Random killers were the hardest to catch; without motive, it was hard to tie killer to victim, or to sift one person out of thousands with the opportunity. With the barbies, the problem would be squared and cubed.

"Again, we don't know.''

Bach sighed. "I want to see the witnesses to the crime. I might as well start interviewing them.''

In short order, thirteen barbies were brought. Bach intended to question them thoroughly to see if their stories were consistent, and if they had changed.

She sat them down and took them one at a time, and almost immediately ran into a stone wall. It took her several minutes to see the problem, frustrating minutes spent trying to establish which of the barbies had spoken to the officer first, which second, and so forth.

"Hold it. Listen carefully. Was this body physically present at the time of the crime? Did these eyes see it happen?''

The barbie's brow furrowed. "Why, no. But does it matter?''

"It does to me, babe. *Hey, twenty-three thousand*!''

The barbie stuck her head in the door. Bach looked pained.

"I need the actual people who were *there*. Not thirteen picked at random."

"The story is known to all."

Bach spent five minutes explaining that it made a difference to her, then waited an hour as 23900 located the people who were actual witnesses.

And again she hit a stone wall. The stories were absolutely identical, which she knew to be impossible. Observers *always* report events differently. They make themselves the hero, invent things before and after they first began observing, rearrange and edit and interpret. But not the barbies. Bach struggled for an hour, trying to shake one of them, and got nowhere. She was facing a consensus, something that had been discussed among the barbies until an account of the event had emerged and then been accepted as truth. It was probably a close approximation, but it did Bach no good. She needed discrepancies to gnaw at, and there were none.

Worst of all, she was convinced no one was lying to her. Had she questioned the thirteen random choices she would have gotten the same answers. They would have thought of themselves as having been there, since some of them had been and they had been told about it. What happened to one, happened to all.

Her options were evaporating fast. She dismissed the witnesses, called 23900 back in, and sat her down. Bach ticked off points on her fingers.

"One. Do you have the personal effects of the deceased?"

"We have no private property."

Bach nodded. "Two. Can you take me to her room?"

"We each sleep in any room we find available at night. There is no—"

"Right. Three. Any friends or co-workers I might . . ." Bach rubbed her forehead with one hand. "Right. Skip it. Four. What was her job? Where did she work?"

"All jobs are interchangeable here. We work at what needs—"

"*Right!*" Bach exploded. She got up and paced the floor. "What the hell do you expect me to *do* with a situation like this? I don't have *anything* to work with, not one snuffin' *thing*. No way of telling *why* she was killed, no way to pick out the *killer*, no way . . . ah, *shit*. What do you expect me to *do*?"

"We don't expect you to do anything," the barbie said, quietly. "We didn't ask you to come here. We'd like it very much if you just went away."

In her anger Bach had forgotten that. She was stopped, unable to move in any direction. Finally, she caught Weil's eye and jerked her head toward the door.

"Let's get out of here." Weil said nothing. He followed Bach out the door and hurried to catch up.

They reached the tube station, and Bach stopped outside their waiting capsule. She sat down heavily on a bench, put her chin on her palm, and watched the ant-like mass of barbies working at the loading dock.

"Any ideas?"

Weil shook his head, sitting beside her and removing his cap to wipe sweat from his forehead.

"They keep it too hot in here," he said. Bach nodded, not really hearing him. She watched the group of barbies as two separated themselves from the crowd and came a few steps in her direction. Both were laughing, as if at some private joke, looking right at Bach. One of them reached under her blouse and withdrew a long, gleaming steel knife. In one smooth motion she plunged it into the other barbie's stomach and lifted, bringing her up on the balls of her feet. The one who had been stabbed looked surprised for a moment, staring down at herself, her mouth open as the knife gutted her like a fish. Then her eyes widened and she stared horror-stricken at her companion, and slowly went to her knees, holding the knife to her as blood gushed out and soaked her white uniform.

"Stop her!" Bach shouted. She was on her feet and running, after a moment of horrified paralysis. It had looked *so* much like the tape.

She was about forty meters from the killer, who moved with deliberate speed, jogging rather than running. She passed the barbie who had been attacked—and who was now on her side, still holding the knife hilt almost tenderly to herself, wrapping her body around the pain. Bach thumbed the panic button on her communicator, glanced over her shoulder to see Weil kneeling beside the stricken barbie, then looked back—

—to a confusion of running figures. Which one was it? *Which one?*

She grabbed the one that seemed to be in the same place and moving in the same direction as the killer had been before she looked away. She swung the barbie around and hit her hard on the side of the neck with the edge of her palm, watched her fall while trying to look at all the other barbies at the same time. They were running in both directions, some trying to get away, others entering the loading dock to see what was going on. It was a madhouse scene with shrieks and shouts and baffling movement.

Bach spotted something bloody lying on the floor, then knelt by the inert figure and clapped the handcuffs on her.

She looked up into a sea of faces, all alike.

The commissioner dimmed the lights, and he, Bach, and Weil faced the big screen at the end of the room. Beside the screen was a department photoanalyst with a pointer in her hand. The tape began to run.

"Here they are," the woman said, indicating two barbies with the tip of the long stick. They were just faces on the edge of the crowd, beginning to move. "Victim right here, the suspect to her right." Everyone watched as the stabbing was re-created. Bach winced when she saw how long she had taken to react. In her favor, it had taken Weil a fraction of a second longer.

"Lieutenant Bach begins to move here. The suspect moves back toward the crowd. If you'll notice, she is watching Bach over her shoulder. Now. Here." She froze a frame. "Bach loses eye contact. The suspect peels off the plastic glove which prevented blood from staining her hand. She drops it, moves laterally. By the time Bach looks back, we can see she is after the wrong suspect."

Bach watched in sick fascination as her image assaulted the wrong barbie, the actual killer only a meter to her left. The tape resumed normal speed, and Bach watched the killer until her eyes began to hurt from not blinking. She would not lose her this time.

"She's incredibly brazen. She does not leave the room for another twenty minutes." Bach saw herself kneel and help the medical team load the wounded barbie into the capsule. The killer had been at her elbow, almost touching her. She felt her arm break out in goose pimples.

She remembered the sick fear that had come over her as she knelt by the injured woman. *It could be any of them. The one behind me, for instance* . . .

She had drawn her weapon then, backed against the wall, and not moved until the reinforcements arrived a few minutes later.

At a motion from the commissioner, the lights came back on.

"Let's hear what you have," he said.

Bach glanced at Weil, then read from her notebook.

" 'Sergeant Weil was able to communicate with the victim shortly before medical help arrived. He asked her if she knew anything pertinent as to the identity of her assailant. She answered no, saying only that it was "the wrath." She could not elaborate.' I quote now from the account Sergeant Weil wrote down immediately after the interview. ' "It hurts, it hurts." "I'm dying, I'm dying." I told her help was on the way. She responded: "I'm dying." Victim became incoherent, and I attempted to get a shirt from the onlookers to stop the flow of blood. No cooperation was forthcoming.' "

"It was the word 'I'," Weil supplied. "When she said that, they all started to drift away."

" 'She became rational once more,' " Bach resumed, " 'long enough to whisper a number to me. The number was twelve-fifteen, which I wrote down as one-two-one-five. She roused herself once more, said "I'm dying." ' " Bach closed the notebook and looked up. "Of course, she was right." She coughed nervously.

"We invoked section 35b of the New Dresden Unified Code, 'Hot Pursuit,' suspending civil liberties locally for the duration of the search. We located component 1215 by the simple expedient of lining up all the barbies and having them pull their pants down. Each has a serial number in the small of her back. Component 1215, one Sylvester J. Cronhausen, is in custody at this moment.

"While the search was going on, we went to sleeping cubicle number 1215 with a team of criminologists. In a concealed compartment beneath the bunk we found these items." Bach got up, opened the evidence bag, and spread the items on the table.

There was a carved wooden mask. It had a huge nose with a hooked end, a mustache, and a fringe of black hair around it. Beside the mask were several jars of powders and creams, grease paint and cologne. One black nylon sweater, one pair black trousers, one pair black sneakers. A stack of pictures clipped from magazines, showing ordinary people, many of them wearing more clothes than was normal in Luna. There was a black wig and a merkin of the same color.

"What was that last?" the commissioner asked.

"A merkin, sir," Bach supplied. "A pubic wig."

"Ah." He contemplated the assortment, leaned back in his chair. "Somebody liked to dress up."

"Evidently, sir." Bach stood at ease with her hands clasped behind her back, her face passive. She felt an acute sense of failure, and a cold determination to get the woman with the gall to stand at her elbow after committing murder before her eyes. She was sure the time and place had been chosen deliberately, that the barbie had been executed for Bach's benefit.

"Do you think these items belonged to the deceased?"

"We have no reason to state that, sir," Bach said. "However, the circumstances are suggestive."

"Of what?"

"I can't be sure. These things *might* have belonged to the victim. A random search of other cubicles turned up nothing like this. We showed the items to component 23900, our liaison. She professed not to know their purpose." She stopped, then added, "I believe she was lying. She looked quite disgusted."

"Did you arrest her?"

"No, sir. I didn't think it wise. She's the only connection we have, such as she is."

The commissioner frowned, and laced his fingers together. "I'll leave it up to you, Lieutenant Bach. Frankly, we'd like to be shut of this mess as soon as possible."

"I couldn't agree with you more, sir."

"Perhaps you don't understand me. We have to have a warm body to indict. We have to have one soon."

"Sir, I'm doing the best I can. Candidly, I'm beginning to wonder if there's anything I *can* do."

"You still don't understand me." He looked around the

office. The stenographer and photoanalyst had left. He was alone with Bach and Weil. He flipped a switch on his desk, turning a recorder *off*, Bach realized.

"The news is picking up on this story. We're beginning to get some heat. On the one hand, people are afraid of these barbies. They're hearing about the murder fifty years ago, and the informal agreement. They don't like it much. On the other hand, there's the civil libertarians. They'll fight hard to prevent anything happening to the barbies, on principle. The government doesn't want to get into a mess like that. I can hardly blame them."

Bach said nothing, and the commissioner looked pained.

"I see I have to spell it out. We have a suspect in custody," he said.

"Are you referring to component 1215, Sylvester Cronhausen?"

"No. I'm speaking of the one you captured."

"Sir, the tape clearly shows she is not the guilty party. She was an innocent bystander." She felt her face heat up as she said it. Damn it, she had tried her best.

"Take a look at this." He pressed a button and the tape began to play again. But the quality was much impaired. There were bursts of snow, moments when the picture faded out entirely. It was a very good imitation of a camera failing. Bach watched herself running through the crowd—there was a flash of white—and she had hit the woman. The lights came back on in the room.

"I've checked with the analyst. She'll go along. There's a bonus in this, for both of you." He looked from Weil to Bach.

"I don't think I can go through with that, sir.

He looked like he'd tasted a lemon. "I didn't say we were doing this today. It's an option. But I ask you to look at it this way, just look at it, and I'll say no more. This is the way *they themselves* want it. They offered you the same deal the first time you were there. Close the case with a confession, no mess. We've already got this prisoner. She just says she killed her, she killed all of them. I want you to ask yourself, is she wrong? By her own rights and moral values? She believes she shares responsibility for the murders, and society demands a culprit. What's wrong with accepting their compromise and letting this all blow over?''

''Sir, it doesn't feel right to me. This is not in the oath I took. I'm supposed to protect the innocent, and she's innocent. She's the *only* barbie I *know* to be innocent.''

The commissioner sighed. ''Bach, you've got four days. You give me an alternative by then.''

''Yes, sir. If I can't, I'll tell you now that I won't interfere with what you plan. But you'll have to accept my resignation.''

Anna-Louise Bach reclined in the bathtub with her head pillowed on a folded towel. Only her neck, nipples, and knees stuck out above the placid surface of the water, tinted purple with a generous helping of bath salts. She clenched a thin cheroot in her teeth. A ribbon of lavender smoke curled from the end of it, rising to join the cloud near the ceiling.

She reached up with one foot and turned on the taps, letting out cooled water and re-filling with hot until the sweat broke out on her brow. She had been in the tub for several hours. The tips of her fingers were like washboards.

There seemed to be few alternatives. The barbies were foreign to her, and to anyone she could assign to interview them. They didn't want her help in solving the crimes. All the old rules and procedures were useless. Witnesses meant nothing; one could not tell one from the next, nor separate their stories. Opportunity? Several thousand individuals had it. Motive was a blank. She had a physical description in minute detail, even tapes of the actual murders. Both were useless.

There was one course of action that might show results. She had been soaking for hours in the hope of determining just how important her job was to her.

Hell, what else did she want to do?

She got out of the tub quickly, bringing a lot of water with her to drip onto the floor. She hurried into her bedroom, pulled the sheets off the bed and slapped the nude male figure on the buttocks.

"Come on, Svengali," she said. "Here's your chance to do something about my nose."

She used every minute while her eyes were functioning to read all she could find about Standardists. When Atlas worked on her eyes, the computer droned into an earphone. She memorized most of the *Book of Standards*.

Ten hours of surgery, followed by eight hours flat on her back, paralysed, her body undergoing forced regeneration, her eyes scanning the words that flew by on an overhead screen.

Three hours of practice, getting used to shorter legs and arms. Another hour to assemble her equipment.

When she left the Atlas clinic, she felt she would pass for a barbie as long as she kept her clothes on. She hadn't gone *that* far.

People tended to forget about access locks that led to the surface. Bach had used the fact more than once to show up in places where no one expected her.

She parked her rented crawler by the lock and left it there. Moving awkwardly in her pressure suit, she entered and started it cycling, then stepped through the inner door into an equipment room in Anytown. She stowed the suit, checked herself quickly in a washroom mirror, straightened the tape measure that belted her loose white jumpsuit, and entered the darkened corridors.

What she was doing was not illegal in any sense, but she was on edge. She didn't expect the barbies to take kindly to her masquerade if they discovered it, and she knew how easy it was for a barbie to vanish forever. Three had done so before Bach ever got the case.

The place seemed deserted. It was late evening by the arbitrary day cycle of New Dresden. Time for the nightly equalization. Bach hurried down the silent hallways to the main meeting room in the temple.

It was full of barbies and a vast roar of conversation. Bach had no trouble slipping in, and in a few minutes she knew her facial work was as good as Atlas had promised.

Equalization was the barbie's way of standardizing experience. They had been unable to simplify their lives to the point where each member of the community experienced the same things every day; the *Book of Standards* said it was a goal to be aimed for, but probably unattainable this side of Holy Reassimilation with Goddess. They tried to keep the available jobs easy enough that each member could do them all. The commune did not seek to make a profit; but air, water, and food had to be purchased, along with replacement parts and services to keep things running. The community had to produce things to trade with the outside.

They sold luxury items: hand-carved religious statues, illuminated holy books, painted crockery, and embroidered tapestries. None of the items were Standardist. The barbies had no religious symbols except their uniformity and the tape measure, but nothing in their dogma prevented them from selling objects of reverence to people of other faiths.

Bach had seen the products for sale in the better shops. They were meticulously produced, but suffered from the fact that each item looked too much like every other. People buying hand-produced luxuries in a technological age tend to want the differences that non-machine production entails, whereas the barbies wanted everything to look exactly alike. It was an ironic situation, but the barbies willingly sacrificed value by adhering to their standards.

Each barbie did things during the day that were as close as possible to what everyone else had done. But someone had to cook meals, tend the air machines, load the freight. Each component had a different job each day. At equalization, they got together and tried to even that out.

It was boring. Everyone talked at once, to anyone that happened to be around. Each woman told what she had done that day. Bach heard the same group of stories a hundred times before the night was over, and repeated them to anyone who would listen.

Anything unusual was related over a loudspeaker so everyone could be aware of it and thus spread out the intolerable burden of anomaly. No barbie wanted to keep a unique experience to herself; it made her soiled, unclean, until it was shared by all.

Bach was getting very tired of it—she was short on sleep—when the lights went out. The buzz of conversation shut off as if a tape had broken.

"All cats are alike in the dark," someone muttered, quite near Bach. Then a single voice was raised. It was solemn; almost a chant.

"We are the wrath. There is blood on our hands, but it is the holy blood of cleansing. We have told you of the cancer eating at the heart of the body, and yet still you cower away from what must be done. *The filth must be removed from us*!"

Bach was trying to tell which direction the words were coming from in the total darkness. Then she became aware of movement, people brushing against her, all going in the same direction. She began to buck the tide when she realized everyone was moving away from the voice.

"You think you can use our holy uniformity to hide among

us, but the vengeful hand of Goddess will not be stayed. The mark is upon you, our one-time sisters. Your sins have set you apart, and retribution will strike swiftly.

"*There are five of you left*. Goddess knows who you are, and will not tolerate your perversion of her holy truth. Death will strike you when you least expect it. Goddess sees the differentness within you, the differentness you seek but hope to hide from your upright sisters."

People were moving more swiftly now, and a scuffle had developed ahead of her. She struggled free of people who were breathing panic from every pore, until she stood in a clear space. The speaker was shouting to be heard over the sound of whimpering and the shuffling of bare feet. Bach moved forward, swinging her outstretched hands. But another hand brushed her first.

The punch was not centered on her stomach, but it drove the air from her lungs and sent her sprawling. Someone tripped over her, and she realized things would get pretty bad if she didn't get to her feet. She was struggling up when the lights came back on.

There was a mass sigh of relief as each barbie examined her neighbor. Bach half expected another body to be found, but that didn't seem to be the case. The killer had vanished again.

She slipped away from the equalization before it began to break up, and hurried down the deserted corridors to room 1215.

She sat in the room—little more than a cell, with a bunk, a chair, and a light on a table—for more than two hours before the door opened, as she had hoped it would. A barbie stepped inside, breathing hard, closed the door, and leaned against it.

"We wondered if you would come," Bach said, tentatively.

The woman ran to Bach and collapsed at her knees, sobbing.

"Forgive us, please forgive us, our darling. We didn't dare come last night. We were afraid that . . . that if . . . that it might have been you who was murdered, and that the wrath would be waiting for us here. Forgive us, forgive us."

"It's all right," Bach said, for lack of anything better. Suddenly, the barbie was on top of her, kissing her with a desperate passion. Bach was startled, though she had expected something of the sort. She responded as best she could. The barbie finally began to talk again.

"We must stop this, we just have to stop. We're so frightened of the wrath, but . . . but the *longing!* We can't stop ourselves. We need to see you so badly that we can hardly get through the day, not knowing if you are across town or working at our elbow. It builds all day, and at night, we cannot stop ourselves from sinning yet again." She was crying, more softly this time, not from happiness at seeing the woman she took Bach to be, but from a depth of desperation. "What's going to become of us?" she asked, helplessly.

"Shhh," Bach soothed. "It's going to be all right."

She comforted the barbie for a while, then saw her lift her head. Her eyes seemed to glow with a strange light.

"I can't wait any longer," she said. She stood up, and began taking off her clothes. Bach could see her hands shaking.

Beneath her clothing the barbie had concealed a few things that looked familiar. Bach could see that the merkin was already in place between her legs. There was a wooden mask much like the one that had been found in the secret panel, and a jar. The barbie unscrewed the top of it and used her middle finger to smear dabs of brown onto her breasts, making stylized nipples.

"Look what *I* got," she said, coming down hard on the

pronoun, her voice trembling. She pulled a flimsy yellow
blouse from the pile of clothing on the floor, and slipped it
over her shoulders. She struck a pose, then strutted up and
down the tiny room.

"Come on, darling," she said. "Tell me how beautiful I
am. Tell me I'm lovely. Tell me I'm the only one for you.
The only one. What's the *matter*? Are you still frightened?
I'm not. I'll dare anything for you, my one and only love."
But now she stopped walking and looked suspiciously at
Bach. "Why aren't you getting dressed?"

"We . . . uh, I can't," Bach said, extemporizing. "They,
uh, someone found the things. They're all gone." She didn't
dare remove her clothes because her nipples and pubic hair
would look too real, even in the dim light.

The barbie was backing away. She picked up her mask and
held it protectively to her. "What do you mean? Was she
here? The wrath? Are they after us? It's true, isn't it? They
can see us." She was on the edge of crying again, near panic.

"No, no, I think it was the police—" But it was doing no
good. The barbie was at the door now, and had it half open.

"You're her! What have you done to . . . no, no, you stay
away." She reached into the clothing that she now held in
her hands, and Bach hesitated for a moment, expecting a
knife. It was enough time for the barbie to dart quickly
through the door, slamming it behind her.

When Bach reached the door, the woman was gone.

Bach kept reminding herself that she was not here to find the
other potential victims—of whom her visitor was certainly
one—but to catch the killer. The fact remained that she
wished she could have detained her, to question her further.

The woman was a pervert, by the only definition that made
any sense among the Standardists. She, and presumably the
other dead barbies, had an individuality fetish. When Bach

had realized that, her first thought had been to wonder why they didn't simply leave the colony and become whatever they wished. But then why did a Christian seek out prostitutes? For the taste of sin. In the larger world, what these barbies did would have had little meaning. Here, it was sin of the worst and tastiest kind.

And somebody didn't like it at all.

The door opened again, and the woman stood there facing Bach, her hair disheveled, breathing hard.

"We had to come back," she said. "We're so sorry that we panicked like that. Can you forgive us?" She was coming toward Bach now, her arms out. She looked so vulnerable and contrite that Bach was astonished when the fist connected with her cheek.

Bach thudded against the wall, then found herself pinned under the woman's knees, with something sharp and cool against her throat. She swallowed very carefully, and said nothing. Her throat itched unbearably.

"She's dead," the barbie said. "And you're next." But there was something in her face that Bach didn't understand. The barbie brushed at her eyes a few times, and squinted down at her.

"Listen, I'm not who you think I am. If you kill me, you'll be bringing more trouble on your sisters than you can imagine."

The barbie hesitated, then roughly thrust her hand down into Bach's pants. Her eyes widened when she felt the genitals, but the knife didn't move. Bach knew she had to talk fast, and say all the right things.

"You understand what I'm talking about, don't you?" She looked for a response, but saw none. "You're aware of the political pressures that are coming down. You know this whole colony could be wiped out if you look like a threat to the outside. You don't want that."

"If it must be, it will be," the barbie said. "The purity is the important thing. If we die, we shall die pure. The blasphemers must be killed."

"I don't care about that anymore," Bach said, and finally got a ripple of interest from the barbie. "I have my principles, too. Maybe I'm not as fanatical about them as you are about yours. But they're important to me. One is that the guilty be brought to justice."

"You have the guilty party. Try her. Execute her. She will not protest."

"*You* are the guilty party."

The woman smiled. "So arrest us."

"All right, all right. I can't, obviously. Even if you don't kill me, you'll walk out that door and I'll never be able to find you. I've given up on that. I just don't have the time. This was my last chance, and it looks like it didn't work."

"We don't think you could do it, even with more time. But why should we let you live?"

"Because we can help each other." She felt the pressure ease up a little, and managed to swallow again. "You don't want to kill me, because it could destroy your community. Myself . . . I need to be able to salvage some self-respect out of this mess. I'm willing to accept your definition of morality and let you be the law in your own community. Maybe you're even right. Maybe you *are* one being. But I can't let that woman be convicted, when I *know* she didn't kill anyone."

The knife was not touching her neck now, but it was still being held so that the barbie could plunge it into her throat at the slightest movement.

"And if we let you live? What do you get out of it? How do you free your 'innocent' prisoner?"

"Tell me where to find the body of the woman you just killed. I'll take care of the rest."

• • •

The pathology team had gone and Anytown was settling down once again. Bach sat on the edge of the bed with Jorge Weil. She was as tired as she ever remembered being. How long had it been since she slept?

"I'll tell you," Weil said, "I honestly didn't think this thing would work. I guess I was wrong."

Bach sighed. "I wanted to take her alive, Jorge. I thought I could. But when she came at me with the knife . . ." She let him finish the thought, not caring to lie to him. She'd already done that to the interviewer. In her story, she had taken the knife from her assailant and tried to disable her, but was forced in the end to kill her. Luckily, she had the bump on the back of her head from being thrown against the wall. It made a black-out period plausible. Otherwise, someone would have wondered why she waited so long to call for police and an ambulance. The barbie had been dead for an hour when they arrived.

"Well, I'll hand it to you. You sure pulled this out. I'll admit it, I was having a hard time deciding if I'd do as you were going to do and resign, or if I could have stayed on. Now I'll never know."

"Maybe it's best that way. I don't really know, either."

Jorge grinned at her. "I can't get used to thinking of *you* being behind that godawful face."

"Neither can I, and I don't want to see any mirrors. I'm going straight to Atlas and get it changed back." She got wearily to her feet and walked toward the tube station with Weil.

She had not quite told him the truth. She did intend to get her own face back as soon as possible—nose and all—but there was one thing left to do.

From the first, a problem that had bothered her had been the question of how the killer identified her victims.

Presumably the perverts had arranged times and places to

meet for their strange rites. That would have been easy enough. Any one barbie could easily shirk her duties. She could say she was sick, and no one would know it was the same barbie who had been sick yesterday, and for a week or month before. She need not work; she could wander the halls acting as if she was on her way from one job to another. No one could challenge her. Likewise, while 23900 had said no barbie spent consecutive nights in the same room, there was no way for her to know that. Evidently room 1215 had been taken over permanently by the perverts.

And the perverts would have no scruples about identifying each other by serial number at their clandestine meetings, though they could not do it in the streets. The killer didn't even have that.

But someone had known how to identify them, to pick them out of a crowd. Bach thought she must have infiltrated meetings, marked the participants in some way. One could lead her to another, until she knew them all and was ready to strike.

She kept recalling the strange way the killer had looked at her, the way she had squinted. The mere fact that she had not killed Bach instantly in a case of mistaken identity meant she had been expecting to see something that had not been there.

And she had an idea about that.

She meant to go to the morgue first, and to examine the corpses under different wavelengths of lights, with various filters. She was betting some kind of mark would become visible on the faces, a mark the killer had been looking for with her contact lenses.

It had to be something that was visible only with the right kind of equipment, or under the right circumstances. If she kept at it long enough, she would find it.

If it was an invisible ink, it brought up another interesting question. How had it been applied? With a brush or spray gun? Unlikely. But such an ink on the killer's hands might look and feel like water.

Once she had marked her victims, the killer would have to be confident the mark would stay in place for a reasonable time. The murders had stretched over a month. So she was looking for an indelible, invisible ink, one that soaked into pores.

And if it was indelible . . .

There was no use thinking further about it. She was right, or she was wrong. When she struck the bargain with the killer she had faced up to the possibility that she might have to live with it. Certainly she could not now bring a killer into court, not after what she had just said.

No, if she came back to Anytown and found a barbie whose hands were stained with guilt, she would have to do the job herself.

COCOON

Greg Egan

"Cocoon" was purchased by Gardner Dozois, and appeared in the May 1994 issue of Asimov's, *with an illustration by Steve Cavallo; the story went on to appear on the Hugo Final Ballot in 1995, and to win both the Ditmar Award and the* Asimov's Readers Award. *Egan has had a string of powerful stories in* Asimov's *throughout the '90s. In fact, it's already a fairly safe bet to predict that Australian writer Greg Egan is going to come to be recognized (if indeed he hasn't* already *been so recognized) as being one of the Big New Names to emerge in SF in the nineties, and one of the most inventive and intriguing of all the new "hard science" writers. His first novel,* Quarantine, *appeared in 1992, to wide critical acclaim, and was followed by a second novel in 1994,* Permutation City, *which won the John W. Campbell Memorial Award. His most recent books are a collection of his short fiction,* Axiomatic, *and a new novel,* Distress. *Upcoming is another new novel,* Diaspora.*

In the powerful story that follows—one of 1994's most controversial—he unravels a suspenseful and provocative mystery that revolves around sexual politics, corporate intrigue, and high-tech eugenics, all set against the background of a troubled future Australia . . .

The explosion shattered windows hundreds of meters away, but started no fire. Later, I discovered that it had shown up on a seismograph at Macquarie University, fixing the time precisely: 3:52 A.M. Residents woken by the blast phoned emergency services within minutes, and our night shift operator called me just after four, but there was no point rushing to the scene when I'd only be in the way. I sat at the terminal in my study for almost an hour, assembling background data and monitoring the radio traffic on headphones, drinking coffee and trying not to type too loudly.

By the time I arrived, the local fire service contractors had departed, having certified that there was no risk of further explosions, but our forensic people were still poring over the wreckage, the electric hum of their equipment all but drowned out by birdsong. Lane Cove was a quiet, leafy suburb, mixed residential and high-tech industrial, the lush vegetation of corporate open spaces blending almost seamlessly into the adjacent national park that straddled the Lane Cove River. The map of the area on my car terminal had identified suppliers of laboratory reagents and pharmaceuticals, manufacturers of precision instruments for scientific and aerospace applications, and no less than twenty-seven biotechnology firms—including Life Enhancement International, the erstwhile sprawling concrete building now reduced to a collection of white powdery blocks clustered around twisted reinforcement rods. The exposed steel glinted in the early light, disconcertingly pristine; the building was only three years old. I could understand why the forensic team had ruled out an accident at their first glance; a few drums of organic solvent could not have done anything remotely like *this*. Nothing legally stored in a residential zone could reduce a modern building to rubble in a matter of seconds.

I spotted Janet Lansing as I left my car. She was surveying the ruins with an expression of stoicism, but she was hugging herself. Mild shock, probably. She had no other reason to be chilly; it had been stinking hot all night, and the temperature was already climbing. Lansing was Director of the Lane Cove complex: forty-three years old, with a Ph.D. in molecular biology from Cambridge, and an M.B.A. from an equally reputable Japanese virtual university. I'd had my knowledge miner extract her details, and photo, from assorted databases before I'd left home.

I approached her and said, "James Glass, Nexus Investigations." She frowned at my business card, but accepted it, then glanced at the technicians trawling their gas chromatographs and holography equipment around the perimeter of the ruins.

"They're yours, I suppose?"

"Yes. They've been here since four."

She smirked slightly. "What happens if I give the job to someone else? And charge the lot of you with trespass?"

"If you hire another company, we'll be happy to hand over all the samples and data we've collected."

She nodded distractedly. "I'll hire you, of course. Since four? I'm impressed. You've even arrived before the insurance people." As it happened, LEI's "insurance people" owned 49 percent of Nexus, and would stay out of the way until we were finished, but I didn't see any reason to mention that. Lansing added sourly, "Our so-called security firm only worked up the courage to phone me half an hour ago. Evidently a fiber-optic junction box was sabotaged, disconnecting the whole area. They're supposed to send in patrols in the event of equipment failure, but apparently they didn't bother."

I grimaced sympathetically. "What exactly were you people making here?"

"Making? Nothing. We did no manufacturing; this was pure R & D."

In fact, I'd already established that LEI's factories were all in Thailand and Indonesia, with the head office in Monaco, and research facilities scattered around the world. There's a fine line, though, between demonstrating that the facts are at your fingertips, and unnerving the client. A total stranger *ought* to make at least one trivial wrong assumption, ask at least one misguided question. I always do.

"So what were you researching and developing?"

"That's commercially sensitive information."

I took my notepad from my shirt pocket and displayed a standard contract, complete with the usual secrecy provisions. She glanced at it, then had her own computer scrutinize the document. Conversing in modulated infrared, the machines rapidly negotiated the fine details. My notepad signed the agreement electronically on my behalf, and Lansing's did the same, then they both chimed happily in unison to let us know that the deal had been concluded.

Lansing said, "Our main project here was engineering improved syncytiotrophoblastic cells." I smiled patiently, and she translated for me. "Strengthening the barrier between the maternal and fetal blood supplies. Mother and fetus don't share blood directly, but they exchange nutrients and hormones across the placental barrier. The trouble is, all kinds of viruses, toxins, pharmaceuticals and illicit drugs can also cross over. The natural barrier cells didn't evolve to cope with AIDS, fetal alcohol syndrome, cocaine-addicted babies, or the next thalidomidelike disaster. We're aiming for a single intravenous injection of a gene-tailoring vector, which would trigger the formation of an extra layer of cells in the appropriate structures within the placenta, specifically designed to shield the fetal blood supply from contaminants in the maternal blood."

"A thicker barrier?"

"Smarter. More selective. More choosy about what it lets

through. We know exactly what the developing fetus actually *needs* from the maternal blood. These gene-tailored cells would contain specific channels for transporting each of those substances. Nothing else would be allowed through.''

''Very impressive.'' *A cocoon around the unborn child, shielding it from all of the poisons of modern society.* It sounded exactly like the kind of beneficent technology a company called Life Enhancement would be hatching in leafy Lane Cove. True, even a layman could spot a few flaws in the scheme. I'd heard that AIDS most often infected children during birth itself, not pregnancy—but presumably there were other viruses that crossed the placental barrier more frequently. I had no idea whether or not mothers at risk of giving birth to children stunted by alcohol or addicted to cocaine were likely to rush out *en masse* and have gene-tailored fetal barriers installed—but I could picture a strong demand from people terrified of food additives, pesticides, and pollutants. In the long term—if the system actually worked, and wasn't prohibitively expensive—it could even become a part of routine prenatal care.

Beneficent, and lucrative.

In any case—whether or not there were biological, economic, and social factors which might keep the technology from being a complete success . . . it was hard to imagine anyone objecting to *the principle of the thing*.

I said, ''Were you working with animals?''

Lansing scowled. ''Only early calf embryos, and disembodied bovine uteruses on tissue-support machines. If it was an animal rights group, they would have been better off bombing an abattoir.''

''Mmm.'' In the past few years, the Sydney chapter of Animal Equality—the only group known to use such extreme methods—had concentrated on primate research facilities. They might have changed their focus, or been misinformed, but LEI still seemed like an odd target; there were plenty of laboratories widely known to use whole, live rats and rabbits as if they were disposable test tubes—many of them quite close by. "What about competitors?"

"No one else is pursuing this kind of product line, so far as I know. There's no race being run; we've already obtained individual patents for all of the essential components—the membrane channels, the transporter molecules—so any competitor would have to pay us license fees, regardless."

"What if someone simply wanted to damage you, financially?"

"Then they should have bombed one of the factories instead. Cutting off our cash flow would have been the best way to hurt us; this laboratory wasn't earning a cent."

"Your share price will still take a dive, won't it? Nothing makes investors nervous quite so much as terrorism."

Lansing agreed, reluctantly. "But then, whoever took advantage of that and launched a takeover bid would suffer the same taint, themselves. I don't deny that commercial sabotage takes place in this industry, now and then . . . but not on a level as crude as this. Genetic engineering is a subtle business. Bombs are for fanatics."

Perhaps. But who would be fanatically opposed to the idea of shielding human embryos from viruses and poisons? Several religious sects flatly rejected any kind of modification to human biology . . . but the ones who employed violence were far more likely to have bombed a manufacturer of abortifacient drugs than a laboratory dedicated to the task of *safeguarding* the unborn child.

Elaine Chang, head of the forensic team, approached us. I introduced her to Lansing. Elaine said, "It was a very professional job. If you'd hired demolition experts, they wouldn't have done a single thing differently. But then, they probably would have used identical software to compute the timing and placement of the charges.'' She held up her notepad, and displayed a stylized reconstruction of the building, with hypothetical explosive charges marked. She hit a button and the simulation crumbled into something very like the actual mess behind us.

She continued, ''Most reputable manufacturers these days imprint every batch of explosives with a trace element signature, which remains in the residue. We've linked the charges used here to a batch stolen from a warehouse in Singapore five years ago.''

I added, ''Which may not be a great help, though, I'm afraid. After five years on the black market, they could have changed hands a dozen times.''

Elaine returned to her equipment. Lansing was beginning to look a little dazed. I said, ''I'd like to talk to you again, later—but I am going to need a list of your employees, past and present, as soon as possible.''

She nodded, and hit a few keys on her notepad, transferring the list to mine. She said, ''Nothing's been lost, really. We had off-site backup for all of our data, administrative and scientific. And we have frozen samples of most of the cell lines we were working on, in a vault in Milson's Point.''

Commercial data backup would be all but untouchable, with the records stored in a dozen or more locations scattered around the world—heavily encrypted, of course. Cell lines sounded more vulnerable. I said, ''You'd better let the vault's operators know what's happened.''

''I've already done that; I phoned them on my way here.'' She gazed at the wreckage. ''The insurance company will pay for the rebuilding. In six months' time, we'll be back on our feet. So whoever did this was wasting their time. The work will go on.''

I said, ''Who would want to stop it in the first place?''

Lansing's faint smirk appeared again, and I very nearly

asked her what she found so amusing. But people often act incongruously in the face of disasters, large or small; nobody had died, she wasn't remotely hysterical, but it would have been strange if a setback like this hadn't knocked her slightly out of kilter.

She said, "*You* tell *me*. That's your job, isn't it?"

Martin was in the living room when I arrived home that evening. Working on his costume for the Mardi Gras. I couldn't imagine what it would look like when it was completed, but there were definitely feathers involved. Blue feathers. I did my best to appear composed, but I could tell from his expression that he'd caught an involuntary flicker of distaste on my face as he looked up. We kissed anyway, and said nothing about it.

Over dinner, though, he couldn't help himself.

"Fortieth anniversary this year, James. Sure to be the biggest yet. You could at least come and watch." His eyes glinted; he enjoyed needling me. We'd had this argument five years running, and it was close to becoming a ritual as pointless as the parade itself.

I said flatly, "Why would I want to watch ten thousand drag queens ride down Oxford Street, blowing kisses to the tourists?"

"Don't exaggerate. There'll only be a thousand men in drag, at most."

"Yeah, the rest will be in sequined jockstraps."

"If you actually came and watched, you'd discover that most people's imaginations have progressed far beyond that."

I shook my head, bemused. "If people's imaginations had *progressed*, there'd be no Gay and Lesbian Mardi Gras at all. It's a freak show, for people who want to live in a cultural ghetto. Forty years ago, it might have been . . . provocative. Maybe it did some good, back then. But *now?* What's the point? There are no laws left to change, there's no politics left to address. This kind of thing just recycles the same moronic stereotypes, year after year.''

Martin said smoothly, ''It's a public reassertion of the right to diverse sexuality. Just because it's no longer a *protest march* as well as a celebration doesn't mean it's irrelevant. And complaining about stereotypes is like . . . complaining about the characters in a medieval morality play. The costumes are code, shorthand. Give the great unwashed heterosexual masses credit for some intelligence; they don't watch the parade and conclude that the average gay man spends all his time in a gold lamé tutu. People aren't that literal-minded. They all learnt semiotics in kindergarten, they know how to decode the message.''

''I'm sure they do. But it's still the wrong message: it makes exotic what ought to be mundane. Okay, people have the right to dress up any way they like and march down Oxford Street . . . but it means absolutely nothing to me.''

''I'm not asking you to join in—''

''Very wise.''

''—but if one hundred thousand straights can turn up, to show their support for the gay community, why can't you?''

I said wearily, ''Because every time I hear the word *community*, I know I'm being manipulated. If there *is* such a thing as *the gay community*, I'm certainly not a part of it. As it happens, I don't want to spend my life watching *gay and lesbian* television channels, using *gay and lesbian* news systems . . . or going to *gay and lesbian* street parades. It's all so . . . proprietary. You'd think there was a multinational corporation who had the franchise rights on homosexuality. And if you don't *market the product* their way, you're some kind of second-class, inferior, bootleg, unauthorized queer.''

Martin cracked up. When he finally stopped laughing, he said, ''Go on. I'm waiting for you to get to the part where you say you're no more proud of being gay than you are of having brown eyes, or black hair, or a birthmark behind your left knee.''

I protested. ''That's true. Why should I be 'proud' of something I was born with? I'm not proud, *or* ashamed. I just *accept* it. And I don't have to join a parade to prove that.''

''So you'd rather we all stayed invisible?''

''*Invisible!* You're the one who told me that the representation rates in movies and TV last year were close to the true demographics. And if you hardly even *notice it* anymore when an openly gay or lesbian politician gets elected, that's because it's *no longer an issue*. To most people, now, it's about as significant as . . . being left or right handed.''

Martin seemed to find this suggestion surreal. ''Are you trying to tell me that it's now a *non-subject?* That the inhabitants of this planet are now absolutely impartial on the question of sexual preference? Your faith is touching—but . . .'' He mimed incredulity.

I said, ''We're equal before the law with any heterosexual couple, aren't we? And when was the last time you told someone you were gay and they so much as blinked? And yes, I know, there are dozens of countries where it's still illegal— along with joining the wrong political parties, or the wrong religions. Parades in Oxford Street aren't going to change *that*.''

''People are still bashed *in this city*. People are *still* discriminated against.''

''Yeah. And people are also shot dead in peak-hour traffic for playing the wrong music on their car stereos, or denied jobs because they live in the wrong suburbs. I'm not talking about the perfection of human nature. I just want you to acknowledge one tiny victory: leaving out a few psychotics, and a few fundamentalist bigots . . . most people *just don't care*.''

Martin said ruefully, ''If only that were true!''

The argument went on for more than an hour—ending in a stalemate, as usual. But then, neither one of us had seriously expected to change the other's mind.

I did catch myself wondering afterward, though, if I really believed all of my own optimistic rhetoric. *About as significant as being left or right handed?* Certainly, that was the line taken by most Western politicians, academics, essayists, talk show hosts, soap opera writers, and mainstream religious leaders . . . but the same people had been espousing equally high-minded principles of racial equality for decades, and the reality still hadn't entirely caught up on *that* front. I'd suffered very little discrimination, myself—by the time I reached high school, tolerance was hip, and I'd witnessed a constant stream of improvements since then . . . but how could I ever know precisely how much hidden prejudice remained? By interrogating my own straight friends? By reading the sociologists' latest attitude surveys? People will always tell you what they think you want to hear.

Still, it hardly seemed to matter. Personally, I could get by without the deep and sincere approval of every other member of the human race. Martin and I were lucky enough to have been born into a time and place where, in almost every tangible respect, we were treated as equal.

What more could anyone hope for?

In bed that night, we made love very slowly, at first just kissing and stroking each other's bodies for what seemed like hours. Neither of us spoke, and in the stupefying heat I lost all sense of belonging to any other time, any other reality. Nothing existed but the two of us; the rest of the world, the rest of my life, went spinning away into the darkness.

The investigation moved slowly. I interviewed every current member of LEI's workforce, then started on the long list of past employees. I still believed that commercial sabotage was the most likely explanation for such a professional job—but blowing up the opposition is a desperate measure; a little civilized espionage usually comes first. I was hoping that someone who'd worked for LEI might have been approached in the past and offered money for inside information—and if I could find just one employee who'd turned down a bribe, they might have learnt something useful from their contact with the presumed rival.

Although the Lane Cove facility had only been built three years before, LEI had operated a research division in Sydney for twelve years before that, in North Ryde, not far away. Many of the ex-employees from that period had moved interstate or overseas; quite a few had been transferred to LEI divisions in other countries. Still, almost no one had changed their personal phone numbers, so I had very little trouble tracking them down.

The exception was a biochemist named Catherine Mendelsohn; the number listed for her in the LEI staff records had been canceled. There were seventeen people with the same surname and initials in the national phone directory; none admitted to being Catherine Alice Mendelsohn, and none looked at all like the staff photo I had.

Mendelsohn's address in the Electoral Roll, an apartment in Newtown, matched the LEI records—but the same address was in the phone directory (and Electoral Roll) for Stanley Goh, a young man who told me that he'd never met Mendelsohn. He'd been leasing the apartment for the past eighteen months.

Credit rating databases gave the same out-of-date address. I couldn't access tax, banking, or utilities records without a warrant. I had my knowledge miner scan the death notices, but there was no match there.

Mendelsohn had worked for LEI until about a year before the move to Lane Cove. She'd been part of a team working on a gene-tailoring system for ameliorating menstrual side-effects, and although the Sydney division had always specialized in gynecological research, for some reason the project was about to be moved to Texas. I checked the industry publications; apparently, LEI had been rearranging all of its operations at the time, gathering together projects from around the globe into new multi-disciplinary configurations, in accordance with the latest fashionable theories of research dynamics. Mendelsohn had declined the transfer, and had been retrenched.

I dug deeper. The staff records showed that Mendelsohn had been questioned by security guards after being found on the North Ryde premises late at night, two days before her dismissal. Workaholic biotechnologists aren't uncommon, but starting the day at two in the morning shows exceptional dedication, especially when the company has just tried to shuffle you off to Amarillo. Having turned down the transfer, she must have known what was in store.

Nothing came of the incident, though. And even if Mendelsohn *had* been planning some minor act of sabotage, that hardly established any connection with a bombing four years later. She might have been angry enough to leak confidential information to one of LEI's rivals ... but whoever had bombed the Lane Cove laboratory would have been more interested in someone who'd worked on the fetal barrier project itself—a project which had only come into existence a year after Mendelsohn had been sacked.

I pressed on through the list. Interviewing the ex-employees was frustrating; almost all of them were still working in the biotechnology industry, and they would have been an ideal group to poll on the question of *who would benefit most* from LEI's misfortune—but the confidentiality agreement I'd signed meant that I couldn't disclose anything about the research in question—not even to people working for LEI's other divisions.

The one thing which I *could* discuss drew a blank: if anyone had been offered a bribe, they weren't talking about it—and no magistrate was going to sign a warrant letting me loose on a fishing expedition through a hundred and seventeen people's financial records.

Forensic examination of the ruins, and the sabotaged fiberoptic exchange, had yielded the usual catalogue of minutiae which might eventually turn out to be invaluable—but none of it was going to conjure up a suspect out of thin air.

Four days after the bombing—just as I found myself growing desperate for a fresh angle on the case—I had a call from Janet Lansing.

The backup samples of the project's gene-tailored cell lines had been destroyed.

The vault in Milson's Point turned out to be directly underneath a section of the Harbor Bridge—built right into the foundations on the north shore. Lansing hadn't arrived yet, but the head of security for the storage company, an elderly man called David Asher, showed me around. Inside, the traffic was barely audible, but the vibration coming through the floor felt like a constant mild earthquake. The place was cavernous, dry and cool. At least a hundred cryogenic freezers were laid out in rows; heavily clad pipes ran between them, replenishing their liquid nitrogen.

Asher was understandably morose, but cooperative. Celluloid movie film had been archived here, he explained, before everything went digital; the present owners specialized in biological materials. There were no guards physically assigned to the vault, but the surveillance cameras and alarm systems looked impressive, and the structure itself must have been close to impregnable.

Lansing had phoned the storage company, Biofile, on the morning of the bombing. Asher confirmed that he'd sent someone down from their North Sydney office to check the freezer in question. Nothing was missing—but he'd promised to boost security measures immediately. Because the freezers were supposedly tamper-proof, and individually locked, clients were normally allowed access to the vault at their convenience, monitored by the surveillance cameras, but otherwise unsupervised. Asher had promised Lansing that, henceforth, nobody would enter the building without a member of his staff to accompany them—and he claimed that nobody had been inside since the day of the bombing, anyway.

When two LEI technicians had arrived that morning to carry out an inventory, they'd found the expected number of culture flasks, all with the correct bar code labels, all tightly sealed—but the appearance of their contents was subtly wrong. The translucent frozen colloid was more opalescent than cloudy; an untrained eye might never have noticed the difference, but apparently it spoke volumes to the cognoscenti.

The technicians had taken a number of the flasks away for analysis; LEI were working out of temporary premises, a subleased corner of a paint manufacturer's quality control lab. Lansing had promised me preliminary test results by the time we met.

Lansing arrived, and unlocked the freezer. With gloved hands, she lifted a flask out of the swirling mist and held it up for me to inspect.

She said, "We've only thawed three samples, but they all look the same. The cells have been torn apart."

"How?" The flask was covered with such heavy condensation that I couldn't have said if it was empty or full, let alone *cloudy* or *opalescent*.

"It looks like radiation damage."

My skin crawled. I peered into the depths of the freezer;

all I could make out were the tops of rows of identical flasks—*but if one of them had been spiked with a radioisotope* . . .

Lansing scowled. "Relax." She tapped a small electronic badge pinned to her lab coat, with a dull gray face like a solar cell: a radiation dosimeter. "*This* would be screaming if we were being exposed to anything significant. Whatever the source of the radiation was, it's no longer in here—and it hasn't left the walls glowing. Your future offspring are safe."

I let that pass. "You think all the samples will turn out to be ruined? You won't be able to salvage anything?"

Lansing was stoical as ever. "It looks that way. There are some elaborate techniques we could use, to try to repair the DNA—but it will probably be easier to synthesize fresh DNA from scratch, and re-introduce it into unmodified bovine placental cell lines. We still have all the sequence data; that's what matters in the end."

I pondered the freezer's locking system, the surveillance cameras. "Are you sure that the source was *inside* the freezer? Or could the damage have been done without actually breaking in—right through the walls?"

She thought it over. "Maybe. There's not much metal in these things; they're mostly plastic foam. But I'm not a radiation physicist; your forensic people will probably be able to give you a better idea of what happened, once they've checked out the freezer itself. If there's damage to the polymers in the foam, it might be possible to use that to reconstruct the geometry of the radiation field."

A forensic team was on its way. I said, "How would they have done it? Walked casually by, and just—?"

"Hardly. A source which could do this in one quick hit would have been unmanageable. It's far more likely to have been a matter of weeks, or months, of low-level exposure."

"So they must have smuggled some kind of device into

their own freezer, and aimed it at yours? But then . . . we'll
be able to trace the effects right back to the source, won't
we? So how could they have hoped to get away with it?''

Lansing said, ''It's even simpler than that. We're talking
about a modest amount of a gamma-emitting isotope, not
some billion-dollar particle-beam weapon. The effective range
would be a couple of meters, at most. If it *was* done from the
outside, you've just narrowed down your suspect list to two.''
She thumped the freezer's left neighbor in the aisle, then did
the same to the one on the right—and said, ''Aha.''

''What?''

She thumped them both again. The second one sounded
hollow. I said, ''No liquid nitrogen? It's not in use?''

Lansing nodded. She reached for the handle.

Asher said, ''I don't think—''

The freezer was unlocked, the lid swung open easily. Lansing's badge started beeping—and, worse, *there was something in there, with batteries and wires.* . . .

I don't know what kept me from knocking her to the
floor—but Lansing, untroubled, lifted the lid all the way. She
said mildly, ''Don't panic; this dose rate's nothing. Threshold
of detectable.''

The thing inside looked superficially like a home-made
bomb—but the batteries and timer chip I'd glimpsed were
wired to a heavy-duty solenoid, which was part of an elaborate shutter mechanism on one side of a large, metallic gray
box.

Lansing said, ''Cannibalized medical source, probably. You
know these things have turned up in *garbage dumps?*'' She
unpinned her badge and waved it near the box; the pitch of
the alarm increased, but only slightly. ''Shielding seems to be
intact.''

I said, as calmly as possible, ''These people have access to
high explosives. You don't have any idea what the fuck might

be in there, or what it's wired up to do. This is the point where we walk out, quietly, and leave it to the bomb-disposal robots.''

She seemed about to protest, but then she nodded contritely. The three of us went up onto the street, and Asher called the local terrorist services contractor. I suddenly realized that they'd have to divert all traffic from the bridge. The Lane Cove bombing had received some perfunctory media coverage—but *this* would lead the evening news.

I took Lansing aside. ''They've destroyed your laboratory. They've wiped out your cell lines. Your data may be almost impossible to locate and corrupt—so the next logical target is you and your employees. Nexus doesn't provide protective services, but I can recommend a good firm.''

I gave her the phone number; she accepted it with appropriate solemnity. ''So you finally believe me? These people aren't commercial saboteurs. They're dangerous fanatics.''

I was growing impatient with her vague references to ''fanatics.'' ''Who exactly do you have in mind?''

She said darkly, ''We're tampering with certain . . . *natural processes*. You can draw your own conclusions, can't you?''

There was no logic to that at all. God's Image would probably want to *force* all pregnant women with HIV infections, or drug habits, to use the cocoon; they wouldn't try to bomb the technology out of existence. Gaia's Soldiers were more concerned with genetically engineered crops and bacteria than trivial modifications to insignificant species like humans—and they wouldn't have used *radioisotopes* if the fate of the planet depended on it. Lansing was beginning to sound thoroughly paranoid—although in the circumstances, I couldn't really blame her.

I said, ''I'm not drawing any conclusions. I'm just advising you to take some sensible precautions, because we have no way of knowing how far this might escalate. But . . . Biofile must lease freezer space to every one of your competitors. A commercial rival would have found it a thousand times easier than any hypothetical sect member to get into the vault to plant that thing.''

A gray armor-plated van screeched to a halt in front of us; the back door swung up, ramps slid down, and a squat, multi-limbed robot on treads descended. I raised a hand in greeting and the robot did the same; the operator was a friend of mine.

Lansing said, ''You may be right. But then, there's nothing to stop a terrorist from having a day job in biotechnology, is there?''

The device turned out not to be booby-trapped at all—just rigged to spray LEI's precious cells with gamma rays for six hours, starting at midnight, every night. Even in the unlikely event that someone had come into the vault in the early hours and wedged themselves into the narrow gap between the freezers, the dose they received would not have been much; as Lansing had suggested, it was the cumulative effect over months which had done the damage. The radioisotope in the box was cobalt 60, almost certainly a decommissioned medical source—grown too weak for its original use, but still too hot to be discarded—stolen from a ''cooling off'' site. No such theft had been reported, but Elaine Chang's assistants were phoning around the hospitals, trying to persuade them to re-inventory their concrete bunkers.

Cobalt 60 was dangerous stuff—but fifty milligrams in a carefully shielded container wasn't exactly a tactical nuclear weapon. The news systems went berserk, though: ATOMIC TERRORISTS STRIKE HARBOR BRIDGE, et cetera. If LEI's enemies *were* activists, with some ''moral cause'' which they hoped to set before the public, they clearly had the worst PR advisers in the business. Their prospects of gaining the slightest sympathy had vanished, the instant the first news reports had mentioned the word *radiation*.

My secretarial software issued polite statements of "No comment" on my behalf, but camera crews began hovering outside my front door, so I relented and mouthed a few news-speak sentences for them which meant essentially the same thing. Martin looked on, amused—and then I looked on, astonished, as Janet Lansing's own doorstop media conference appeared on TV.

"These people are clearly ruthless. Human life, the environment, radioactive contamination . . . all mean nothing to them."

"Do you have any idea who might be responsible for this outrage, Dr. Lansing?"

"I can't disclose that, yet. All I can reveal, right now, is that our research is at the very cutting edge of preventative medicine—and I'm not at all surprised that there are powerful vested interests working against us."

Powerful vested interests? What was *that* meant to be code for—if not the rival biotechnology firm whose involvement she kept denying? No doubt she had her eye on the publicity advantages of being the victim of ATOMIC TERRORISTS—but I thought she was wasting her breath. In two or more years' time, when the product finally hit the market, the story would be long forgotten.

After some tricky jurisdictional negotiations, Asher finally sent me six months' worth of files from the vault's surveillance cameras—all that they kept. The freezer in question had been unused for almost two years; the last authorized tenant was a small IVF clinic which had gone bankrupt. Only about 60 percent of the freezers were currently leased, so it wasn't particularly surprising that LEI had had a conveniently empty neighbor.

I ran the surveillance files through image-processing software, in the hope that someone might have been caught in the act of opening the unused freezer. The search took almost an hour of supercomputer time—and turned up precisely nothing. A few minutes later, Elaine Chang popped her head into my office to say that she'd finished her analysis of the damage to the freezer walls: the nightly irradiation had been going on for between eight and nine months.

Undeterred, I scanned the files again, this time instructing the software to assemble a gallery of every individual sighted inside the vault.

Sixty-two faces emerged. I put company names to all of them, matching the times of each sighting to Biofile's records of the use of each client's electronic key. No obvious inconsistencies showed up; nobody had been seen inside who hadn't used an authorized key to gain access—and the same people had used the same keys, again and again.

I flicked through the gallery, wondering what to do next. *Search for anyone glancing slyly in the direction of the radioactive freezer?* The software could have done it—but I wasn't quite ready for barrel-scraping efforts like that.

I came to a face which looked familiar: a blonde woman in her mid-thirties, who'd used the key belonging to Federation Centennial Hospital's Oncology Research Unit, three times. I was certain that I knew her, but I couldn't recall where I'd seen her before. It didn't matter; after a few seconds' searching, I found a clear shot of the name badge pinned to her lab coat. All I had to do was zoom in.

The badge read: C. MENDELSOHN.

There was a knock on my open door. I turned from the screen; Elaine was back, looking pleased with herself.

She said, "We've finally found a place who'll own up to having lost some cobalt 60. What's more . . . the activity of our source fits their missing item's decay curve, exactly."

"So where was it stolen from?"
"Federation Centennial."

I phoned the Oncology Research Unit. Yes, Catherine Mendelsohn worked there—she'd done so for almost four years—but they couldn't put me through to her; she'd been on sick leave all week. They gave me the same canceled phone number as LEI—but a different address, an apartment in Petersham. The address wasn't listed in the phone directory; I'd have to go there in person.

A cancer research team would have no reason to want to harm LEI, but a commercial rival—with or without their own key to the vault—could still have paid Mendelsohn to do their work for them. It seemed like a lousy deal to me, whatever they'd offered her—if she was convicted, every last cent would be traced and confiscated—but bitterness over her sacking might have clouded her judgment.

Maybe. Or maybe that was all too glib.

I replayed the shots of Mendelsohn taken by the surveillance cameras. She did nothing unusual, nothing suspicious. She went straight to the ORU's freezer, put in whatever samples she'd brought, and departed. She didn't glance slyly in any direction at all.

The fact that she had been inside the vault—on legitimate business—proved nothing. The fact that the cobalt 60 had been stolen from the hospital where she worked could have been pure coincidence.

And anyone had the right to cancel their phone service.

I pictured the steel reinforcement rods of the Lane Cove laboratory, glinting in the sunlight.

On the way out, reluctantly, I took a detour to the basement. I sat at a console while the armaments safe checked my fingerprints, took breath samples and a retinal blood spectrogram, ran some perception-and-judgment response time tests, then quizzed me for five minutes about the case. Once it was satisfied with my reflexes, my motives, and my state of mind, it issued me a nine-millimeter pistol and a shoulder holster.

Mendelsohn's apartment block was a concrete box from the 1960s, front doors opening onto long shared balconies, no security at all. I arrived just after seven, to the smell of cooking and the sound of game show applause, wafting from a hundred open windows. The concrete still shimmered with the day's heat; three flights of stairs left me coated in sweat. Mendelsohn's apartment was silent, but the lights were on.

She answered the door. I introduced myself, and showed her my ID. She seemed nervous, but not surprised.

She said, "I still find it galling to have to deal with people like you."

"People like—?"

"I was opposed to privatizing the police force. I helped organize some of the marches."

She would have been fourteen years old at the time—a precocious political activist.

She let me in, begrudgingly. The living room was modestly furnished, with a terminal on a desk in one corner.

I said, "I'm investigating the bombing of Life Enhancement International. You used to work for them, up until about four years ago. Is that correct?"

"Yes."

"Can you tell me why you left?"

She repeated what I knew about the transfer of her project to the Amarillo division. She answered every question directly, looking me straight in the eye; she still appeared nervous, but she seemed to be trying to read some vital piece of information from my demeanor. *Wondering if I'd traced the cobalt?*

"What were you doing on the North Ryde premises at two in the morning, two days before you were sacked?"

She said, "I wanted to find out what LEI was planning for the new building. I wanted to know why they didn't want me to stick around."

"Your job was moved to Texas."

She laughed drily. "The work wasn't *that* specialized. I could have swapped jobs with someone who wanted to travel to the States. It would have been the perfect solution—and there would have been plenty of people more than happy to trade places with me. But no, that wasn't allowed."

"So . . . did you find the answer?"

"Not that night. But later, yes."

I said carefully, "So you knew what LEI was doing in Lane Cove?"

"Yes."

"How did you discover that?"

"I kept an ear to the ground. Nobody who'd stayed on would have told me directly, but word leaked out, eventually. About a year ago."

"*Three years after you'd left?* Why were you still interested? Did you think there was a market for the information?"

She said, "Put your notepad in the bathroom sink and run the tap on it."

I hesitated, then complied. When I returned to the living room, she had her face in her hands. She looked up at me grimly.

"*Why was I still interested?* Because I wanted to know why *every project* with any lesbian or gay team members was being transferred out of the division. I wanted to know if that was pure coincidence. Or not."

I felt a sudden chill in the pit of my stomach. I said, "If you had some problem with discrimination, there are avenues you could have—"

Mendelsohn shook her head impatiently. "LEI was never *discriminatory*. They didn't sack anyone who was willing to move—and they always transferred the entire team; there was nothing so crude as picking out *individuals* by sexual preference. And they had a rationalization for everything: projects were being re-grouped between divisions to facilitate 'synergistic cross-pollination.' And if that sounds like pretentious bullshit, it was—but it was plausible pretentious bullshit. Other corporations have adopted far more ridiculous schemes, in perfect sincerity.''

''But if it wasn't a matter of discrimination . . . why should LEI want to force people out of one particular division—?''

I think I'd finally guessed the answer, even as I said those words—but I needed to hear her spell it out, before I could really believe it.

Mendelsohn must have been practicing her version for non-biochemists; she had it down pat. ''When people are subject to *stress*—physical or emotional—the levels of certain substances in the bloodstream increase. Cortisol and adrenaline, mainly. Adrenaline has a rapid, short-term effect on the nervous system. Cortisol works on a much longer time frame, modulating all kinds of bodily processes, adapting them for hard times: injury, fatigue, whatever. If the stress is prolonged, someone's cortisol can be elevated for days, or weeks, or months.

''High enough levels of cortisol, in the bloodstream of a pregnant woman, can cross the placental barrier and interact with the hormonal system of the developing fetus. There are parts of the brain where embryonic development is switched into one of two possible pathways, by hormones released by the fetal testes or ovaries. The parts of the brain which control body image, and the parts which control sexual preference. Female embryos usually develop a brain wired with a self-image of a female body, and the strongest potential for sexual attraction toward males. Male embryos, vice versa. And it's the sex hormones in the fetal bloodstream which let the growing neurons *know* the gender of the embryo, and which wiring pattern to adopt.

"Cortisol can interfere with this process. The precise interactions are complex, but the ultimate effect depends on the timing; different parts of the brain are switched into gender-specific versions at different stages of development. So stress at different times during pregnancy leads to different patterns of sexual preference and body image in the child: homosexual, bisexual, transsexual.

"Obviously, a lot depends on the mother's biochemistry. Pregnancy *itself* is stressful—but everyone responds to that differently. The first sign that cortisol might have an effect came in studies in the 1980s, on the children of German women who'd been pregnant during the most intense bombing raids of World War II—when the stress was so great that the effect showed through despite individual differences. In the nineties, researchers thought they'd found a gene which determined male homosexuality . . . but it was always maternally inherited—and it turned out to be influencing *the mother's stress response*, rather than acting directly on the child.

"If maternal cortisol, and other stress hormones, were kept from reaching the fetus . . . then the gender of the brain would always match the gender of the body in every respect. All of the present variation would be wiped out."

I was shaken, but I don't think I let it show. Everything she said rang true; I didn't doubt a word of it. I'd always known that sexual preference was decided before birth. I'd known that I was gay, myself, by the age of seven. I'd never sought out the elaborate biological details, though—because I'd never believed that the tedious mechanics of the process could ever matter to me. What turned my blood to ice was not finally learning *the neuroembryology of desire*. The shock was discovering that LEI planned to reach into the womb and take *control* of it.

I pressed on with the questioning in a kind of trance, putting my own feelings into suspended animation.

I said, "LEI's barrier is for filtering out *viruses and toxins.* You're talking about a natural substance which has been present for millions of years—"

"LEI's barrier will keep out everything they deem *nonessential.* The fetus doesn't *need* maternal cortisol in order to survive. If LEI doesn't explicitly include transporters for it, it won't get through. And I'll give you one guess what their plans are."

I said, "You're being paranoid. You think LEI would invest millions of dollars just to take part in a conspiracy to rid the world of homosexuals?"

Mendelsohn looked at me pityingly. "It's not a *conspiracy.* It's a *marketing opportunity.* LEI doesn't give a shit about the sexual politics. They could put in cortisol transporters, and sell the barrier as an anti-viral, anti-drug, anti-pollution screen. Or, they could leave them out, and sell it as all of that—plus a means of guaranteeing a heterosexual child. *Which do you think would earn the most money?*"

That question hit a nerve; I said angrily, "And you had so little faith in people's choice that you *bombed the laboratory* so that no one would ever have the chance to decide?"

Mendelsohn's expression turned stony. "I did *not* bomb LEI. Or irradiate their freezer."

"No? We've traced the cobalt 60 to Federation Centennial."

She looked stunned for a moment, then she said, "Congratulations. Six thousand other people work there, you know. I'm obviously not the only one of them who'd discovered what LEI is up to."

"You're the only one with access to the Biofile vault. What do you expect me to believe? That having learnt about this project, you were going to do absolutely nothing about it?"

"Of course not! And I still plan to publicize what they're doing. Let people know what it will mean. Try to get the issue debated before the product appears in a blaze of misinformation."

"You said you've known about the work for a year."

"Yes—and I've spent most of that time trying to verify all the facts, before opening my big mouth. Nothing would have been stupider than going public with half-baked rumors. I've only told about a dozen people so far, but we were going to launch a big publicity campaign to coincide with this year's Mardi Gras. Although now, with the bombing, everything's a thousand times more complicated." She spread her hands in a gesture of helplessness. "But we still have to do what we can, to try to keep the worst from happening."

"The worst?"

"Separatism. Paranoia. Homosexuality redefined as *pathological*. Lesbians and sympathetic straight women looking for their *own* technological means to *guarantee* the survival of the culture . . . while the religious far-right try to prosecute them for *poisoning their babies* . . . with a substance *God's* been happily 'poisoning' babies with for the last few thousand years! Sexual tourists traveling from wealthy countries where the technology is in use, to poorer countries where it isn't."

I was sickened by the vision she was painting—but I pushed on. "These dozen friends of yours—?"

Mendelsohn said dispassionately, "Go fuck yourself. I've got nothing more to say to you. I've told you the truth. I'm not a criminal. And I think you'd better leave."

I went to the bathroom and collected my notepad. In the doorway, I said, "If you're not a criminal, why are you so hard to track down?"

Wordlessly, contemptuously, she lifted her shirt and showed me the bruises below her rib cage—fading, but still an ugly sight. Whoever it was who'd beaten her—an ex-lover?—I could hardly blame her for doing everything she could to avoid a repeat performance.

On the stairs, I hit the REPLAY button on my notepad. The software computed the frequency spectrum for the noise of the running water, subtracted it out of the recording, and then amplified and cleaned up what remained. Every word of our conversation came through crystal clear.

From my car, I phoned a surveillance firm and arranged to have Mendelsohn kept under twenty-four-hour observation.

Halfway home, I stopped in a side street, and sat behind the wheel for ten minutes, unable to think, unable to move.

In bed that night, I asked Martin, "You're left-handed. How would you feel if no one was ever born left-handed again?"

"It wouldn't bother me in the least. Why?"

"You wouldn't think of it as a kind of . . . genocide?"

"Hardly. What's this all about?"

"Nothing. Forget it."

"You're shaking."

"I'm cold."

"You don't feel cold to me."

As we made love—tenderly, then savagely—I thought: *This is our language, this is our dialect. Wars have been fought over less. And if this language ever dies out, a people will have vanished from the face of the Earth.*

I knew I had to drop the case. If Mendelsohn was guilty, someone else could prove it. To go on working for LEI would destroy me.

Afterward, though . . . that seemed like sentimental bullshit. I belonged to no tribe. Every human being possessed their own sexuality—and when they died, it died with them. If no one was ever born gay again, it made no difference to *me*.

And if I dropped the case *because I was gay*, I'd be abandoning everything I'd ever believed about my own equality, my own identity . . . not to mention giving LEI the chance to announce: *Yes, of course we hired an investigator without regard to sexual preference—but apparently, that was a mistake.*

Staring up into the darkness, I said, "Every time I hear the word *community*, I reach for my revolver."

There was no response; Martin was fast asleep. I wanted to wake him, I wanted to argue it all through, there and then—but I'd signed an agreement, I couldn't tell him a thing.

So I watched him sleep, and tried to convince myself that when the truth came out, he'd understand.

I phoned Janet Lansing, brought her up to date on Mendelsohn—and said coldly, "Why were you so coy? *'Fanatics'? 'Powerful vested interests'?* Are there some words you have trouble pronouncing?"

She'd clearly prepared herself for this moment. "I didn't want to plant my own ideas in your head. Later on, that might have been seen as prejudicial."

"Seen as prejudicial by *whom*?" It was a rhetorical question: the media, of course. By keeping silent on the issue, she'd minimized the risk of being seen to have launched a witch-hunt. Telling me to go look for *homosexual terrorists* might have put LEI in a very unsympathetic light . . . whereas my finding Mendelsohn—for other reasons entirely, despite my ignorance—would come across as proof that the investigation had been conducted without any preconceptions.

I said, "You had your suspicions, and you should have disclosed them. At the very least, you should have told me what the barrier was *for*."

"The barrier," she said, "is for protection against viruses and toxins. But anything we do to the body has side effects. It's not my role to judge whether or not those side effects are acceptable; the regulatory authorities will insist that we publicize *all* of the consequences of using the product—and then the decision will be up to consumers.''

Very neat: the government would twist their arm, ''forcing them'' to disclose their major selling point!

''And what does your market research tell you?''

''That's strictly confidential.''

I very nearly asked her: *When exactly did you find out that I was gay? After you'd hired me—or before?* On the morning of the bombing, while I'd been assembling a dossier on Janet Lansing . . . had *she* been assembling dossiers on all of the people who might have bid for the investigation? And had she found the ultimate PR advantage, the ultimate seal of impartiality, just too tempting to resist?

I didn't ask. I still wanted to believe that it made no difference: she'd hired me, and I'd solve the crime like any other, and nothing else would matter.

I went to the bunker where the cobalt had been stored, at the edge of Federation Centennial's grounds. The trapdoor was solid, but the lock was a joke, and there was no alarm system at all; any smart twelve-year-old could have broken in. Crates full of all kinds of (low-level, shortlived) radioactive waste were stacked up to the ceiling, blocking most of the light from the single bulb; it was no wonder that the theft hadn't been detected sooner. There were even cobwebs—but no mutant spiders, so far as I could see.

After five minutes poking around, listening to my borrowed dosimetry badge adding up the exposure, I was glad to get out . . . whether or not the average chest X-ray would have done ten times more damage. *Hadn't Mendelsohn realized that: how irrational people were about radiation, how much harm it would do her cause once the cobalt was discovered? Or had her own—fully informed—knowledge of the minimal risks distorted her perception?*

The surveillance teams sent me reports daily. It was an expensive service, but LEI was paying. Mendelsohn met her friends openly—telling them all about the night I'd questioned her, warning them in outraged tones that they were almost certainly being watched. They discussed the fetal barrier, the options for—legitimate—opposition, the problems the bombing had caused them. I couldn't tell if the whole thing was being staged for my benefit, or if Mendelsohn was deliberately contacting only those friends who genuinely believed that she hadn't been involved.

I spent most of my time checking the histories of the people she met. I could find no evidence of past violence or sabotage by any of them—let alone experience with high explosives. But then, I hadn't seriously expected to be led straight to the bomber.

All I had was circumstantial evidence. All I could do was gather detail after detail, and hope that the mountain of facts I was assembling would eventually reach a critical mass—or that Mendelsohn would slip up, cracking under the pressure.

Weeks passed, and Mendelsohn continued to brazen it out. She even had pamphlets printed, ready to distribute at the Mardi Gras—condemning the bombing as loudly as they condemned LEI for its secrecy.

The nights grew hotter. My temper frayed. I don't know what Martin thought was happening to me, but I had no idea how we were going to survive the impending revelations. I couldn't begin to face up to the magnitude of the backlash there'd be once ATOMIC TERRORISTS met GAY BABY-POISONERS in the daily murdochs—and it would make no difference whether it was Mendelsohn's arrest which broke the news to the public, or her media conference blowing the whistle on LEI and proclaiming her own innocence; either way, the investigation would become a circus. I tried not to think about any of it; it was too late to do anything differently, to drop the case, to tell Martin the truth. So I worked on my tunnel vision.

Elaine scoured the radioactive waste bunker for evidence, but weeks of analysis came up blank. I quizzed the Biofile guards, who (supposedly) would have been watching the whole thing on their monitors when the cobalt was planted, but nobody could recall a client with an unusually large and oddly shaped item, wandering casually into the wrong aisle.

I finally obtained the warrants I needed to scrutinize Mendelsohn's entire electronic history since birth. She'd been arrested exactly once, twenty years before, for kicking an—unprivatized—policeman in the shin, during a protest he'd probably, privately, applauded. The charges had been dropped. She'd had a court order in force for the last eighteen months, restraining a former lover from coming within a kilometer of her home. (The woman was a musician with a band called Tetanus Switchblade; she had two convictions for assault.) There was no evidence of undeclared income, or unusual expenditure. No phone calls to or from known or suspected dealers in arms or explosives, or their known or suspected associates. But everything could have been done with pay phones and cash, if she'd organized it carefully.

Mendelsohn wasn't going to put a foot wrong while I was watching. However careful she'd been, though, she could not have carried out the bombing alone. What I needed was someone venal, nervous, or conscience-stricken enough to turn informant. I put out word on the usual channels: I'd be willing to pay, I'd be willing to bargain.

Six weeks after the bombing, I received an anonymous message by datamail:

Be at the Mardi Gras. No wires, no weapons. I'll find you.
29:17:5:31:23:11

I played with the numbers for more than an hour, trying to

make sense of them, before I finally showed them to Elaine.

She said, "Be careful, James."

"Why?"

"These are the ratios of the six trace elements we found in the residue from the explosion."

Martin spent the day of the Mardi Gras with friends who'd also be in the parade. I sat in my air-conditioned office and tuned in to a TV channel which showed the final preparations, interspersed with talking heads describing the history of the event. In forty years, the Gay and Lesbian Mardi Gras had been transformed from a series of ugly confrontations with police and local authorities, into a money-spinning spectacle advertised in tourist brochures around the world. It was blessed by every level of government, led by politicians and business identities—and the police, like most professions, now had their own float.

Martin was no transvestite (or muscle-bound leather-fetishist, or any other walking cliché); dressing up in a flamboyant costume, one night a year, was as false, as artificial, for him as it would have been for most heterosexual men. But I think I understood why he did it. He felt guilty that he could "pass for straight" in the clothes he usually wore, with the speech and manner and bearing which came naturally to him. He'd never concealed his sexuality from anyone—but it wasn't instantly apparent to total strangers. For him, taking part in the Mardi Gras was a gesture of solidarity with those gay men who *were* visible, obvious, all year round—and who'd borne the brunt of intolerance because of it.

As dusk fell, spectators began to gather along the route. Helicopters from every news service appeared overhead, turning their cameras on each other to prove to their viewers that this was An Event. Mounted crowd-control personnel—in something very much like the old blue uniform that had vanished when I was a child—parked their horses by the fast-food stands, and stood around fortifying themselves for the long night ahead.

I didn't see how the bomber could seriously expect to find me once I was mingling with a hundred thousand other people—so after leaving the Nexus building, I drove my car around the block slowly, three times, just in case.

By the time I'd made my way to a vantage point, I'd missed the start of the parade; the first thing I saw was a long line of people wearing giant plastic heads bearing the features of famous and infamous queers. (Apparently the word was back in fashion again, officially declared non-perjorative once more, after several years out of favor.) It was all so Disney I could have gagged—and yes, there was even Bernadette, the world's first lesbian cartoon mouse. I only recognized three of the humans portrayed—Patrick White, looking haggard and suitably bemused, Joe Orton, leering sardonically, and J. Edgar Hoover, with a Mephistophelian sneer. Everyone wore their names on sashes, though, for what that was worth. A young man beside me asked his girlfriend, "Who the hell was Walt Whitman?"

She shook her head. "No idea. Alan Turing?"

"Search me."

They photographed both of them, anyway.

I wanted to yell at the marchers: *So what? Some queers were famous. Some famous people were queer. What a surprise! Do you think that means you own them?*

I kept silent, of course—while everyone around me cheered and clapped. I wondered how close the bomber was, how long he or she would leave me sweating. Panopticon—the surveillance contractors—were still following Mendelsohn and all of her known associates, most of whom were somewhere along the route of the parade, handing out their pamphlets.

None of them appeared to have followed me, though. The bomber was almost certainly someone outside the network of friends we'd uncovered.

An anti-viral, anti-drug, anti-pollution barrier, alone—or a means of guaranteeing a heterosexual child. Which do you think would earn the most money? Surrounded by cheering spectators—half of them mixed-sex couples with children in tow—it was *almost* possible to laugh off Mendelsohn's fears. Who, here, would admit that they'd buy a version of the cocoon which would help wipe out the source of their entertainment? But applauding the freak show didn't mean wanting your own flesh and blood to join it.

An hour after the parade had started, I decided to move out of the densest part of the crowd. If the bomber couldn't reach me through the crush of people, there wasn't much point being here. A hundred or so leather-clad women on—noise-enhanced—electric motorbikes went riding past in a crucifix formation, behind a banner which read DYKES ON BIKES FOR JESUS. I recalled the small group of fundamentalists I'd passed earlier, their backs to the parade route lest they turn into pillars of salt, holding up candles and praying for rain.

I made my way to one of the food stalls, and bought a cold hot dog and a warm orange juice, trying to ignore the smell of horse turds. The place seemed to attract law enforcement types; J. Edgar Hoover himself came wandering by while I was eating, looking like a malevolent Humpty Dumpty.

As he passed me, he said, "Twenty-nine. Seventeen. Five."

I finished my hot dog and followed him.

He stopped in a deserted side street, behind a supermarket parking lot. As I caught up with him, he took out a magnetic scanner.

I said, "No wires, no weapons." He waved the device over me. I was telling the truth. "Can you talk through that thing?"

"Yes." The giant head bobbed strangely; I couldn't see any eye holes, but he clearly wasn't blind.

"Okay. Where did the explosives come from? We know they started off in Singapore, but who was your supplier here?"

Hoover laughed, deep and muffled. "I'm not going to tell you that. I'd be dead in a week."

"So what *do* you want to tell me?"

"That I only did the grunt work. Mendelsohn organized everything."

"No shit. But what have you got that will prove it? Phone calls? Financial transactions?"

He just laughed again. I was beginning to wonder how many people in the parade would know who'd played J. Edgar Hoover; even if he clammed up now, it was possible that I'd be able to track him down later.

That was when I turned and saw six more, identical, Hoovers coming around the corner. They were all carrying baseball bats.

I started to move. Hoover One drew a pistol and aimed it at my face. He said, "Kneel down slowly, with your hands behind your head."

I did it. He kept the gun on me, and I kept my eyes on the trigger, but I heard the others arrive, and close into a half-circle behind me.

Hoover One said, "Don't you know what happens to traitors? Don't you know what's going to happen to you?"

I shook my head slowly. I didn't know what I could say to appease him, so I spoke the truth. "How can I be a traitor? What is there to betray? Dykes on Bikes for Jesus? The William S. Burroughs Dancers?"

Someone behind me swung their bat into the small of my back. Not as hard as they might have; I lurched forward, but I kept my balance.

Hoover One said, "Don't you know any history, Mr. Pig? Mr. *Polizei?* The Nazis put us in their death camps. The Reaganites tried to have us all die of AIDS. And here you are now, Mr. Pig, working for the fuckers who want to wipe us off the face of the planet. That sounds like betrayal to *me.*"

I knelt there, staring at the gun, unable to speak. I couldn't dredge up the words to justify myself. The truth was too difficult, too gray, too confusing. My teeth started chattering. *Nazis. AIDS. Genocide.* Maybe he was right. Maybe I deserved to die.

I felt tears on my cheeks. Hoover One laughed. "Boo hoo, Mr. Pig." Someone swung their bat onto my shoulders. I fell forward on my face, too afraid to move my hands to break the fall; I tried to get up, but a boot came down on the back of my neck.

Hoover One bent down and put the gun to my skull. He whispered, "Will you close the case? Lose the evidence on Catherine? You know, your boyfriend frequents some dangerous places; he needs all the friends he can get."

I lifted my face high enough above the asphalt to reply. "Yes."

"Well done, Mr. Pig."

That was when I heard the helicopter.

I blinked the gravel out of my eyes and saw the ground, far brighter than it should have been; there was a spotlight trained on us. I waited for the sound of a bullhorn. Nothing happened. I waited for my assailants to flee. Hoover One took his foot off my neck.

And then they all laid into me with their baseball bats.

I should have curled up and protected my head, but curiosity got the better of me; I turned and stole a glimpse of the chopper. It was a news crew, of course, refusing to do anything unethical like spoil a good story just when it was getting telegenic. That much made perfect sense.

But the goon squad made no sense at all. Why were they sticking around, now that the cameras were running? Just for the pleasure of beating me for a few seconds longer?

Nobody was *that* stupid, that oblivious to PR.

I coughed up two teeth and hid my face again. *They wanted it all to be broadcast.* They *wanted* the headlines, the backlash, the outrage. ATOMIC TERRORISTS! BABY-POISONERS! BRUTAL THUGS!

They wanted to demonize the enemy they were pretending to be.

The Hoovers finally dropped their bats and started running. I lay on the ground drooling blood, too weak to lift my head to see what had driven them away.

A while later, I heard hoofbeats. Someone dropped to the ground beside me and checked my pulse.

I said, "I'm not in pain. I'm happy. I'm delirious."

Then I passed out.

On his second visit, Martin brought Catherine Mendelsohn to the hospital with him. They showed me a recording of LEI's media conference, the day after the Mardi Gras—two hours before Mendelsohn's was scheduled to take place.

Janet Lansing said, "In the light of recent events, we have no choice but to go public. We would have preferred to keep this technology under wraps for commercial reasons, but innocent lives are at stake. And when people turn on their own kind—"

I burst the stitches in my lips laughing.

LEI had bombed their own laboratory. They'd irradiated their own cells. And they'd hoped that I'd cover up for Mendelsohn, once the evidence led me to her, out of sympathy with her cause. Later, with a tip-off to an investigative reporter or two, the cover-up would have been revealed.

The perfect climate for their product launch.

Since I'd continued with the investigation, though, they'd had to make the best of it: sending in the Hoovers, claiming to be linked to Mendelsohn, to punish me for my diligence.

Mendelsohn said, "Everything LEI leaked about me—the cobalt, my key to the vault—was already spelt out in the pamphlets I'd printed, but that doesn't seem to cut much ice with the murdochs. I'm the Harbor Bridge Gamma Ray Terrorist now."

"You'll never be charged."

"Of course not. So I'll never be found innocent, either."

I said, "When I'm out of here, I'm going after them." *They wanted impartiality? An investigation untainted by prejudice? They'd get exactly what they paid for, this time. Minus the tunnel vision.*

Martin said softly, "Who's going to employ you to do that?"

I smiled, painfully. "LEI's insurance company."

When they'd left, I dozed off.

I woke suddenly, from a dream of suffocation.

Even if I proved that the whole thing had been a marketing exercise by LEI—even if half their directors were thrown in prison, even if the company itself was liquidated—the technology would still be owned by *someone*.

And one way or another, in the end, it would be *sold*.

That's what I'd missed, in my fanatical neutrality: you can't sell a cure without a disease. So even if I was right to be neutral—even if there was no difference to fight for, no difference to betray, no difference to preserve—the best way to *sell* the cocoon would always be to invent one. And even if it would be no tragedy at all if there was nothing left but heterosexuality in a century's time, the only path which could lead there would be one of lies, and wounding, and vilification.

Would people buy that, or not?

I was suddenly very much afraid that they would.

THE GORGON FIELD

Kate Wilhelm

*"The Gorgon Field" was purchased by Shawna Mc-
Carthy, and appeared in the August 1985 issue of
Asimov's, with a cover by J. K. Potter and an interior illustration by Stephen L. Gervais. Wilhelm is
another writer who doesn't appear in Asimov's as
often as we'd like, but each appearance has been
significant, including her story "The Girl Who Fell
into the Sky," which won a Nebula Award in 1987.
Kate Wilhelm began publishing in 1956, and by now
is widely regarded as one of the best of today's writers. Wilhelm won a Nebula Award in 1968 for her
short story, "The Planners," took a Hugo in 1976
for her novel* Where Late the Sweet Birds Sang, *and
won yet another Nebula in 1988 for her story "Forever Yours, Anna." Her many books include the novels* Margaret and I, Fault Lines, The Clewisten Test,
Juniper Time, Welcome, Chaos, Oh, Susannah!,
Huysman's Pets, *and* Cambio Bay, *and the collections* The Downstairs Room, Somerset Dreams, The
Infinity Box, Listen, Listen, Children of the Wind,
and And the Angels Sing. *Wilhelm and her husband,
writer Damon Knight, ran the famous Milford
Writer's Conference for many years, and both were
involved for many years in the operation of the* Clar-
ion *workshop for new young writers. She lives with
her family in Eugene, Oregon.*

Wilhelm's work has never been limited to the strict boundaries of the field, and she has published mainstream thrillers and comic novels as well as science fiction. In recent years, she has become particularly well-known as a mystery novelist, with a long series of novels and stories about the detecting team of Constance Leidl and Charlie Meiklejohn, a series that started in the pages of Asimov's *with the story "With Thimbles, with Forks, with Hope," and has gone on to include well-known mystery novels such as* The Hamlet Trap, Smart House, Seven Kinds of Death, The Dark Door, *and* Sweet, Sweet Poison. *The Leidl and Meiklejohn stories have been collected in* A Flush of Shadows. *Wilhelm's other mystery novels include* Death Qualified, The Best Defense, *and* Justice for Some.*

In the engrossing story that follows, one of the best of the Leidl and Meiklejohn stories, she shows us that although it's a detective's duty to follow a path into the heart of even the most complex of mazes, getting out of the labyrinth again once you get in may turn out to be the most difficult and dangerous part of the job . . .

Constance took the call that morning; when she hung up there was a puzzled expression on her face. "Why us?" she asked rhetorically.

"Why not us?" Charlie asked back.

She grinned at him and sat down at the breakfast table where he was finishing his French toast.

"That," she said, pouring more coffee, "was Deborah Rice, née Wyandot, heiress to one of the world's great fortunes. She wants to come talk to us this afternoon, and she lied to me."

His interest rose slightly, enough to make him look up from the newspaper. "About what?"

"She claims we know people in common and that we probably met in school. I knew she was there, it would be like trying to hide Prince Charles, I should think, but I never met her, and she knows it.''

''So why did you tell her to come on out?''

''I'm not sure. She wanted us to come to her place in Bridgeport and when I said no, she practically pleaded for an appointment here. I guess that did it. I don't think she pleads for many things, or ever has.''

It was April; the sun was warm already, the roses were budding, the daffodils had come and gone, and the apple trees were in bloom. Too pretty to leave right now, Constance thought almost absently, and pushed a cat away from under the table with her foot. It was the evil cat Brutus who had always been a city cat, still wanted to be a city cat, and didn't give a damn about the beauty of the country in April. He wanted toast, or bacon, anything that might land on the floor. The other two cats were out hunting, or sunning themselves, or doing something else catlike. Brutus was scrounging for food. And Charlie, not yet showered and shaved, his black hair like a bush, a luxuriant overnight growth of bristly beard like a half mask on his swarthy face, making him look more like a hood than a country gentleman, cared just about as much for the beautiful fresh morning as the cat. Constance admitted this to herself reluctantly. He had been glad to leave the city after years on the police force, following as many years as a fire marshal, but she felt certain that he did not see what she saw when he looked out the window at their miniature farm. On the other hand, she continued the thought firmly, he slept well, and he looked wonderful and felt wonderful. But he did miss the city. She had been thinking for weeks that they should do something different, get away for a short time, almost anything. There had been several cases they could have taken, but nothing that seemed worth the effort of shattering the state of inertia they had drifted into.

Maybe Deborah Rice would offer something different, she thought then, and that was really why she had told her to come on out.

"My father," Deborah Rice said that afternoon, "is your typical ignorant multi-millionaire."

"Mother," Lori Rice cried, "stop it! It isn't fair!"

Constance glanced at Charlie, then back to their guests, mother and daughter. Deborah Rice was about fifty, wearing a fawn-colored cashmere suit with a silk blouse the exact same color. Lori was in jeans and sneakers, and was thirteen. Both had dusky skin tones, although their eyes were bright blue. The automobile they had arrived in, parked out in the driveway, was a baby-blue Continental, so new that probably it never had been washed.

"All right," Deborah said to her daughter. "It isn't fair, nevertheless it's true. He never went past the sixth grade, if that far. He doesn't know anything except business, his business." She turned to Constance. "He's ignorant, but he isn't crazy."

"Mrs. Rice," Charlie said then in his drawly voice that made him sound half asleep, or bored, "exactly what is it you wanted to see us about?"

She nodded. "Do you know who my father is, Mr. Meiklejohn?"

"Carl Wyandot. I looked him up while we were waiting for you to arrive."

"He is worth many millions of dollars," she said, "and he has kept control of his companies, all of them, except what he got tired of. And now my brother is threatening to cause a scandal and accuse my father of senility."

Charlie was shaking his head slowly; he looked very unhappy now. "I'm afraid you need attorneys, not us."

He glanced at Constance. Her mouth had tightened slightly, probably not enough to be noticeable to anyone else, but he saw it. She would not be interested either, he knew. No court appearance as a tame witness, a prostitute, paid to offer testimony proving or disproving sanity, not for her. Besides, she was not qualified; she was a psychologist, retired, not a psychiatrist. For an instant he had an eerie feeling that the second thought had been hers. He looked at her sharply; she was studying Deborah Rice with bright interest. A suggestion of a smile had eased the tightness of her mouth.

And Deborah seemed to settle deeper in her chair. "Hear me out," she said. Underlying the imperious tone was another tone that might have been fear. "Just let me tell you about it. Please."

Constance looked at Lori, who was teasing Brutus, tickling his ears, restoring his equanimity with gentle strokes, then tickling again. Lori was a beautiful child, and if having access to all the money in the world had spoiled her, it did not show. She was just beginning to curve with adolescence, although her eyes were very aware. She knew the danger in teasing a full-grown, strange cat.

"We'll listen, of course," Constance said easily to Deborah Rice, accepting for now the presence of the girl.

"Thank you. My father is eighty," she said, her voice becoming brisk and businesslike. "And he is in reasonably good health. Years ago he bought a little valley west of Pueblo, Colorado, in the mountains. Over the last few years he's stayed there more and more, and now he's there almost all the time. He has his secretary, and computers, modems, every convenience, and really there's no reason why he can't conduct business from the house. The home office is in Denver and there are offices in New York, California, England. But he's in control. You have to understand that. There are vice-presidents and managers and God knows what to carry out his orders, and it's been like that for twenty-five years. Nothing has changed in that respect. My brother can't make a case that he's neglecting the business."

Charlie watched Brutus struggle with indecision, and finally decide that he was being mistreated. He did not so much jump from Lori's lap as flow off to the floor; he stretched, hoisted his tail, and stalked out without a backward glance. Lori began to pick at a small scab on her elbow. The fragrance of apple blossoms drifted through the room. Charlie swallowed a yawn.

"I live in Bridgeport," Deborah was saying. "My husband is the conductor of the symphony orchestra, and we're busy with our own lives. Admittedly I haven't spent a great deal of time with Father in the last years, but neither has Tony, my brother. Anyway, last month Tony called me to say Father was having psychological problems. I flew out to Colorado immediately. Lori went with me." She turned her gaze toward her daughter. She took a deep breath, then continued. "Father was surrounded by his associates, as usual. People are always in and out. They use the company helicopter to go back and forth. At first I couldn't see anything at all different, but then . . . There's a new man out there. He calls himself Ramón, claims he's a Mexican friend of a friend, or something, and he has a terrible influence over my father. This is what bothered Tony so much."

Constance and Charlie exchanged messages in a glance. Hers was, *they'll go away pretty soon, be patient*. His was, *let's give them the bum's rush*. Deborah Rice was frowning slightly at nothing in particular. And now, Constance realized, Lori was putting on an act, pretending interest in a magazine she had picked up. She was unnaturally still, as if she was holding her breath.

Finally Deborah went on. "Tony believes Ramón was responsible for the firing of two of his, Tony's, subordinates at the house. It's like a little monarchy," she said with some bitterness. "Everyone has spies, intrigues. The two people Father fired alerted Tony about Ramón. Tony's office is in New York, you see."

"That hardly seems like enough to cause your brother to assume your father's losing it," Charlie said bluntly.

"No, of course not. There are other things. Tony's convinced that Father is completely dominated by Ramón. He's trying to gather evidence. You see, Ramón is . . . strange."

"He's a shaman," Lori said, her face flushed. She ducked her head and mumbled, "He can do magic and Grandpa knows it." She leafed through the magazine, turning pages rapidly.

"And do you know it, too?" Charlie asked.

"Sure. I saw him do magic."

Deborah sighed. "That's why I brought her," she said. "Go on and tell them."

It came out in a torrent; obviously this was what she had been waiting for. "I was at the end of the valley, where the stone formations are, and Ramón came on a horse and got off it and began to sing. Chant, not really sing. And then he was on top of one of the pillars and singing to the setting sun. Only you can't get up there. I mean, they just go straight up, hundreds of feet up. But he was up there until the sun went down and I ran home and didn't even stop."

She turned another page of the magazine. Very gently Charlie asked, "Did Ramón see you when he rode up on his horse?"

She continued to look at the pages. "I guess he saw me run. From up there you could see the whole valley." Her face looked pinched when she raised her head and said to Charlie, "You think I'm lying? Or that I'm crazy? Like Uncle Tony thinks Grandpa is crazy?"

"No, I don't think you're crazy," he said soberly. "Of course, I'm not the expert in those matters. Are you crazy?"

''No! I saw it! I wasn't sleeping or dreaming or smoking dope or having an adolescent fantasy!'' She shot a scornful look at her mother, then ducked her head again and became absorbed in the glossy advertising.

Deborah looked strained and older than her age. ''Will you please go out and bring in the briefcase?'' she asked quietly. ''I brought pictures of the formations she's talking about,'' she added to Constance and Charlie.

Lori left them after a knowing look, as if very well aware that they wanted to talk about her.

''Is it possible that she was molested?'' Constance asked as soon as she was out of the house.

''I thought of that. She ran in that day in a state of hysteria. I took her to her doctor, of course, but there was no evidence that anything like that happened.''

''Mrs. Rice,'' Charlie said then, ''that was a month ago. Why are you here now, today?''

She bit her lip and took a deep breath. ''Lori is an accomplished musician, violin and flute, piano. She can play almost any instrument she handles. It's a real gift. Recently, last week, I kept hearing this weird, that's the only word I can think of, weird music. Over and over, first on one instrument, then another. I finally demanded that she tell me what she was up to, and she admitted she was trying to recreate the chant Ramón had sung. She's obsessed with it, with him, perhaps. It frightened me. If one encounter with him could affect her that much, what is he doing to my father? Maybe Tony's right. I don't know what I think anymore.''

''Have you thought of counseling for her?'' Constance asked.

''Yes. She didn't cooperate, became defensive, accused me of thinking she's crazy. It's so ridiculous and at the same time terrifying. We had a good relationship until this happened.

She always was close to her father and me until this. Now
... You saw the look she gave me.''

And how much of that was due to adolescent string cutting,
how much due to Ramón? Constance let it go when Lori
returned with the briefcase.

"One last question," Charlie said a little later, after ex-
amining the photographs of the valley. Lori had gone outside
to look for the cats; she had asked permission without prompt-
ing, apparently now bored with the conversation. "Why us?
Your brother has hired detectives, presumably, to check on
Ramón." She nodded. "And you could buy a hospital and
staff it with psychiatrists, if you wanted that. What do you
want us to do?''

She looked embarrassed suddenly. She twisted her watch
band and did not look directly at them now. "Tony had a
woman sent out, a detective," she said hesitantly. "Within a
week she left the valley and refused to go back. I think she
was badly frightened." She glanced at Charlie then away. "I
may be asking you to do something dangerous. I just don't
know. But I don't think the detectives looking for Ramón's
past will come up with anything. They haven't yet. Whatever
secret he has, whatever he can or can't do, is out there in the
valley. Expose him, discredit him, or ... or prove he is what
he claims. Father named the valley. The Valley of Gorgons.
I said he's ignorant and he is. He didn't know who the Gorgons were. He named the valley after the formations, thinking,
I suppose, the people turned to stone were the Gorgons. He
hasn't read any of the literature about shamanism, either, none
of the Don Juan books, nothing like that. But Ramón has
studied them all, I'd be willing to bet. It will take someone
as clever as he is to expose him and I just don't think Tony's
detectives will be capable of it.''

"Specifically what do you want us to do?" Charlie asked
in his sleepy voice. Constance felt a chill when she realized

that he had taken on the case already no matter what exactly Deborah was asking of them.

"Go out there and spend a week, two weeks, however long it takes and find out what hold he has on my father. Find out how he fools so many people into believing in his magic. Prove he's a charlatan out for my father's money. I'll be there. You can be my guests. I've done that before, had guests at the house."

"Will you take Lori?" Charlie asked.

"No! She'll never see him again! This fascination will pass. She'll forget him. I'm concerned for my father."

Their tickets had arrived by special delivery the day following Deborah's visit, first class to Denver, where, she had told them, they would be met. Their greeter at Stapleton had been a charming, dimpled young woman who had escorted them to a private lounge and introduced Captain Smollet, who was to fly them to Pueblo in the company plane, as soon as their baggage was available. In Pueblo they had been met again, by another lovely young woman who gave them keys to a Cadillac Seville and a map to the Valley of Gorgons and wished them luck in finding it.

And now Charlie was driving the last miles, according to the map, which had turned out to be much better than the road maps he was used to. Deborah had offered to have them met by the company helicopter which could take them all the way to the house, and Constance had refused politely, and adamantly. She would walk first. The scenery was breathtaking, sheer cliffs with high trees on the upper reaches, piñons and stunted desert growth at the lower elevations, and, watered by the run-off of spring, green everywhere. All the peaks gleamed with snow, melt-water streams cascaded down the precipitous slopes, and it seemed that the world was covered with columbines in profuse bloom, more brilliant that Constance had dreamed they could be.

At the turn they came to next they were warned by a neat sign that this was a dead-end road, private property, no admittance. The woods pressed closer here, made a canopy overhead. In the perpetual shadows snow lingered in drifts that were only faintly discolored. They climbed briefly, made a sweeping turn, and Charlie braked.

"Holy Christ!" he breathed.

Constance gasped in disbelief as he brought the Cadillac to a stop on the side of the mountain road. Below was the Valley of Gorgons. It looked as if a giant had pulled the mountain apart to create a deep, green Eden with a tiny stream sparkling in the sunshine, groves of trees here and there, a small dam and a lake that was the color of the best turquoise. A meadow was in the center of the valley, with horses that looked like toys. Slowly Charlie began to drive again, but he stopped frequently and the houses and outbuildings became more detailed, less doll-like. And finally they had gone far enough to be able to turn and see for the first time the sandstone formations that had given the valley its name. It was late afternoon; the sunlight shafted through the pillars. They looked like frozen flames—red, red-gold, red with black streaks, yellow. . . . Frozen flames leaping toward the sky.

The valley, according to the map, was about six miles long, tapered at the east end to a blunt point, with two leg-like projections at the western end, one of them nearly two miles long, the other one and a half miles, both roughly fifty feet wide, and in many places much narrower. The lake and several buildings took up the first quarter of the valley, then the main house and more buildings, with a velvety lawn surrounding them all, ended at the half-way point. The meadow with the grazing horses made up the next quarter and the sandstone formations filled the rest. At the widest point the valley was two miles across, but most of it was less than that. The stream was a flashing ribbon that clung close to the base of the cliffs. There was no natural inlet to the valley except for the tumbled rocks the stream had dislodged. A true hidden valley, Constance thought, awed by the beauty, the perfect containment of a small Eden.

Deborah met them at the car. Close behind her was a slender young Chicano. She spoke rapid Spanish to him and he nodded. "Come in," she said to Constance and Charlie then. "I hope your trip was comfortable, not too tiring. I'm glad you're here. This is Manuel. He'll be at your beck and call for the duration of your visit, and he speaks perfect English, so don't let him kid you about that." Manuel grinned sheepishly.

"How do you do?" Constance said to the youth. "Just Manuel?"

"Just Manuel, Señora," he said. His voice was soft, the words not quite slurred, but easy.

Charlie spoke to him and went behind the car to open the trunk, get out their suitcases.

"Please, Señor," he said, "permit me. I will place your things in your rooms."

"You might as well let him," Deborah said with a shrug. "Look." She was looking past them and the car toward the end of the valley.

The golden globe of the sun was balanced on the highest peak of the formations. It began to roll off; the pillars turned midnight black with streaks of light blazing between them too bright to bear. Their fire had been extinguished and the whole world flamed behind them. No one spoke or moved until the sun dropped behind the mountain peak in the distance and the sky was awash in sunset colors of cerise and green and rose-gold; the pillars were simply dark forms against the gaudy backdrop.

Charlie was the first one to move. He had been holding the keys; now he extended them toward Manuel, and realized that the boy was regarding Constance with a fixed gaze. When Charlie looked at her, there were tears in her eyes. He touched her arm. "Hey," he said gently. "You okay?"

She roused with a start. "I must be more tired than I realized."

"Sí," Manuel said then and took the keys.

Deborah led them into the house. The house kept changing, Charlie thought as they entered. From up on the cliff it had not looked very large or imposing. The bottom half was finished in gray stone the color of the granite cliffs behind it. The upper floor had appeared to be mostly glass and pale wood. Above that a steep roof had gleamed with skylights. It had grown as they approached until it seemed to loom over everything else; none of the other buildings was two stories high. But as soon as they were inside, everything changed again. They were in a foyer with a red tile floor; there were many immense clay pots with greenery: trees, bushes, and flowering plants perfumed the air. Ahead, the foyer widened, became an indoor courtyard, and the light was suffused with the rose tints of sunset. The proportions were not inhuman here; the feeling was of comfort and simplicity and warmth. In the center of the courtyard was a pool with a fountain made of greenish quartz and granite.

"Father said it was to help humidify the air," Deborah said. "But actually he just likes it."

"Me too," Charlie agreed.

"It's all incredible," Constance said. They were moving toward a wide, curving staircase, and stopped when a door opened across the courtyard and a man stepped out, leaning on a gnarly cane. He was wearing blue jeans and a chamois shirt and boots. His hair was silver.

"Father," Deborah said, and motioned for Charlie and

Constance to come. "These are my friends I mentioned. They got here in time for the sunset."

"I know," he said. "I was upstairs watching too." His eyes were on Constance. They were so dark they looked black, and his skin was deeply tanned.

Deborah introduced them. He did not offer to shake hands, but bowed slightly. "Mi casa es su casa," he said. "Please join me for supper." He bowed again and stepped back into what they could now see was an elevator. "And you, of course," he added to his daughter and the door closed on him.

"Well," Deborah said with an undercurrent of unease, "aren't you the honored ones? Sometimes people are here a week before they even see him, much less have a meal with him." She gave Constance a searching look. "He was quite taken with you."

"Does he have rheumatoid arthritis?" Constance asked as they resumed their way toward the stairs, started up.

"Yes. Most of the time it's under control, but it is painful. He says he feels better here than anywhere else. I guess the aridity helps."

The courtyard soared to the skylights. On the second floor a wide balcony overlooked it; there were Indian rugs on the walls between doors, and on the floor. It was bright and informal and lovely, Constance thought again. It did not surprise her a bit that Carl Wyandot felt better here than anywhere else.

Deborah took them to two rooms at the south-east corner of the house. There was a spacious bathroom with a tub big enough to lie down in and float. If they wanted anything, she told them, please ring. She had not been joking about Manuel being at their disposal. He was their personal attendant for the duration of their visit. Dinner would be at seven. She would come for them shortly before that. "And don't dress up," she added at the door. "No one ever does here. I'll keep on what I'm wearing." She was dressed in chinos and a cow-boy shirt with pointed flaps over the breast pockets, and a wide belt with a huge silver buckle.

As soon as she was gone and the door firmly closed, Charlie took Constance by the shoulders and studied her face intently. "What is it, honey? What's wrong?"

"Wrong? Nothing. That's what's wrong, nothing is. Does that make any sense?"

"No," he said bluntly, not releasing her.

"Didn't you feel it when we first got out of the car?" Her pale blue eyes were sparkling, there was high color on her fair cheeks, as if she had a fever. He touched her forehead and she laughed. "I felt something, and then when the sunset flared, it was like an electric jolt. Didn't you feel that?"

"I wish to hell we were home."

"Maybe we are. Maybe I'll never want to leave here." She spoke lightly, and now she moved away from his hands to go to the windows. "I wish we could have had a room on the west side. But I suppose he has that whole end of the house. I would if it were mine."

"It's just a big expensive house on an expensive piece of real estate," he said. "All it takes is enough money."

She shook her head. "Oh, no. That's not it. All the money on earth wouldn't buy what's out there."

"And what's that?"

"Magic. This is a magic place."

They dined in Carl Wyandot's private sitting room. Here too were the decorative Indian and Mexican rugs, the wall hangings, the pots with lush plants. And here the windows were nearly floor to ceiling with drapes that had been opened all the way. He had the entire western side of the second floor, as Constance had guessed he would. When she saw how he handled his silverware, she knew Deborah had been right;

they were being honored. His hands were misshapen with arthritis, drawn into awkward angles, the knuckles enlarged and sore looking. He was a proud man; he would not permit many strangers to gawk.

The fifth member of the party was Ramón. Thirty, forty, older? Constance could not tell. His eyes were a warm brown, his face smooth, his black hair moderately short and straight. He had a lithe, wiry build, slender hands. And, she thought, if she had to pick one word to use to describe him, it would be stillness. Not rigidity or strain, but a natural stillness. He did not fidget or make small talk or respond to rhetorical questions, and yet he did not give the impression of being bored or withdrawn. He was dressed in jeans and a long-sleeved plaid shirt; in this establishment it appeared that only the servants dressed up. The two young men who waited on them wore black trousers, white dress shirts and string ties. They treated Ramón with perhaps a shade more reverence than they showed Wyandot.

Charlie was telling about the day he had run into one of the arsonists he had put away who was then out of prison. "He introduced me to his pals, told them who I was, what I had done, all of it, as if he was proud. Then we sat down and had a beer and talked. He wasn't resentful, but rather pleased to see me again."

Carl Wyandot nodded. "Preserving the order of the cosmos is always a pleasing experience. He had his role, you had yours. But you can't really be retired after being so active, not at your age!"

He was too shrewd to lie to, Charlie decided, and he shook his head. "I do private investigations now and then. And Constance writes books and does workshops sometimes. We stay busy."

Deborah was the only one who seemed shocked by this disclosure.

"Actually I'm planning a book now," Constance said. "It will deal with the various superstitions that continue to survive even in this super-rational age. Like throwing coins into a fountain. That goes so far back that no one knows for certain when it began. We assume that it was to propitiate the Earth Goddess for the water that the people took from her. It has variations throughout the literature."

"To what end?" Carl Wyandot asked. "To debunk or explain or what?"

"I don't debunk things of that sort," she said. "They are part of our heritage. I accept the theory that the archetypes are patterns of possible behavior, they determine how we perceive and react to the world, and usually they can't be explained or described. They come to us as visions, or dream images, and they come to all of us in the same forms over and over. Civilized, educated Westerner, African native who has never seen a book, they have the same dream images, the same impulses in their response to the archetypes. If we try to bury them, deny them, we are imperiling our own psyches."

"Are you not walking the same ground that Carl Jung plowed?" Ramón asked. He spoke with the polite formality of one whose English was a second language, learned in school.

"It's his field," Constance said. "But it's a very big field and he opened it to all. His intuition led him to America, you know, to study the dreams of the Hopi, but he did not pursue it very far. One lifetime was not long enough, although it was a very long and very productive lifetime."

"Did he not say that good sometimes begets evil? And that evil necessarily begets evil."

"Where did he say that? I don't recall it."

"Perhaps I am mistaken. However, he knew that this inner

voyage of discovery can be most dangerous. Only the very brave dare risk it, or the very foolish.''

Constance nodded soberly. "He did say the brighter the light, the darker the shadow. The risk may be in coming across the shadow that is not only darker than you expected, but larger, large enough to swallow you."

Ramón bowed slightly. "We shall talk again, I hope, before your visit comes to an end. Now, please forgive me, Don Carlos, but it is late."

"Yes, it is," the old man said. "Our guests have had a very long day." One of the servants appeared behind his chair; others seemed to materialize, and the evening was over.

"Thank you, Mr. Wyandot," Constance said. "It was a good evening."

"For me as well," he said, and he looked at Ramón. "You heard what he called me. Please, you also, call me that. It sounds less formal, don't you agree?"

Deborah walked to their room with them. At the door she said abruptly, "May I come in and have a drink?"

Someone had been there. The beds were turned down in one room, and in the other a tray had been brought up with bottles, glasses, an ice bucket. Charlie went to examine the bottles and Constance said she wanted coffee. Deborah rang and it seemed only an instant before there was a soft knock; she asked Manuel to bring coffee and then sat down and accepted the drink Charlie had poured for her.

"You just don't realize what happened tonight," she said after taking a long drink. "Father doesn't usually see strangers at all. He doesn't ask them to dinner. He doesn't introduce them to Ramón. And he doesn't take a back seat and watch others engage in conversation. Skoal!" She drank again, then added, "And Ramón was as gabby as a school girl. Another first. He said more to you tonight than he's ever said to me."

Manuel came back with coffee and Deborah finished her

drink and stood up. "Tomorrow when you wake up, just ring for breakfast. That's what we all do. No one but the managers and people like that eat in the dining room. Wander to your heart's content and I'll see you around noon and give you the grand tour. Okay?"

As soon as she was gone, Charlie turned to Constance. "He was warning you loud and clear," he said.

"I know."

"I don't like it."

"I think we're keeping order in the cosmos," she said thoughtfully. "And I think it's better that way. Now for those books."

They had asked Deborah for everything in the house about her father, the history of the area, geology, whatever was available. Deborah had furnished a dozen books at least. Reluctantly Charlie put his drink aside and poured coffee for himself. It would be a while before they got to bed.

It was nearly two hours later when Constance closed her book with a snap, and saw that Charlie was regarding her with brooding eyes.

"Wow," he said softly.

"The biography?"

"Yeah. Want me to paraphrase the early years?" At her nod, he took a deep breath and started. "Tom Wyandot had a falling out with his family, a good, established English family of lawyers back in Virginia. He headed west, looked for gold in California and Mexico, got married to a Mexican woman, had a son, Carl. He heard there was a lot of gold still in Colorado, and headed for the mountains with his wife, Carl, two Mexican men, an Indian guide, and the wife of one of the men. At some point a gang of outlaws got on their trail and the Indian brought the party to the valley to hide. A few nights later the outlaws made a sneak attack and killed everyone but Tom Wyandot and the child Carl. Tom managed to

hide them among the formations. The next day he buried the
rest of the group, including his wife, and he and the boy
started out on foot, forty miles to Pueblo, with no supplies,
horses, anything else. They got there almost dead. Carl was
five.''

Constance's eyes were distant, unfocused. He knew she was
visualizing the scenes; he continued. ''For the next eight years
Tom prowled the mountains, sometimes taking Carl, sometimes alone. Then he died, and it's a little unclear just how.
Carl was with him, on one of their rambles, and Carl returned
alone. He said his father had fallen over a cliff. He led a
search party to the location and they recovered the body, buried him in Pueblo, and Carl took off. He turns up next a year
later in Texas, where he later struck it rich in oil.''

Constance pulled herself back with a sigh. ''Oh dear,'' she
murmured. ''Carl bought the valley in nineteen thirty. He
started construction in nineteen forty.'' She frowned. ''I wonder just when he located the valley again.''

''Me too. But right now, what I'm thinking is that my body
seems to believe it's way past bedtime. It won't have any
truck with clocks.''

''The idea is to bake yourself first and then jump into the
lake,'' Constance said the next day, surveying the sauna with
approval.

''No way. You have any idea of the temperature of the
lake?''

''I know, but it'll have to do. There just isn't any snow
around.''

''That isn't exactly what I meant,'' he said acidly.

''Oh?'' Her look of innocence was a parody; they both
laughed. ''I'm not kidding, you'll really be surprised. You'll
love it.''

They wandered on. Swimming pool, steam room, gymna-

sium, Jacuzzi, a boathouse with canoes and rowboats . . . One
of the other buildings held offices, another was like a motel
with its own coffee shop. There were other outbuildings for
machinery, maintenance equipment, garages, and a hangar.
The helicopter, Charlie remembered. It was impossible to es-
timate the size of the staff. They kept catching glimpses of
servants—the males in black trousers and white shirts, the
females in gaily patterned dresses or skirts and blouses. They
introduced themselves to several of the men Deborah had
called the managers, all in sports clothes, all looking as if
they were wearing invisible gray suits.

"It's a whole damn city," Charlie complained. They had
left the main complex and were walking along a path that was
leading them to a grove of cottonwood trees. Ahead were
several cottages, well separated, very private. They stopped.
Ramón was coming toward them.

"Good morning," Constance called to him. "What a
lovely morning!"

He nodded. "Good morning. I intended finding you, to in-
vite you to dinner in my house. It would give me honor."

Charlie felt a flash of irritation when Constance agreed
without even glancing toward him. He would have said yes
also, but usually they consulted silently, swiftly. And why was
Ramón making it easy? he wondered glumly. He knew damn
well they were there to investigate him. Ramón bowed slightly
and went back the way he had come, and they turned to go
the other way. Charlie's uneasiness increased when it occurred
to him that Ramón had stalled their unannounced visit very
neatly.

When Deborah met them at noon, she had a jeep waiting
to take them to the gorgons. The first stop was at a fenced
area at the far end of the meadow. Inside the fence, smooth,
white river stones had been laid in a mound. A bronze plaque
had been placed there. There were the names: Beatrix Wy-

andot, Pablo and Maria Marquesa, Juan Moreno, and Julio Tallchief. Under them the inscription: Massacred July 12, 1906.

"Father left space for his grave," Deborah said. "He's to be buried there alongside his mother. Then no one else."

This was the widest part of the valley, two miles across. The mountains rose very steeply on both sides in unscalable cliffs at this end, exactly as if a solid mass of granite had been pulled open to reveal the sandstone formations. They started fifty yards from the graves.

Constance studied the columns and pillars; when Deborah started to talk again, she moved away from the sound of her voice. She had read about the formations. The largest of them was one hundred eighty feet high with a diameter of forty-eight feet. The pillars soared into the brilliant blue sky with serene majesty. They appeared even redder than they had at a distance. The rubble around the bases was red sand with silvery sagebrush here and there. Larger pieces had fallen off, had piled up in some places like roots pushing out of the ground. She had the feeling that the formations had not been left by the erosion of the surrounding land, but that they were growing out of the earth, rising of their own will, reaching for the sky. The silence was complete here. No wind stirred the sage or blew the sand; nothing moved.

There was a right way; there was a wrong way. She took a step, then another, another. She retreated, went a different way. She was thinking of nothing, not able to identify what it was she felt, something new, something compelling. Another step. The feeling grew stronger. For a moment she held an image of a bird following a migratory pattern; it slipped away. Another step.

Suddenly Charlie's hand was on her arm, shaking her. "For God's sake, Constance!"

Then the sun was beating down on her head, too hot in this

airless place, and she glanced about almost indifferently. "I was just on my way back," she said.

"Did you hear me calling you?"

"I was thinking."

"You didn't hear a thing. You were like a sleepwalker."

She took his hand and started to walk. "Well, I'm awake now and starved. Is it lunch yet?"

Charlie's eyes remained troubled all afternoon and she did not know what to say, what to tell him, how to explain what she had done. She had wandered all the way back through the gorgons to the opposite side, a mile and a half at least, and if he had not actually seen her, she might still be wandering, because she had not heard him, had not even thought of him. She felt that she had entered a dream world where time was not allowed, that she had found a problem to solve, and the problem could not be stated, the solution, even if found, could never be explained.

Late in the afternoon Constance coaxed Charlie into the sauna with her, and then into the lake, and he was as surprised as she had known he would be, and as delighted. They discovered the immense tub in their suite was large enough for two people. They made love languorously and slept for nearly an hour. A good day, all things considered, he decided when they went to Ramón's cottage for dinner. It had not escaped his attention that Constance had timed things in order to be free to stand outside and watch the sunset flame the gorgons.

Tonight, Ramón told them, they would have peasant food. He had cooked dinner—a pork stew with cactus and tomatillos and plantains. It was delicious.

They sipped thick Mexican coffee in contentment. Throughout dinner they had talked about food, Mexican food, how it differed from one section of the country to another, how it differed from Central and South American food. Ramón talked charmingly about childhood in Mexico, the festivals, the feasts.

Lazily Charlie said, "You may know peasant food but you're not a peasant. Where did you go to school?"

Ramón shrugged. "Many places. University of Mexico, UCLA, the Sorbonne. I am afraid I was not a good student. I seldom attended regular classes. Eventually each school discovered this and invited me to go away."

"You used the libraries a lot, I expect," Charlie said almost indifferently.

"Yes. Señor, it is understood that you may want to ask me questions."

"Did Mrs. Rice tell you she hired us?"

"No, señor. Don Carlos told me this."

"Did he also tell you why?"

"The little girl, Lori, saw something that frightened her very much. It worries her mother. And Señor Tony is very unhappy with my presence here."

In exasperation Charlie asked, "Are you willing to simply clear up any mystery about yourself? Why haven't you already done it?"

"Señor, there is no mystery. From the beginning I have stated what I desire. First to Don Carlos, then to anyone who asked."

"And what is that?"

"To own the valley. When Don Carlos lies beside his mother, then I shall own the valley."

For a long time Charlie stared at him silenced, disbelieving. Finally he said, "And you think Don Carlos will simply give it to you?"

"Sí."

"Why?"

"I cannot say, Señor. No man can truly say what is in the heart of another."

Charlie felt the hairs on his arms stirring and turned to Constance. She was signaling. No more, not now. Not yet. Abruptly he stood up. "We should go."

"Thank you," Constance said to Ramón. "We really should go now."

He walked out with them. The night air was cold, the sky very clear with more stars visible than they had ever seen in New York state. A crescent moon hung low in the eastern sky, its mountains clear, jagged. The gorgons were lost in shadows now. But the moon would sail on the sun path, Constance thought, and set over the highest pinnacle and silver light would flow through the openings. . . .

"Good night, Señora," Ramón said softly, and left them.

They did not speak until they were in their room. "May we have coffee?" Constance asked Manuel. There were many more books to read, magazine articles to scan.

"It's blackmail," Charlie said with satisfaction when Manuel had vanished. "So what does he have on Don Carlos?"

Constance gave him a disapproving look. "That's too simple."

"Maybe. But I've found that the simplest explanation is usually the right one. He's too damn sure of himself. It must be something pretty bad."

She moved past him to stand at the window. She would have to be out at sunrise, she was thinking, when the sun would appear above the tumbled rocks of the stream and light up the gorgons with its first rays. Something nagged at her memory. They had looked up the rough waterway, not really a waterfall, but very steep, the water flashing in and out of the granite, now spilling down a few feet, to pour over rocks again. It was as if the sunlight, the moonlight had cut through the cliff, opened a path for the tumbling water. The memory that had tried to get through receded.

Manuel brought their coffee and they settled down to read.

A little later Charlie put down his book with disgust and started to complain, when he saw that she was sleeping. He took her book from her lap; she roused only slightly and he took her by the hand to the bedroom, got her into bed. Almost instantly she was sleeping soundly. He returned to his books.

He would poke around in the library and if he didn't find something written about Wyandot by someone who had not idolized him, he would have to go to Denver, or somewhere, and search further. Wyandot and his past, that was the key, he felt certain. Blackmail. Find the leverage and confront both blackmailer and victim and then get the hell out of here. He nodded. And do it all fast.

The next morning he woke up to find Constance's bed empty. He started to get up, then lay down again staring at the ceiling. She had gone out to look at the formations by sunrise, he knew. He waited, tense and unhappy, until she returned quietly, undressed and got back in bed. He pretended to be asleep and in a short while he actually fell asleep again. Neither of them mentioned it that day.

She insisted on going to the gorgons again in the afternoon. "Take some books along," she said in an offhand manner. "I want to explore and I may be a while." She did not look at him when she said this. Today they planned to ride horses and eat sandwiches and not return until after sundown.

He had binoculars this time and before the afternoon ended he found himself birdwatching. Almost angrily he got to his feet and started to walk among the gorgons, looking for Constance. She had been gone for nearly two hours. Abruptly he stopped, even more angrily. She had asked him to wait, not come after her. He glanced about at the formations; it was like being in a red sandstone forest with the trunks of stone trees all around him casting long black shadows, all pointing together at the other end of the valley, pointing at the spillway the stream had cut. It was too damn quiet in here. He found his way out and stood in the shade looking at the entire valley lying before him. The late sun turned the cascading stream into gold. He was too distant to see its motion; it looked like a vein of gold in the cliffs. He raised the binoculars and examined the valley slowly, and even more slowly studied the spillway. He swore softly, and sat down in the shade to wait for Constance and think.

When she finally appeared she was wan and abstracted. "Satisfied?" he asked and now there was no anger in his voice, only concern.

She shook her head. "I'm trying too hard. Want to start back?"

Manuel came with the horses, guaranteed gentle and safe, he had assured them earlier, and he had been right. They rode slowly, not talking. Night fell swiftly here after the sun went down. It was nearly dark when they reached the house and their room again. Would they like dinner served in their room? Manuel had asked, and after looking at Constance, Charlie had nodded.

"Can you tell me what you're doing?" he asked her after Manuel had left them.

"I don't know."

"Okay. I thought so. I think I'm onto something, but I have to go to Denver. Will you fly out in the helicopter, or should we plan a couple of days and drive?"

"I can't go," she said quietly, and added, "don't press me, please."

"Right. I'll be back by dark. I sure as hell don't want to try to fly in here blind." He grinned with the words. She responded with a smile belatedly.

He summoned Manuel who nodded when Charlie asked about the helicopter trip. "Sí. When do you want to go?"

And Manuel was not at all surprised that he was going alone, he thought grimly, after making the arrangements. Constance went to bed early again. He stood regarding her as she slept and under his breath he cursed Deborah Rice and her father and Ramón. "You can't have her!" he said silently.

The managers had been in the swimming pool; others had been in the dining room and library. Constance finally had started to gather her books to search for some place quiet. Manuel gently took them from her. "Please, permit me," he said softly. "It is very noisy today."

She had had lunch with Deborah Rice. Tony was coming tomorrow, she had said, and he was both furious and excited. He had something. There would be a showdown, she had predicted gloomily, and her father had never lost a showdown in his life. Deborah was wandering about aimlessly and would intrude again, Constance knew, would want to talk to no point, just to have something to do, and Constance had to think. It seemed that she had not thought anything through since arriving at the Valley of Gorgons. That was the punishment for looking, she thought, wryly: the brain turned to stone.

She was reluctant to return to her rooms. Without Charlie they seemed too empty. "I'll go read out under the gorgons," she said finally. At least out there no one bothered her, and she had to think. She felt that she almost knew something, could almost bring it to mind, but always it slipped away again.

"Sí," Manuel said. "We should take the jeep, Señora. It is not good to ride home after dark."

She started to say she would not be there that long, instead she nodded.

Charlie had been pacing in the VIP lounge for half an hour before his pilot, Jack Wayman, turned up. It was seven-fifteen.

"Where the hell have you been?" Charlie growled. "Let's get going."

"Mr. Meiklejohn, there's a little problem with one of the rotors. I've been trying to round up a part, but no luck. Not until morning."

He was a fresh-faced young man, open, ingenuous. Charlie found his hands balling, took a step toward the younger man, who backed up. "I'll get it airborne by seven in the morning, Mr. Meiklejohn. I'm sure of it. I called the house and explained the problem. You have a room at the Hilton—"

Charlie spun around and left him talking. He tried to buy a seat on another flight to Pueblo first and when that failed, no more flights out that night, he strode to the Hertz Rental desk.

"I'm going to rent a plane for Pueblo," he said, "and I'll want a car there waiting. Is that a problem?"

The young man behind the desk shrugged. "Problem, sir. They close up at seven down there."

"I'll rent a car here and drive down," Charlie said in a clipped, hard voice. "Is *that* a problem?"

"No, sir!"

By a quarter to eight he was leaving the airport. He felt exactly the way he had felt sometimes, especially in his last few years with the fire department, when he knew with certainty the fire had been set, the victim murdered. It was a cold fury, a savage rage made even more dangerous because it was so deep within that nothing of it showed on the surface, but an insane desire, a need, fueled it, and the need was to strike out, to lash out at the criminal, the victims, the system, anything. He knew now with the same certainty that the pilot had waited deliberately until after seven to tell him that he was stranded in Denver. And he was equally certain that by now the pilot had called the valley to warn them that he was driving, that he would be there by midnight. And if they had done anything to Constance, he knew, he would blow that whole valley to hell along with everyone in it.

"Manuel," Constance said when they arrived at the gorgons, "go on back to the house. You don't have to stay out here with me."

"Oh, no, Señora. I will stay."

"No, Manuel. I have to be alone so I can think. That's why I came out here, to think. There are too many people wandering around the house, too many distractions. If I know I'm keeping you out here, waiting, that would be distracting, too. I really want to be alone for a few hours."

"But, Señora, you could fall down, or get lost. Don Carlos would flay me if an accident happened."

She laughed. "Go home, Manuel. You know I can't get lost. Lost where? And I've been walking around more years than you've been alive. Go home. Come back for me right after sunset."

His expression was darkly tragic. "Señora, it is possible to get lost in your own house, in your own kitchen even. And out here it is possible even more."

"If you can't find me," she said softly, "tell Ramón. He'll find me."

"Sí," Manuel said, and walked to the jeep unhappily.

She watched the jeep until it disappeared among cottonwood trees that edged the stream at the far end of the meadow, and only when she could no longer see it did she feel truly alone. Although the mornings and nights were cold, the afternoons were warm; right now shade was welcome. She selected a spot in the shade, brushed sand clear of rocks and settled herself to read.

First a history of the area. These were the Sangre de Cristo Mountains, named by the Spanish, long since driven out, leaving behind bits and pieces of their language, bits of architecture. She studied a picture of petroglyphs outside Pueblo, never deciphered, not even by the first Indians the Spaniards had come across. Another people driven out? Leaving behind bits and pieces of a language? She lingered longer over several pictures of the Valley of the Gods west of Colorado Springs. Formations like these, but more extensive, bigger, and also desecrated. She frowned at that thought, then went on to turn pages, stopping only at pictures now. An Oglala Sioux medicine lodge, then the very large medicine wheel in Wyoming, desecrated. The people who constructed the medicine lodges could not explain the medicine wheel, she read, and abruptly snapped the book shut. That was how history was written, she told herself. The victors destroy or try to destroy the gods of the vanquished, and as years go by, the gods themselves fade into the dust. The holy places that remain are turned into tourist attractions, fees are charged, guided tours conducted, books written about the significance of the megaliths, or the pyramids, or the temples, or the ground drawings. And when the dust stirs, the gods stir also, and they wait.

She began to examine a different book, this one done by a small press, an amateur press. The text was amateurish also, but the photographs that accompanied it were first rate. The photographer had caught the gorgons in every possible light. Brilliant sunlight, morning, noon, sunset . . . Moonlight, again, all phases. During a thunderstorm. She drew in a sharp breath at a picture of lightning frozen on the highest peak. There was one with snow several feet deep; each gorgon wore a snow cap. The last section was a series of aerial pictures, approaching from all directions, with stiletto shadows, no shadows at all. . . . Suddenly she felt vertiginous.

She had come to the final photograph taken from directly above the field of gorgons at noon. There were no shadows, the light was brilliant, the details sharp and clear. Keeping her gaze on the picture, she felt for her notebook and tore out a piece of paper, positioned it over the photograph. The note paper was thin enough for the image to come through. She picked up her pencil and began to trace the peaks, not trying to outline them precisely, only to locate them with circles. When she was done she studied her sketch and thought, of course, that was how they would be.

She put her pencil point on the outermost circle and started to make a line linking each circle to the next. When she finished, her pencil was in the center of the formations; she had drawn a spiral. A unicursal labyrinth.

Slowly she stood up and turned toward the gorgons. She had entered in the wrong place before, she thought absently, and she had not recognized the pattern. Knowing now what it was, it seemed so obvious that she marveled at missing it before.

She walked very slowly around the gorgons to the easternmost pillar. Facing the valley, she saw that the low sun had turned the stream to gold; the shadows at her feet reached for it. She entered the formations. There was a right way, and a wrong way, but now the right way drew her; she did not have to think about it. A step. Another.

She did not know how long she had been hearing the soft singing, chanting, but it was all around her, drawing her on, guiding her even more than the feeling of being on the right path. She did not hesitate this time, nor did she retrace any steps. Her pace was steady. When the light failed, she stopped.

I could continue, she said silently in her head.

Sí, Ramón's voice replied, also in her head.

Will it kill me?

I do not know.

I will go out now.

Sí. There was a note of deep regret in the one syllable.

It doesn't matter how I leave, does it?

No, Señora. It does not matter.

She took a step, but now she stumbled, caught herself by clutching one of the gorgons. It was very dark; she could see nothing. There was no sound. Suddenly she felt panic welling up, flooding her. She took another step and nearly fell over a rock. Don't run! she told herself, for God's sake, don't try to run! She took a deep breath, not moving yet. Her heartbeat subsided.

"Please, Señora, permit me." Ramón's soft voice was very near.

She felt his hand on her arm, guiding her, and she followed gratefully until they left the formations and Manuel ran up to her in a greater panic than she had felt.

"Gracias, Madre! Gracias!" he cried. "Oh, Señora, thank goodness, you're safe! Come, let us return to the house!"

She looked for Ramón to thank him, but he was no longer there. Tiredly she went to the jeep and got in. Although it was dark, there was not the impenetrable black that she had experienced within the formations. They swallowed light just as they swallowed sound, she thought without surprise. She leaned back and closed her eyes, breathing deeply.

At the house they were met by a young woman who took Constance by the arm. "Señora, please permit me. I am Felicia. Please allow me to assist you."

Manuel had explained the problem with the helicopter and she was glad now that Charlie was not on hand to see her drag herself in in this condition. He would have a fit, she thought, and smiled gratefully at Felicia.

"I am a little bit tired," she admitted. "And very hungry."

Felicia laughed. "First, Don Carlos said, you must have a drink, and then a bath, and then dinner. Is that suitable, Señora?"

"Perfect."

•   •   •

Charlie was cursing bitterly, creeping along the state road looking for a place where he could turn around. He had overshot the private road, he knew. He had driven over forty miles since leaving Pueblo, and the turn was eight to ten miles behind him, but there was no place to turn. He had trouble accepting that he had missed the other road, and the neat sign warning that this was private property, dead end, but it was very black under the trees and he had missed it. And now he had to turn, go back even slower and find it. It was fifteen more minutes before there was a spot flat enough, wide enough to manuever around to head back, and half an hour after that before he saw the sign.

No one could work with the New York fire department and then the police department as many years as he had done without developing many senses that had once been latent only. Those senses could take him through a burned-out building, or into an alleyway, or toward a parked car in a state of alertness that permitted him to know if the next step was a bad one, or if there was someone waiting in the back seat of the car. He had learned to trust those senses without ever trying to identify or isolate them. And now they were making him drive with such caution that he was barely moving; finally he stopped altogether. A mountain road in daylight, he told himself, would look very different from that same road at night. But this different? He closed his eyes and drew up an image of the road he had driven over before—narrow, twisting, climbing and descending steeply, but different from this one that met all those conditions.

This road was not as well maintained, he realized, and it was narrower than the other one. On one side was a black drop-off, the rocky side of the mountain on the other, and not enough space between them to turn around.

"Well, well," he murmured and took a deep breath. This road could meander for miles and end up at a ranch, or a mining camp, or a fire tower, or in a snowbank. It could just peter out finally. He let the long breath out in a sigh. Two more miles, and if he didn't find a place where he could turn, he would start backing out. His stomach felt queasy and his palms were sweating now. He began a tuneless whistle, engaged the gears and started forward again.

"You know about the holy places on earth, don't you?" Don Carlos asked Constance. He had invited her to his apartment for a nightcap. Ramón was there, as she had known he would be.

"A little," she said. "In fact, I visited a couple of them some years ago. Glastonbury Tor was one. It was made by people in the megalithic period and endures yet. A three-dimensional labyrinth. I was with a group and our guide was careful to point out that simply climbing the hill accounted for all the physiological changes we felt. Shortness of breath, a feeling of euphoria, heightened awareness."

Ramón's stillness seemed to increase as if it were an aura that surrounded him and even part of the room. If one got close enough to him, she thought, the stillness would be invasive.

"I saw Croagh Patrick many years ago," Don Carlos said. "Unfortunately I was a skeptic and refused to walk up it barefooted. I've always wondered what that would have been like."

"The labyrinth is one of the strongest mystical symbols," Ramón said. "It is believed that the evil at the center cannot walk out because of the curves. Evil flows in straight lines."

"Must one find only evil there?" Constance asked.

"No. Good and evil dwell there side by side, but it is the evil that wants to come out."

"The Minotaur," she murmured. "Always we find the Minotaur, and it is ourself."

"You don't believe that good and evil exist independently of human agencies?" Ramón asked.

She shook her head.

"Señora, imagine a pharmacy with shelves of bright pills, red, blue, yellow, all colors, some sugarcoated. You would not allow a child to wander there and sample. Good and evil side by side, sometimes in the same capsule. Every culture has traveled the same path from the simplest medicines to the most sophisticated, but they all have this in common: side by side, in the same medicine, evil and good dwell forever intertwined."

"I have read," she said slowly, "that when the guru sits on his mountain top, he increases his power, his knowledge, every time a supplicant makes the pilgrimage to him. In the same way, when children dance the maypole, the center gathers the power. At one time the center was a person who became very powerful this way."

Ramón nodded. "And sometimes sacrificed at the conclusion of the ceremony."

"Did you try to lure the child Lori to the center of the gorgons?" Her voice sounded harsh even to her own ears.

"No, Señora."

"You tried to coax me in."

"No, Señora. I regretted that you stopped, but I did not lure you."

"Don Carlos is a believer. Why don't you use him?"

"I wanted to," Don Carlos said simply. "I can't walk that far."

"There will be others. Manuel. Or the girl Felicia. There must be a lot of believers here."

"Perhaps because they believe, they fear the Minotaur too much," Ramón said.

"And so do I," she said flatly.

"No, Señora. You do not believe in independent evil. You

will meet your personal Minotaur, and you do not fear yourself.''

Abruptly she stood up. ''I am very tired. If you'll excuse me, I'd like to go to bed now.''

Neither man moved as she crossed the room. Then Ramón said almost too softly to hear, ''Señora, I was not at the gorgons this evening. I have spent the entire evening here with Don Carlos.''

She stopped at the door and looked back at them. Don Carlos nodded soberly.

''Constance,'' he said, ''if you don't want to go all the way, leave here tomorrow. Don't go back to the formations.''

''You've been here for years,'' she said. ''Why didn't you do it a long time ago?''

For a moment his face looked mummified, bitter; the expression changed, became benign again. ''I was the wrong one,'' he said. ''I couldn't find the way. I felt it now and then, but I couldn't find my way.''

There was a right way and a wrong way, she thought, remembering. A right person and a wrong person. ''Good night,'' she said quietly, and left them.

She stood by her windows in the dark looking out over the valley, the lake a silver disc in moonlight, the dark trees, pale granite cliffs. ''Charlie,'' she whispered to the night, ''I love you.'' She wished he were with her, and closed her eyes hard on the futile wish. Good night, darling, she thought at him then. Sleep well. When she lay down in bed, she felt herself falling gently into sleep.

Charlie pulled on the hand brake and leaned forward to rest his head on the steering wheel, ease the strain in his neck from watching so closely behind him with his head out the open door. Suddenly he lifted his head, listening. Nothing, hardly even any wind to stir the trees. All at once he admitted to himself that he would not be able to back out in the dark. The backup lights were too dim, the road too curvy with switchbacks that were invisible, and a drop-off too steep, the rocky mountain too close. He had scraped the car several times already, and he had stopped too many times with one or two wheels too close to the edge or even over it. He had thought this before, but each time he had started again; now he reached out and turned off the headlights. The blackness seemed complete at first; gradually moonlight filtered through the trees. It was all right, he thought tiredly. He could rest for a while and at dawn start moving again. He pulled the door shut, cracked the window a little, and leaned back with his eyes closed and slept.

When Charlie drove in the next morning, Constance met him and exclaimed at his condition. "My God, you've been wrestling with bears! Are you all right?"

"Hungry, tired, dirty. All right. You?"

"Fine. Manuel, a pot of coffee right now and then a big breakfast, steak, eggs, fruit, everything. Half an hour."

Charlie waited until they were in their room to kiss her. She broke away shaking her head. "You might have fought off bears, but you won. I'm going to run a bath while you strip. Come on, hop!"

He chuckled and started to peel off his clothes. She really was fine. She looked as if she had slept better than he had anyway. Now the ordeal of trying to get back seemed distant and even ludicrous.

Manuel brought coffee while he was bathing; she took it the rest of the way and sat by the tub while he told her his adventures.

"You really think someone moved the sign?" she asked incredulously. "Why?"

"Why do I think it, or why did they do it?"

"Either. Both."

"It was gone this morning, back where it belonged. I think Ramón didn't want me here last night. What happened?"

"Nothing. That must be breakfast." She nearly ran out.

Nothing? He left the tub and toweled briskly, got on his robe and went to the sitting room where Manuel was finishing arranging the dishes.

When they were alone again, and his mouth full of steak, he said, "Tell me about it."

Constance took her coffee to the window and faced out. "I don't know what there is to tell. I had a nightcap with Don Carlos and Ramón and went to bed pretty early and slept until after eight." She came back and sat down opposite him. "I really don't know what happened," she said softly. "Something important, but I can't say what it was. There's power in the gorgons, Charlie. Real power. Anyone who knows the way can tap into it. That sounds so . . . stupid, doesn't it? But it's true. Let me sort it out in my own mind first, okay? I can't talk about it right now. What did you find?"

"Enough to blow Ramón's boat out of the water," he said. At her expression of dismay, he added, "I thought that's what we came here for."

There was a knock on the door and she went to answer it. Deborah was there, looking pale and strained.

"All hell's about to break loose today," she said when Constance waved her in. "Charlie, I'm glad you're back. Father's in conference, and then he's sending his associates to Denver to get together with company attorneys or something. And Tony's due in by two. Father wants to clear the decks before then for the showdown. You're invited. Three, in his apartment."

An exodus began and continued all day. The helicopter came and went several times; a stream of limousines crept up

the mountain road, vanished. The loud laughter was first subdued, then gone. Yesterday the managers had all been su-
premely confident, clad in their invisible gray suits; today, the
few that Constance had seen had been like school boys caught
doing nasty things in the lavatory.

And now Charlie was probably the only person within
miles who was relaxed and comfortable, wholly at ease,
watching everything with unconcealed, almost childish interest. They were in Don Carlos's apartment, waiting for the
meeting to start. Tony Wyandot was in his mid-forties, trim
and athletic, an executive who took his workouts as seriously
as his mergers. He was dark, like his father and sister, and
very handsome. Constance knew his father must have looked
much like that at his age. He had examined her and Charlie
very briefly when they were introduced, and, she felt certain,
he knew their price, or thought he did. After that he dismissed
them.

Charlie sat easily at the far edge of the group, watchful,
quiet. Ramón stood near the windows, also silent. Carl Wyandot entered the sitting room slowly, leaning on his cane,
nodded to everyone and took his leather chair that obviously
had been designed for his comfort. And Deborah sat near him,
as if to be able to reach him if he needed help. She and Tony
ignored Ramón.

Tony waited until his father was seated, then said, "I asked
for a private meeting. I prefer not to talk business or family
matters before strangers."

Charlie settled more easily into his chair. He would do, he
thought of Tony. Direct, straight to the point, not a trace of
fear or subservience, but neither was there the arrogance that
his appearance hinted at. Equal speaking to equal.

"I doubt we have many secrets," his father said. "You
hired detectives and so did your sister." He inclined his head
fractionally toward Charlie. "Go on."

Tony accepted this without a flicker. "First, I am relieved that you've ordered the reorganization study to commence. I'll go to Denver, naturally, and stay as long as it's necessary. Three months should be enough time." He paused. "And I find it very disturbing that you've already signed papers about the dispensation of the valley." His level tone did not change; he kept his gaze on his father, but the room felt as if a current had passed through it.

His father remained impassive and silent.

"You have sole ownership, and you can dispose of your property as you see fit," Tony went on, "but a case can be made that this is an unreasonable act."

Deborah made a sound, cleared her throat perhaps, or gasped. No one looked at her.

"I did not believe that you could be so influenced by a stranger that you would behave in an irrational way," Tony said, his gaze unwavering. "That's why I hired the detectives, to find out exactly why you were doing this. And I found out." He paused again, in thought, then said, "I think we should speak in private, Father. I did find out."

"Just say it."

He bowed slightly. "Ramón is your son. The trail is tenuous, not easy to find, but once found, it leads only to that conclusion. He came here and claimed his share of your estate, and that's why you're giving him this valley."

This time Deborah cried out. "That's a lie!"

Tony shook his head. "I wish it were. I had my agency check and double-check. It's true. Father, you were trying to keep the past buried, protect us, yourself, and there's no need. You provided well for him over the years, took care of his mother, saw that he had opportunities. You owe him nothing. A yearly allowance, if you feel you have to, but no more than that."

Ramón had not moved. Constance glanced at him; his face

was in deep shadow with the windows behind him. She recalled her own words: the brighter the light, the darker the shadow. Deborah was twisting her hands around and around; she looked at Charlie despairingly, and he shrugged and nodded.

"Father," Tony said then, his voice suddenly gentle, "I think I can understand. There's no record of the marriage of your father and mother. You were illegitimate, weren't you?"

For the first time Don Carlos reacted. His face flushed and his mouth tightened.

"But don't you see that it's unimportant now?"

"Haven't I provided for you and your sister?"

"We all know you've been more than generous. No one disputes that."

"And you would turn the valley into, what did you call it? a corporate resort? Knowing I detest the idea, you would do that."

"Not right away," his son said with a trace of impatience. "Places like this are vanishing faster all the time. You can hardly find a secluded spot even today. I'm talking about twenty years from now, fifteen at least."

Don Carlos shook his head. "The business will be yours. I have provided a trust for Deborah. Ramón can have the valley. Do you want to pursue this in court?" His face might have been carved from the granite of the cliffs. His eyes were narrowed; they caught the light and gleamed.

He would welcome a fight, Constance realized, watching him. And he would win. Tony flinched away finally and stood up. He had learned well from his father; nothing of his defeat showed in his face or was detectable in his voice when he said, "As you wish, Father. You know I would not willingly do anything to hurt you."

When he walked from the room, Deborah jumped up and

ran after him. Now Charlie rose lazily from his chair, grinning. "Is he really finished?" he asked.

Don Carlos was looking at the door thoughtfully; he swung around as if surprised to find anyone still in the room. "He isn't done yet," he admitted. "Not quite yet."

"Congratulations," Charlie said, still grinning. "A masterful job of creating a new heir. I would not like to be your adversary."

The old man studied him, then said in a quiet voice, "Are you exceedingly brave, or simply not very smart? I wonder. You are on my land where I have numerous servants who are, I sometimes think, too fanatically loyal."

Constance was looking from one to the other in bewilderment.

"Let me tell a different story," Charlie said. "A group of people arrives at the top of the cliff, where the stream starts to tumble down into the valley. Two Mexican men, two Mexican women, a child, a white man, and an Indian guide. They can't bring horses down that cut, not safely, so they hobble them up there and come down on foot. Looking for gold? A holy place? What? Never mind. A fight breaks out and the white man and the child survive, but when he climbs back out, the horses are gone, and from that bit of thievery, he gets the idea for the whole story he'll tell about bandits. It works; people accept his story. And now his only problem is that he can't find the valley again. He dies without locating it again. Why didn't he kill the child Carlos?"

Don Carlos sighed. "Please sit down. I want a drink. I seldom do anymore, but right now that's what I want."

Ramón mixed drinks for all of them, and then he sat down for the first time since the meeting had started.

Don Carlos drank straight bourbon followed by water. "Have you told Deborah any of this?"

"No."

"It was as you guessed," Don Carlos said finally. "I was back in the formations and didn't even hear the shots. I came out and he was the only one; the others were lying in blood. He raised the gun and aimed at me, and then he put it down again and started to dig graves. I don't know why he didn't shoot. He said from then on I was to be his son and if I ever told anyone he would shoot me too. I believed him. I was five."

"He killed your mother," Constance said, horrified, "and your father."

"Yes."

"How terrible for you. But I don't understand what that has to do with the present."

Don Carlos shrugged. "How much more have you guessed, or learned?" he asked Charlie.

"He couldn't find the valley again, but you did. I suspect there was gold and that it's under the lake today." Don Carlos nodded slightly. "Yes. You took away enough to get your start, and later you bought the valley, and the first thing you did was dam the stream, to hide the gold vein under many feet of water." Again the old man nodded.

Charlie's voice sobered when he continued. "Years passed and you preserved the valley until one day Ramón appeared. Was he hired as a servant? A business associate? It doesn't matter. He read that history and looked at the waterway and drew the same conclusions I did. You felt that the gorgons had saved your life, there was a mystical connection there. And he found how to capitalize on it." He was aware that Constance was signaling, but this time he ignored it and said bluntly, "I have as much right to call you Daddy as he does."

Don Carlos smiled faintly and lifted his glass, finished his bourbon. "You're a worthy adversary," he said to Charlie. "Will the others unravel it also? How did you discover this so quickly?"

"Ramón left a good trail, just hidden enough to make it look good, not so much that it can't be found. He did a fine job of it." He added dryly, "If you spend enough money you can make the world flat again, enough to convince most people anyway. I spent only a little bit and learned everything Tony's detectives had uncovered, and it hit me that if a man of your wealth really wants to hide anything, it gets hidden. I didn't believe a word of it."

Constance looked at Ramón in wonder. "You left false evidence that makes it appear that you are his son? Is that what you did?"

"Sí."

"When?"

"For the last two years we have been working on this."

She felt completely bewildered now. "But why? What on earth for?"

"I knew Tony would investigate Ramón," Don Carlos said. "As soon as he found out I intended to leave the valley to Ramón he would hire investigators to find out why. I tried to come up with something else, but I couldn't think of anything different that he would accept as a good enough reason. He won't talk in public about his father's illicit sex life. I don't want a fight or publicity about this."

"And if you told the truth," Constance said in a low voice, "they could press for a sanity hearing, and probably win." She felt a wave of disgust pass through her at the thought of the hearing, the taunting questions, the innuendoes.

"They might have won such a hearing," Don Carlos said just as quietly as she had spoken.

"And maybe they should have had that chance." Charlie sounded harsh and brusque. "This valley is worth ten million at least, and you're giving it away because he says there's power in the gorgons. Maybe Tony should have his chance."

"Señor," Ramón said, "come to the gorgons at sundown

today. And you, Señora. This matter is not completed yet, not yet.'' He bowed to Don Carlos and Constance and left the room.

They stood up also, Charlie feeling helpless with frustration. ''We won't be able to make that,'' he said to Don Carlos. ''Give him our regrets. We're leaving.''

''We'll be there,'' Constance said clearly.

Don Carlos nodded. ''Yes, we'll all be there.'' He looked at Charlie. ''I ask only that you say nothing to my daughter or son today. Tomorrow it will be your decision. I ask only for today.''

''You're not even offering to buy us,'' Charlie said bitterly.

''Mr. Meiklejohn, I am extremely wealthy, more than you realize. But over the years I have learned that there are a lot of things I can't buy. That was a surprise to me, as it must be to you, if you believe it at all.''

Charlie's frustration deepened; wordlessly he nodded and stalked from the room with Constance close behind him.

''That was brilliant,'' Constance said, walking by Charlie's side along the lake front.

''Yeah, I know.''

''We're really not finished here.'' She was not quite pleading with him.

''Right.''

She caught his arm and they came to a stop. ''I'm sorry,'' she said. ''I have to see it through and I can't say why.''

He nodded soberly. ''That's what scares me.'' He never had doubted her, never had thought of her with another man, never had a moment's cloud of jealousy obscure his vision of her. And he knew she felt the same way about him. Their trust in each other was absolute, but . . . He knew there were areas in her psychic landscape that he could not enter, areas where she walked alone, and he knew that when she walked those infinite and infinitely alien paths the things that occupied her mind were also alien and would not permit translation into his mundane world. Standing close to her in the warm sunlight, a gleaming lake at one side of them, luxurious buildings all around, cars, helicopters, computers, servants by the score available, he felt alone, abandoned, lost. She was beyond reach even though her hand was on his arm.

He lifted her hand and kissed the palm. "It's your party."

She blinked rapidly. "We should go back to the house. Tony scares me right now."

They stopped when Tony and Deborah came into view, heading for the area behind the boathouse. Tony was carrying a rifle; Deborah was almost running to keep up, clutching his arm.

She saw Charlie and Constance and turned to them instead. Tony continued, stony-faced.

"What's up?" Charlie asked pleasantly.

"He's going to do target practice. Kill time." She laughed with a tinge of hysteria in her voice.

"Well, I'm looking for a drink," he said, so relaxed and quiet that he appeared lazy.

She walked with them, studying the path they were on. "Tony's so much like Father. It's uncanny how alike they are."

They all started a few seconds later when a shot sounded, echoing and chasing itself around the granite walls of the valley for a long time.

"He's as violent as Father must have been when he was younger," Deborah said as they started to walk again. "More so, maybe. Father is said to have killed a man back in the twenties. I don't know how true it is, but it doesn't really matter. People who tell the story know it was quite possible. He would kill to protect his interests, his family. And so would Tony."

"So would I," Charlie commented.

Constance shivered. Years ago Charlie had insisted that she take self defense classes far past the point where she felt comfortable with them. "If anyone ever hurts you," he had said, "you'd better take care of him, because if you don't I'll kill the son of a bitch and that will be murder."

Another shot exploded the quiet and then several more in quick succession. It sounded like thunder in the valley. They paused at the house listening, feeling the vibrations in the air, and then entered.

The fountain splashed; the red tiles on the floor glowed; an orange tree in a pot had opened a bloom or two overnight, and filled the air with a heady fragrance. It was very still.

Deborah paused at the fountain and stared at the water. They had started up the wide stairs; her low voice stopped them.

"When Tony and I used to come here, we just had each other, we were pretty close in those days. He was Lori's age when he . . . when something happened out there. He wouldn't talk about it. He was ashamed because he ran and left me behind, and everything changed with us after that. Just like with Lori. I don't think he's ever gone back. And he shouldn't go back. That target practice . . . he claims an eagle has been snatching chickens. He says he'll shoot it on sight." She bowed her head lower. "How I've prayed for an earthquake to come and shake them all down, turn them to dust!" She jammed her hands into her pockets and walked away without looking back at them.

In their room Constance watched silently as Charlie unlocked his suitcase and brought out his thirty-eight revolver. She went to the window then. "Charlie, just for a minute, accept that there might be some force out there, some power. Tony said places like this are vanishing, remember? He was more right than he knew. They are. What if there are places where you can somehow gain access to the power people sometimes seem to have, like the inhuman strength people sometimes have when there's an emergency, a fire, or something like that.''

He made a grunting noise. She continued to look out the window. The sun was getting low, casting long shadows now.

''If people can manipulate that kind of power, why don't they?'' he demanded.

She shrugged. ''New priests drive out the old priests. New religions replace the old. The conquerors write the books and decide what's true, what's myth. Temples are turned into marketplaces. Roads are built. Admission is charged to holy places and the gum wrappers appear, the graffiti . . . But the stories persist in spite of it all. They persist.''

She looked at him when she heard the sound of ice hitting a glass. His face was stony, unknowable.

''When we lose another animal species,'' she said, almost desperate for his understanding now, ''no one knows exactly what we've lost forever. When a forest disappears, no one knows what marvels we might have found in it. Plants that become extinct are gone forever. What drugs? What medicines? What new ways of looking at the universe? We can't really know what we've lost. And this valley's like that. Maybe we can't know what it means today, or even next year, but it exists as a possibility for us to know some day, as long as it remains and is not desecrated.''

He picked up the two glasses and joined her at the window where he put the glasses on a table and took her into his arms. He held her very close and hard for a minute or two and then kissed her. ''Let's have our drink,'' he said afterward. ''And then it'll be about time to mosey on downstairs.'' And he tried to ignore the ice that was deep within him, radiating a chill throughout his body.

• • •

Manuel drove them without a word. He was subdued and
nervous. Ahead of the jeep was a Land Rover moving cautiously, avoiding the ruts in the tracks, easing into and out of
the holes. Deborah and her father were in it. Also ahead of
them was Tony on a horse, in no hurry either. He had a scabbard with the rifle jutting out.

Manuel stopped near the stream where he had parked before, but Deborah drove her father closer to the formations
and parked within fifty feet of them. Manuel got a folding
chair from the car and set it up; he brought a large Indian
blanket and placed it on the back of the chair and then looked
at Deborah with a beseeching expression. She shook her head.
Silently he went back to the jeep, turned it and drove toward
the house. Tony was tying his horse to a hitching post near
the mound of the graves.

Don Carlos walked slowly over the rocky ground; there was
a line of sweat on his upper lip when he reached the chair
and sat down. No one offered to help him, but they all
watched until he was settled. Probably, Charlie thought, they
knew better than to try to help. If he wanted help he would
ask for it politely, matter-of-factly, and unless he did, they
waited. A worthy adversary, he thought again. He had no
doubt that Don Carlos had killed, maybe more than once, and
that he would not hesitate to kill again if he had to. Don
Carlos knew, as Charlie did, that the world was not always a
nice place.

Tony drew nearer. He and Charlie eyed each other like two
alley cats confined in a too-small space, Constance thought,
watching everyone, everything closely.

She heard a faint singing and glanced about to see if the
others were listening too, to see if Ramón had approached
from behind the gorgons. Charlie's expression of lazy inat-
tention did not change; no one moved. They didn't hear it,

she realized. The singing was more like chanting, and louder. The earth rolled away from the sun and caught the light in the stream at the far end of the valley and turned the water to gold. A dagger of golden light slicing through the cliffs, pointing the way.

It was time. She touched Charlie's arm. When he looked at her, she said softly, "Don't let them follow me. Please wait. I'll be back."

The ice flowed through him, tingled his fingers and toes, froze his heart. He nodded silently. Their gaze held for another moment, then she turned and walked toward the entrance of the gorgons. He had known this was her part, just as she had known; he had been braced, waiting for this. He had not known he would be frozen by the icy fear that gripped him now. She did not look back at him when she reached the right place. She took another step and was out of view. He let out his breath.

A right way, a wrong way. Her pace was steady this time, unhesitating. It was as if the wrong way was barred to her, as if she were being channeled only the right way. The chanting was all around her, inside her; it had an exultant tone.

I'm here, Ramón.

Sí, Señora. I was waiting for you.

Sunlight flowed between the highest pillars, spilled like molten gold downward to touch the path before her. Then the sunlight dimmed and the shadows became deep purple. She continued to walk steadily.

"Look!" Deborah cried, and pointed toward the top of the gorgons.

For a second Charlie thought he saw a human figure; it changed, became an eagle. That damn story she had told, he thought angrily. When he looked back at the others, Tony was at the scabbard, hauling out the rifle. The twilight had turned violet, the shadows very deep and velvety. Charlie watched Tony for a second; very soon it would be too dark to see him. He drew his revolver and fired it into the air. Deborah screamed. Tony straightened, holding the rifle.

"Drop it," Charlie said. "Just let it fall straight down and then get back over here."

Tony walked toward him with the rifle in the crook of his arm.

"Put it down," Charlie said softly.

"I'm going to shoot that goddamn eagle," Tony said. His face was set in hard lines, his eyes narrowed. He took another step.

"No way," Charlie said harshly. "My wife's in there and I don't want any bullets headed anywhere near those formations. Understand?" Tony took another step toward him. Charlie raised the revolver, held it with both hands now. His voice was still soft, but it was not easy or lazy sounding. "One more step with that gun and I'll drop you. Put it down!"

He knew the instant that Tony recognized death staring at him, and the muscles in his neck relaxed, his stomach unclenched. Tony put the rifle down on the ground carefully and straightened up again.

"Over by your father," Charlie said. He glanced at Don Carlos and Deborah; they were both transfixed, staring at the gorgons behind him. Tony had stopped, also staring. Deborah was the first to move; she sank to the ground by her father's chair. His hand groped for her, came to rest on her head. He took a deep breath and the spell was over.

"It's going to be dark very soon," Charlie said, hating them all, hating this damn valley, the goddamn gorgons. "Until the moon comes up I'm not going to be able to see a damn thing and what that means is that I'll have to listen pretty hard. Tony, will you please join your father and sister? You'd better all try to make yourselves as comfortable as you can because I intend to shoot at any noise I hear of anyone moving around.''

Deborah made a choking noise. ''Father, please, let's go back to the house. Someone's going to be killed out here!''

Tony began to walk slowly toward them. ''You shouldn't have interfered,'' he said. He sounded very young, very frightened. ''I would have ended it.''

''Tony, I'm sorry. I'm sorry I brought them here. I wish I'd never seen them, either of them.'' Deborah was weeping, her face on her father's knee, his hand on her head. ''This isn't what I wanted. Dear God, this isn't what I wanted.''

Charlie sighed. He felt a lot of sympathy for Tony Wyandot who had come face to face with something he could not handle, could not explain, could not buy or control. In Tony's place he would have done exactly the same thing: try to shoot it out of the sky, protect his property, his sister and father, his sister's child. He would have brought the rifle, but he would have used it, and that made the difference. Don Carlos would have used it, too, if he had decided it was necessary. He had seen Tony take defeat before, with dignity, but this was not like that. He knew that no matter what else happened out here tonight, Tony would always remember that he had not fired the rifle.

Tony reached his father's side and sat on the ground with his knees drawn up, his arms around them. The crisis was over.

The light had long since faded, and with darkness there had come other changes. Constance did not so much think of the differences as feel them, experience and accept them. Her feet seemed far away, hardly attached to her, and her legs were leaden. Each step was an effort, like wading in too-deep water. The air had become dense, a pressure against her that made breathing laborious. She walked with one hand out-stretched, not to feel her way, but almost as if she was trying to part the air before her. She saw herself falling forward and the thick air supporting her, wafting her as it might a feather, setting her down gently, an end of the journey, an end of the torture of trying to get enough air.

Señora.

I'm here, Ramón.

Sí.

It is very hard, Ramón. I'm very tired.

Sí. But you must not stop now.

I know.

Another step. It was agony to lift her foot, to find her foot and make it move. Agony to draw in enough air and then expel it. And again. She was becoming too heavy to move. Too heavy. Stonelike.

"I have to stand up," Don Carlos said. "I'm getting too stiff."

"Do you want to go to the car?" Charlie asked. "You could turn on the heater." They could have turned on the lights, he thought, and knew that even if it had occurred to him earlier he would not have done it.

"No, no. I just want to stand for a minute and then wrap up in the blanket."

"Father," Tony said then, "let me take you back to the house. Keeping vigil in the cold can't be good for you."

"I'm all right," his father said gruffly. "It won't be much longer, I'm sure."

"Father," Tony said after a moment, "don't you see how they're manipulating you? Ramón obviously offered Meikle-john and his wife more than Deborah agreed to pay them. This isn't going to prove anything, freezing our butts off out here in the cold. Meiklejohn," he said in a louder voice, "I'm going to the car for a flashlight. I intend to go haul your wife out of there and be done with this.'' There was the sound of shoes scraping rocks.

Charlie sighed. ''Tony, knock it off, will you?'' he said wearily. ''You know I won't let you do that or anything else.''

''Sit down, Tony,'' his father said. It was a father-to-son command, a voice that expected to be obeyed.

Silence hung over them all. ''Whatever you say,'' Tony finally agreed. ''This is the stupidest thing I've ever seen.''

Charlie loosened his grip on his revolver. Tony was vacillating from the kid who had had his universe shaken to the middle-aged man who could not allow himself to embrace a new belief system, and it obviously was a painful jolt with each switch. He had tried to destroy it and failed, now he had to work even harder to deny it. Charlie couldn't stop feeling that Tony was more in the right than his father. So Constance and Ramón would stroll out eventually and what the hell would that prove? He scowled into the darkness. Meanwhile he intended to preserve order in the cosmos.

There were more stars every time he looked up, as if veil after veil were being removed; he never had known there were so many of them. The moon hung over the house, fattening up nicely night after night. And what if she didn't come back? He checked the thought, but there it was, fully formed, articulated in spite of his efforts to suppress it.

What if she found something, after all? Something so wonderful that she couldn't turn her back on it. What if the power she was looking for turned out to be malevolent? He closed his eyes for a moment and then looked at the moon again, trying to make the jagged edge turn into mountains instead of badly torn paper.

She had not completed a movement for a very long time. She had started another step, but it seemed not to end no matter

how she struggled. And now she could hardly breathe and the
lack of air made her head feel as distant as her feet and hands,
and everywhere in her body there was pain, more pain than
she had known she could endure.

Will she die?

I do not know.

She didn't know how hard it would be.

One never knows that.

But you did it.

*Sí. Over a long period of time. Each time the way one has
gone before is easier.*

You took the photographs of the gorgons, didn't you?

Sí. And I told Manuel to make certain you saw them.

*Twenty-eight pillars. A lunar month. That is very holy, isn't
it?*

Most holy.

*And one must start at sunset and arrive in moonlight. Is
that right?*

That is correct.

*She's taking another step. Actually she hasn't really
stopped yet. But it's so slow and so hard.*

She forced her leg to move again. Another step. Each step
now was a victory in slow motion. So much resistance to
overcome. Again she saw herself falling, floating down, down
and she yearned to rest in the heavy air, not to move, not to
hurt. Another step. The chanting was in her bones; she wanted
to chant, too, but she had no breath. The image of herself
letting go, falling, was becoming realer each time it came
back. It would be so good, so good to let go, to let the heavy
air float her to the ground where she could rest.

"What on earth will he do with the valley?" Deborah asked.
"Not a resort or anything like that. But what?"

"He'll start a school," Don Carlos said. He sounded faint, his voice quavering a bit.

Charlie thought of Ramón teaching kids how to walk among the gorgons. His hands clenched hard and he consciously opened them again, flexed his fingers.

"And Constance," Deborah said, almost plaintively, almost jealously, "why her? What is she doing in there with him?"

"She felt the power and didn't run away," Don Carlos said in his faint voice, as if from a great distance, as if his strength were failing too fast for the words to be said. "She is willing to accept the power that she doesn't understand, and through her Ramón will . . . He needed someone to walk the path while he waits. And I . . . I'll be able to rest knowing the valley is in his hands. Good hands. He'll see that it isn't desecrated, he'll have the strength to take care of it. After tonight he'll be able to teach others."

"What difference does it make?" Tony demanded. "Let him do what he wants with the rotten valley. I sure don't intend to spend any time here ever again."

Charlie nodded. The denial was complete. Tony had saved his soul the only way he could. Everyone was clearly visible with the moon almost directly overhead and brilliant. The dimensions kept changing with the changing light, he thought. Right now the valley looked as wide as a plain, and the house close enough to touch. His eyes were playing tricks. He had slept so little the night before, and the altitude was strange.

For nearly an hour he had been fighting the idea that she really would not come back, that when it became daylight he would have to go in after her, and he would find her huddled at the base of one of those pillars. Twice he had started to go in, and each time he had forced himself to stop, to wait. He got up and stretched and started to walk toward the meadow, anything was better than sitting on the rock much longer.

• • •

When I was a little girl I was so certain that if I could be Beauty, I'd recognize the nobility of the Beast with no trouble at all. How I wanted to be Beauty.

I am sure you recognize evil very well.

Not as well as I should. What if she does this thing tonight, and uses what she gains for evil?

His laugh was gentle. *We talked to you Señora. We measured your reverence for the power here. If we were wrong then one of us will certainly die this night.*

Is this an evil thing, Ramón? To let her walk the path in ignorance, is that evil?

You are not ignorant.

But I'm here and she's there alone.

That is your choice.

No. I can be one or the other.

There is no other, only the one.

Now she knew she had to stop, she could not go on. She shuddered. She put out both hands so that they would break her fall. And she heard her own voice very clearly, "Another step, Constance. One more. Come on!"

One more. Suddenly she was dazzled by silvery light. It struck her in the face like a physical substance and she could see out over the valley in all directions. She laughed.

At the hitching post Charlie turned and came to a dead stop, even his heart stopped. In the center of the formations, on top of the highest of the gorgons, were two figures, Constance and Ramón, shining in the moonlight. He felt the world swim out from under him and caught the post for support, closed his eyes very hard. When he opened them again, the figures were gone. He raced back toward the gorgons. When he got there, Ramón was emerging carrying Constance.

Very gently he transferred her to Charlie's arms. Charlie

watched him walk to Don Carlos and lean over him. It was very clear in the moonlight. After a moment, Don Carlos stood up.

"I didn't ask for this," he whispered, and his voice carried as if he were shouting. "I made no demands, asked for nothing."

"It is given," Ramón said. "Now we must get the Señora to the house and to bed."

"Is she going to be all right?" Don Carlos asked.

"Sí. She is suffering from shock right now."

And Don Carlos moved without his cane, Charlie realized. Constance stirred and pressed her face against his chest. She sighed a long plaintive breath.

Are you sure, Señora? You don't have to go back now. You can stay here.

Oh no! I give it all to you, Ramón. I don't want it. I told Charlie I'd come back. That's what I want.

You can never give it all away, Señora. Some of the power will cling to you forever. Some day perhaps you will come home again.

She took another deep breath, inhaling the familiar smell of Charlie's body, and she let herself go, let herself fall into the sleep she yearned for. Charlie walked to the car with her in his arms almost blinded by tears he could not explain or stop.

RITES OF SPRING

Lisa Goldstein

*"Rites of Spring" was purchased by Gardner Do-
zois, and appeared in the March 1994 issue of Asimov's, with an illustration by Steve Cavallo. Lisa
Goldstein is a Bay Area writer who won the American Book Award for her first novel,* The Red Magi-
cian, *and who has subsequently gone on to become
one of the most critically acclaimed novelists of her
day with books such as* Tourists, The Dream Years,
A Mask for the General, Strange Devices of the Sun
and Moon *and* Summer King, Winter Fool. *Her most
recent book is the novel* Waking the Labyrinth.*
She is less prolific at shorter lengths, although her
elegant and incisive stories, many of which have appeared in* Asimov's, *and which were recently collected in* Travellers in Magic, *are well worth waiting
for—as is true of the wry story that follows, in which
a detective hot on the trail of a Missing Person finds
that that trail leads into territory very far indeed from
the kind of Urban Mean Streets that Private Eyes are
accustomed to travel . . .*

I'm sitting at my desk catching up on paperwork when there's
a knock on my office door. "Come in," I say.

The door opens and a woman steps inside. "Have a seat,"
I say, filing one last piece of paper.

"Are you Ms. Keller?" she asks.

"Liz Keller. And you are—"

"Dora Green." Wisely, she picks the more comfortable of the two office chairs. "I want you to find my daughter."

I look across the desk at her. She has an oval face, dark gray eyes. Her hair is medium-length and black, with a little gray at the temples. She doesn't look much like a parent of a missing child. She doesn't play with the handles of her purse, or light a cigarette. I nod, encouraging her to go on.

"My daughter's name is Carolyn—Carolyn Green," Ms. Green says. "At least it was. I suppose her husband's made her change it."

I try not to frown. In most missing children cases the child is much younger. "Are you sure she wants to be found?" I ask.

"I'm certain. Her husband forced her into the marriage, you see."

"Was she pregnant?"

She doesn't flinch. "No."

I look over this possible client for a moment. She's very well dressed—she wears a soft green pullover and a skirt with a print of entwining leaves and vines and flowers. I remember that it's St. Patrick's Day today, though I would bet that she's not Irish. She smells a little like some flower too, a subtle, expensive perfume. Golden earrings dangle from her ears.

"Look," I say. "Before I can take your money I need you to be clear about some things. I can promise to do my best to find your daughter. Whether she wants to be found is up to her. I'll give her a message from you, whatever—"

"She has to get away from him."

"I can't do that. Your daughter's of legal age—She is of legal age, isn't she?"

"Yes."

"All right then. If she tells me herself that she wants to end the marriage—"

"She does—"

"Then I'll help her. But not otherwise. If she won't leave him I can give her the name of a women's shelter. I know a counselor there. Do you understand?"

"Yes."

"Okay. I need to know some things about your daughter— her husband's name, their last address if you know it. Do you have a picture of them?"

She does. The photograph she shows me must have been taken shortly after the two eloped: the daughter is wearing what looks like a bridal wreath, a circlet of flowers. She is beautiful, with light brown hair and blue eyes. I can't tell what she's thinking; she has the vacant expression of the very young. Her mother seems to have gotten all the wisdom in the family.

Her husband looks nearly twice her age. He is unsmiling, almost grim. He has long greasy hair, a short beard, and wears a black leather vest over a T-shirt. He stands a little in front of her, casting her partly in shadow. "What does she do?" I ask.

"Nothing, as far as I know," Ms. Green says. "He won't let her leave the house."

"What about him? He looks like a Hell's Angel."

"I wouldn't be surprised." For the first time she looks away from me, down toward her lap. She smoothes her busy skirt. "I don't like to think about it."

"How long has she been with him?"

"About four months. They got married right after they met."

"Where did she meet him?"

Ms. Green looks away again. "She says it was in a park."

We talk a little more, and then I give her my standard

contract and explain about my fees. She signs the contract and writes a check for my retainer.

As soon as she leaves the nausea I've been fighting the past few weeks returns. I run down the hallway to the bathroom and make it just in time to throw up into the toilet. As I stand and catch my breath I wonder why the hell they call it morning sickness. Mine seems to go on all day.

I make my way back to the office. I've got to do something about this, I think. I've got to decide. I flip through the calendar on my desk. The doctor's appointment is in two days, on March 19.

Dora Green had given me the last address she had for Carolyn and her husband, and had told me that her daughter had been taking classes at the university. It's past four o'clock, though, and in this sleepy northern California town the university is probably closed for the day. I decide to visit Carolyn's neighborhood.

Before I leave I call a contact in the Department of Motor Vehicles and ask her to run a check on Jack Hayes, Carolyn's husband; on Carolyn Green; and on Carolyn Hayes. Then I pick up my coat and purse, lock the office door, and step out into the hallway.

The landing smells even worse than usual, frying grease and floor polish. They say that your sense of smell improves when you're pregnant, but in the past few weeks I've discovered that this doesn't nearly go far enough. What I think actually happens is that your entire skin becomes a giant olfactory gland.

The temperature outside is in the thirties, and the sun is barely visible through the clouds. It's the coldest March people in this town can remember. Wind burns my ears. My well-dressed client, I remember, wore a plush padded overcoat. I wrap my thin cloth coat around me and get into my car.

The car's heater kicks in just as I drive up to Carolyn's address. I sit in the car a moment longer before going out to face the cold. Iron bars front the windows of some of the houses around me; other houses are boarded up or burned out or covered with graffiti. Five or six teenage boys walk down the street, drinking something from a paper bag and laughing loudly. An old man stands at a bus stop, talking angrily to himself.

I turn off the car and step outside. The wind chills me almost instantly, and I huddle into my coat. The address Ms. Green gave me is an apartment building, and I see the apartment I want facing the landing on the second floor. I climb the outside stairs and knock. Music plays from the first floor.

There is no answer. I knock again, louder. The door to the nearest apartment opens and a man steps out. "What the hell do you want?" he asks. "Can't a man get a little sleep around here?"

Despite his words he is not angry—he sounds weary, as if he has been certain something would wake him up sooner or later. His blond hair is lank and greasy, his face an unhealthy white. People pay a lot of money to get jeans as scuffed as his are, with just those holes at the knees. He might—just might—have a night job, but the odds are against it.

"Do you know Jack Hayes?" I ask. "Or Carolyn Hayes?"

"No. Who the hell are they?"

"They live here, in this apartment. Or they did."

"Oh, those guys." He leans against his doorjamb, suddenly disposed to talk. I see now that he is younger than I first thought, in his early twenties. A child somewhere in the building cries, and someone shouts for quiet. "Those guys were weird, let me tell you. They belonged to some cult or something. Satanists."

"Satanists?"

"Yeah. They had all these people coming and going at all

hours of the day or night, all of them wearing black. Lots of chanting, lots of strange smells. Incense, maybe.''

I sniff the air. There is a whiff of something, though it's harsher than incense. My stomach roils.

"You said 'had,' " I say. "Past tense. Are they gone?"

"I don't know, man," he says. "Now that you mention it I haven't seen them around for a couple of days. Weeks, maybe. You a bill collector?"

I give him one of my cards. He squints at it, as though he has grown unused to reading. "Private investigator, huh?" he says. "Isn't that dangerous, you being a woman and all?" He smiles, as if he thinks he's said something witty.

"Asking personal questions is always dangerous," I say. He squints again; he knows that I've insulted him, but for the moment he doesn't get how. "Call me if they come back, all right?"

He mumbles something and retreats back into his apartment. I try Carolyn Green's doorknob, but the door is locked.

I drive back to the office. There is a message on my machine from my contact at the DMV: she can find nothing for any of the names I gave her. I frown. It's hard to get around in this town without a car, though it is just barely possible. So much for the Hell's Angel theory—I had specifically asked her to check for motorcycle licenses. Maybe they're using aliases, I think, and I frown again.

I had been looking forward to finding Carolyn, to discovering why she had run away with such an unsuitable man. One thing I learned in this business is that people are far stranger than you would ever think, that they almost never do what you would expect. Now I wonder if I'll ever get to meet her.

The next day I wrap myself in my coat and two scarves and head out toward the university. It's even colder than yesterday, and a heavy rain begins while I'm driving. The rain turns into snow as I pull up to a parking garage. It hasn't snowed in this town since I moved here ten years ago.

I show the woman at the registrar's office my PI's license and ask about Carolyn Green. "I'm sorry," she says, shaking her head. "It's against university policy to give out information on students."

She doesn't look sorry at all; she seems delighted to be able to enforce a rule and cause trouble at the same time. Her face is unremarkable, with faded blue eyes and sprayed straw-colored hair, but her glasses are unfortunate—narrow and black, with upswept tips. She must have been in a terrible mood the day she visited the optometrist.

The office is overheated; I shed first one and then the other scarf, and open my coat. I try an appeal to the woman's emotions—missing daughter, frantic mother—but she is unmoved.

It feels good to leave the office, to walk down the hall and push open the door to the cold outside. The snow has stopped. Students are scraping up the thin snow and trying to make snowballs. Someone slips on the grass and goes down; his friends laugh. I'm not foolish enough to think that I'll run into Carolyn Green, but just in case I stop several people and show them her picture. No one recognizes her.

I go to the student store to buy a pair of gloves, and then return to the registrar's office. I'm in luck—Ms. University Policy has left, probably for lunch, and a young woman who looks like a student has come in to replace her. Her eyes widen as I show her my license, and before I even finish my story she is calling up Carolyn's name on the computer.

"Here—I'll give you a print-out of her schedule," the young woman says. "And here's her address, at the top."

The address is the one Ms. Green gave me, but the list of classes could be useful. I thank the woman and leave.

The first class on Carolyn's schedule is Classical Literature, taught by Professor Burnford. Once again I am amazed at how strange people are, how complex. Who would have thought that the woman in the photograph would be interested in such a thing?

I find the building where Carolyn studies Classical Literature and go inside. Professor Burnford's office is on the third floor; a sign on the door says that his office hours are from 12:00 to 2:00. It's five to 12. I lean against the wall to wait.

A few minutes later the professor comes toward me, followed by a student who tries in vain to keep up with his long strides. Burnford says something over his shoulder to the student following him. "Rabbits!" I hear him say as he reaches the door. "Rabbits are fertility symbols!"

Burnford nods to me as I step forward, and without stopping he says, "I can see you after I talk to Joe here. Late Etruscan burial customs, isn't it?"

It isn't, but before I get a chance to tell him so he's unlocked his door and ushered poor Joe inside. I wait a bit more, and then wander down the hallway and read the notices and cartoons posted on office doors. It's all fairly interesting, in a sort of anthropological way. I never finished college myself.

Five minutes later Professor Burnford's door opens and Joe emerges, looking wrung out. He does not meet my eyes as he leaves.

"Sit down," Burnford says as I enter. His hair, eyes and skin are very nearly the same sandy color, and he wears a sand and black hound's-tooth coat. I wonder if he matched his coat deliberately to his face or if it's just a coincidence.

"I hope you don't mind if I eat my lunch while we talk," he says. He opens a brown paper bag and takes out a plastic-wrapped peanut butter sandwich. "I have no time otherwise."

The mention of lunch, and the smell of peanut butter, make

my stomach turn again. The doctor's appointment is tomorrow, I think.

"I'm sorry," he says, taking a bite of the sandwich. "I don't remember your name."

"I'm not a student here, Dr. Burnford," I say. I take out my license and show it to him. "I'm looking for one of your students. Carolyn Green, or Carolyn Hayes."

He nods, his mouth full of peanut butter.

"Do you know her?" I ask.

"Of course I know her. Brilliant girl. You don't get too many under-graduates that good in ancient Greek."

Brilliant? I show him the photograph. "Yes, that's her," he says, taking it from me. "Don't know who the man is, though."

"That's her husband," I say. "Jack Hayes."

"Husband?" He puts down his sandwich, for which I am grateful, and wipes his mouth with a napkin. "So that's what happened to her. I'm sorry to hear it."

"What do you mean?"

"She stopped coming to class a few months ago. I don't usually stick my nose in my students' business, but I was worried about her and I went to the registrar's office to get her phone number. She doesn't have a phone, it turns out."

I nod. I had already noticed that.

"So I thought, that was that," he says. "Husband, you say. Sometimes you get a man who'll pull his wife out of school, even in this day and age."

I say nothing. He'd be surprised if he knew what goes on in this day and age.

He gives me the photograph back. "Shame," he says, shaking his head.

"Do you know anything about her?" I ask. "Any friends you might have seen her with? Acquaintances?"

"No. I never saw her outside of the classroom or my office."

I thank him and leave. The professors of her other two classes aren't in, so I scribble something on the backs of two business cards and push them under the doors. As I drive back to the office I turn on the radio; someone is explaining how to put on snow-chains.

There are two messages waiting for me at the office. A company I've worked for before asks me to run a credit check, and a friend wants to go see a movie tonight.

I should call both of them back. Instead I take out a legal pad and write down columns of numbers. Stroller, car seat, crib, play-pen. So much for clothing, so much for medical expenses. College, and classes in Classical Literature with Professor Burnford. I'm staring at the pad of paper when the phone rings.

I let the machine catch it. "I'm sorry I was angry with you the other day," a voice says, much to my surprise. "We should talk. Please call me."

It's my mother. She's wrong, though; we have nothing to talk about.

"Your test results came back," the doctor says. "They're positive."

I take a deep breath. "That was quick," I say.

"Oh, we're very efficient these days," she says. She smiles; I guess she's trying to put me at ease. "We don't have to kill rabbits anymore."

For some reason this makes me think of Dr. Burnford, shouting at his student about rabbits and fertility symbols.

"Can I ask—" The doctor pauses. "Is this welcome news?"

I've checked the box marked "Single" on the intake form. "I don't know," I say slowly. "It was a one-night stand, really. A friend came into town unexpectedly. I don't—''

The vastness of what I've gotten into hits me; I have to stop and take another breath. I'm not going to break down in front of this woman, though; I'm not going to treat her the way my clients sometimes treat me, as if she's a wise-woman capable of solving all my problems. If I start I'll end up telling her about the screaming fight with my mother, about all my doubts, about God knows what else. ''I'd just like some time to think about it,'' I say.

The doctor nods. She puts me up in those awful cold stirrups and examines me, and then, when I'm dressed, gives me some vitamins and a list of foods I should and shouldn't eat, and a pamphlet on abortion. ''Do you need to talk to someone?'' she asks. ''I can recommend a good counselor.''

I can't remember the number of times I've said the same thing to my clients. I've always prided myself on my ability to manage my own life, to stay out of the kinds of messes my clients seem to get into. I shake my head.

Dora Green is waiting for me in front of my office. I nod to her and unlock the door. ''I wanted to know if you made any progress,'' she says.

I feel very weary. It's far too early for her to expect results. I motion her inside the office and sit at my desk. ''I'm sorry,'' she says, taking the chair opposite me. Today she's wearing a green print dress that's even busier than her skirt, more leaves and flowers and what looks like little animals peering through the foliage. ''I should have waited.''

''Your daughter seems to have moved, and she's stopped going to classes,'' I say. ''Other than that, I can't tell you anything yet.''

She nods. Her calm expression does not change. I wonder if she's had the same thought I had, that her daughter is dead, killed by her husband. Satanic rituals, I think.

"I'm meeting someone for lunch," she says. "You must be hungry too. Can I get you something to eat?"

You're supposed to eat enough for two when you're pregnant, but at the same time you're usually sick to your stomach. Just another example, I think, of how impossible the whole thing is. "I've already eaten," I say.

For a moment I think she knows I'm lying; worse, that she knows everything about me, including where I went this morning. I have never felt this way about any of my clients; usually it's the clients who feel the need to justify their behavior.

"Come with me anyway," she says, smiling a little.

The animals on her print dress are moving. I shake my head, trying to focus, but the hallucination doesn't go away. A badger or something shoulders aside a flowering vine and pads forward, its nose twitching.

I look away. I'd better eat something. "All right," I say, and we head out into the street.

She stops at a restaurant a few blocks from my office, and we go inside. I have never seen this place before; probably it's new. There are posters of flowers on the walls, and vases filled with bright flowers at the table.

Her friend is already there. "This is Mickey," Ms. Green says as we sit down. "Mickey, this is Liz Keller."

Mickey nods at me, amused at something. He is slender, with curly blond hair and light gray eyes. There is a slight family resemblance, and for a moment I think he is Carolyn's brother. But surely Ms. Green would have told me if there were others in the family. I wonder who he is, how they know each other.

The waitress comes soon afterward. I study the menu, trying to remember the list of foods the doctor gave me. I could use a cup of coffee, but I'm almost certain the doctor would disapprove. "I'll have some tea," I say.

The waitress takes the rest of the orders and leaves. "How do you know Ms. Green?" I ask Mickey.

"We're related," he says. "Cousins. What about you? How do you know her?"

"She's hired me in a professional capacity," I say. It's all I can tell him without breaking my client's confidentiality.

"Ah," Mickey says. "You're the new detective."

"New detective?" I say, looking at Ms. Green. The animals on her dress are motionless now, thank God. "You didn't tell me about this. What happened to the old one?"

"She wasn't very good," Ms. Green says.

"And time is running out, isn't it?" Mickey says.

"What do you mean?" I ask.

We're interrupted by the waitress, bringing food for Mickey and Ms. Green and a teapot and cup for me. "So," Mickey says. He reaches over and pours me some tea. "What have you found so far?"

"I can't discuss it without my client's permission," I say.

"Oh, Mickey's family," Ms. Green says. "You can tell him anything you tell me."

I sip my tea, enjoying the warmth. My stomach feels fine now. I remember the first time I met Ms. Green, when she came to my office to hire me, and how the nausea had disappeared then too.

I tell Mickey about my trip to Carolyn's old apartment, my visit to the university. He's still smiling. I'm almost certain he's hiding something, that Ms. Green is wrong to trust him. He seems to feel very little concern for his missing cousin.

He pours me another cup of tea. "What do you plan to do now?" he asks.

It's a good question. I've pretty much run out of leads, but it doesn't do to say so in front of the person paying your salary. I take a sip of tea. "Did you know her husband?" I ask him.

"A little," he says.

"Did you like him?"

Mickey laughs. "Like him? The boyfriend from hell?"

"Why do you think she married him?"

He shrugs.

"They seem very different," I say, pushing him.

He pours more tea. I look at the small teapot; it can't possibly hold that much. I lift the lid. It is filled to the brim.

I look up quickly at Mickey. He's grinning, as if daring me to confront him. "How did you do that?" I ask.

"Do what?" he says.

He must have switched teapots somehow, maybe while I was looking at Ms. Green. "Got to fly," he says. He stands and kisses Ms. Green on the cheek. "It was good seeing you."

I watch him go. My earlier suspicions of him become a certainty; he knows something he's not telling. "I've got to go too," I say. I stand and hurry through the restaurant, trying to keep him in sight.

He hasn't gotten that far ahead of me. He turns left out the door and heads east. A few miles farther on is Carolyn's old apartment. I drop back a little, keeping him in sight. Surely he doesn't intend to walk the entire distance.

He continues on for about a mile. The neighborhood slowly changes; the shopfronts here are dingier, and several of them are boarded up. Some of the buildings are painted three or four colors in a vain attempt to cover the graffiti; they look as if they have mange. A man moves to block me, his hand held out. "Spare change?" he asks.

I sidestep him and continue on. Mickey is still in front of me. He is hurrying a little, as if he's getting closer to his destination.

He comes to a corner. He stops for a moment, as if trying

to make up his mind. Then he turns and looks directly at me, grins, and goes right.

I take the corner after him. I've never had anyone spot me, never, not in any of the dozens of tails I've done. How had he known?

There is no one at all on the street. Grimy warehouses face each other, some protected by corrugated doors or iron gratings, all of them locked. One warehouse has rows of tiny windows on the second floor; about half of them are broken, as if they'd been the target in some game. Trees with branches like sticks line the street. No one seems to work here.

I walk up and down the street for over an hour, looking for Mickey in likely and unlikely places, but he is gone.

I go back to my office to get Ms. Green's phone number. I need Mickey's address, need to ask him a few questions.

The phone rings as I'm paging through my files. I pick it up. "Liz Keller, Private Investigations," I say.

"Liz?" the voice at the other end asks.

It's my mother. I don't need this right now. "What?" I say.

"Did you get my message?"

"Yeah."

"I want to talk to you. I want—I changed my mind. I had no right to interfere with anything you do. It's your life."

"I've always thought so."

"Did you see a doctor?"

She promises not to interfere, and then the first thing she says is interfering. "Yeah," I say.

"What did—"

"The test is positive." Even over the phone lines I can feel her straining to ask a question. "I haven't decided what to do yet."

"Did you think about what I said?"

"No."

"If you're going to have a child—"

"I thought you said you weren't going to interfere."

"Well, I just thought that you could take less dangerous work for a while. At least until the child is born."

"I've told you before. This is what I want to do."

"I know that. I'm not saying you should stop being a detective. But maybe you could take different cases—"

I sigh loudly. My mother has never held a job in her life, and yet she thinks she knows everything about everything. If she meets a jeweler she'll talk with great authority about gemstones. If she meets a car mechanic she'll go on about what the best makes of cars are. You can't correct her misconceptions; she feels absolutely no embarrassment when she finds out she's wrong.

Now she wants to tell me how to run a detective agency. "There are no safe cases," I say. "You can never tell how a case will turn out."

"Well, then, maybe you can stop—"

"No."

"I've talked it over with your father—we can afford—"

I hang up. Next thing she'll suggest I move back in with her and my father, into the old bedroom they've kept for me all these years.

Angry now, I pull Dora Green's file. I start to dial her number and then change my mind. I'm going to go visit her. If Mickey's been hiding something then who's to say she hasn't been? What do I really know about her anyway?

I put on my coat and two scarves and leave the office, slamming the door behind me. My stomach has started to feel queasy again.

There are huge plants on Ms. Green's lawn, pushing up against her outside wall. Somehow they have managed to put forth a few leaves, though the trees on the sidewalk are bare. I ring her doorbell, wondering what it is about this woman and flowers.

Her house is light and warm, with wooden beams and hardwood floors, and, of course, pots of plants placed to catch the sun. Red and green and blue weavings cover the backs of white couches and hang from the walls. She leads me to one of the couches and sits across from me.

Once again I notice how calm she is, how composed. There is a stateliness to her that I don't associate with the parents of missing children. "Have you found my daughter?" she asks.

"No, not yet. But I have found—well, I wonder how much you know about Mickey."

"Mickey?"

"Yes, your cousin. He didn't seem very concerned about Carolyn at the restaurant. I wonder if he's holding something back."

"Mickey." She sits back on the couch and smoothes down the edge of the weaving. "I've been thinking the same thing myself. I think that's one of the reasons I asked you to lunch, so you could meet him and form your own impressions. I don't think he's telling me everything he knows."

"Do you have his address?"

"Yes, of course." She recites his address from memory. It's in a very mixed part of town, with apartment buildings and middle-class houses and small neighborhood shops all jumbled together. It's miles from the warehouse district he led me to this afternoon.

I thank her and start to leave. "Take care of yourself," she says.

Once again I get the unsettling feeling that she knows all about me. For a moment I want to tell her everything, to pour out the things I held back from my mother and the doctor.

Why on earth did Carolyn Green run away from a mother like this?

Suddenly I realize that it's not the financial aspects of having a child I'm worried about. That would be tough, but I can handle it. What I'm terrified of is being the kind of mother my own mother was, interfering, small-minded, unable to let go. What other example do I have?

As I go back to my car I see that the streetlights are starting to come on. I've wasted more time than I thought following Mickey. I go home, and turn the heat up as high as it will go.

The next day I am parked across the street from Mickey's house. There is a car in the driveway, a late model Mercury. He might be out on one of his long walks, but I gamble that the car means he's still home.

Time passes slowly. My car is freezing, but I can't risk turning on the engine to start the heater. Finally the front door opens and Mickey steps out. He passes the car in the driveway and heads for the sidewalk. Another walk today, I think.

I let him get half a block ahead of me and then ease open the car door. This time I am certain he hasn't seen me. He walks slowly, as though he has no destination in mind; it is easy enough to keep him in sight.

He continues this way for several miles. He shows no sign of stopping. Finally he turns down a main street and I see that he is heading toward the warehouse district he visited yesterday. He is moving faster now.

I follow, hurrying to keep him in sight. He comes to the corner at which I lost him and turns. I take the corner after him. He is still in front of me, moving very fast now, almost running.

The rain starts again, lashing the bare trees. He goes halfway down the street and pushes on one of the warehouse doors. I run after him, but by the time I get there the door is closed. I try it; it opens with only the slightest squeak of rusty metal.

I step inside and close the door quickly. The first thing I notice is the smell of corroded metal. I can see nothing; even minutes after I have shut the door the warehouse is pitch dark. I can hear nothing either, not Mickey, not anyone he has come to meet. After a few minutes I make out the distant sound of water dripping on metal.

A flare burns suddenly across the room, too dim to reach me. I move toward it cautiously, keeping close to the shadows by the wall.

As I get nearer I see two huge chairs made of rusted metal. One is empty; a man sits in the other. It is too dark to tell, and I am too far away, but I am almost certain he is the man in the photograph, Carolyn's husband. The sight of the empty chair makes me uneasy.

The light flares higher, and now I see Mickey among the shadows, standing before the man in the chair. The man wears a crown made of iron; its points catch the flames and glow red.

I feel the nudge of an elusive memory, a story I once heard or a lesson I learned in school. I know this place: the dark hall, the two chairs, the harsh smell of rusting metal. But before I can remember it fully the man in the chair speaks.

"Greetings, cousin," he says. "What news do you bring me from the upper world?"

"She knows nothing," Mickey says. "She is unable to find her daughter."

"Good. Her daughter is mine, gained by lawful means."

"Of course," Mickey says.

The red light erupts again. The shadows fall back. The man in the chair looks up and sees me. "Who is that woman?" he asks.

I turn and run. I find the door to the outside, but it is stuck, locked. I am still pulling on it when Mickey comes up behind me.

"Come, Liz," he says. "This is no fit way to greet the King of Hell."

I turn and face him, look beyond him to Jack Hayes. "King of Hell," I say scornfully. "Is that King Jack, or King Hayes?"

"Hades," he says. It is a while before I realize that he is correcting my pronunciation.

"Where is Carolyn?" I ask.

"My wife is safe."

"Where is Carolyn?" I ask again.

"She is not Carolyn," Hayes says. "Her name is Kore. Some call her Persephone."

"I don't have time—"

"I will tell you where she is," he says. "I first saw her many years ago. She was gathering flowers, and she had wandered too far from her companions. I fell in love with her then—I saw that she would bring light to my dark lands. I rode my chariot up from Hell, and I seized her and bore her down to my kingdom. Her mother Demeter searched all the earth for her but could not find her, and in her sorrow called down the chilling winter. It was Hermes who led Demeter to her daughter, that first winter so long ago."

"Hermes?"

Mickey bows toward me mockingly. "The Romans called me Mercury. The messenger, the quick-witted one, the god of commerce. And also—" he grins "—the trickster, the god of thieves."

I wonder if they are both crazy. But it doesn't really matter; the important thing is making sure that Carolyn is safe. "Where is she?"

"You *are* persistent," Mickey says. "She chose well for a change, Demeter did."

"What do you mean?"

"Demeter searches every year for her daughter. She will not end her winter until Kore is found, and we made the search more difficult than usual this year." Mickey shakes his head, almost in admiration. "This is the first time she's hired a private investigator, though. I made sure that the one she found was incompetent, but apparently she tried again without my help."

"Why didn't you just tell her where her daughter is?"

"Some years I do, some years I don't. You can't trust me, really." He grins engagingly. "You know the Little Ice Age, during the Middle Ages? That was my doing. And now—she should have gone to you sooner. She's left it far too late."

"Where—"

Jack Hayes raises his hand to stop me, then waves to a corner of the room still in shadow. Carolyn comes toward us. She is very pale; even her blue eyes seem paler, and there are dark circles under her eyes. Her long white dress is torn and dirty.

Suddenly I remember the rest of the Greek legend. "You've had your time with her," I say to Hayes. "She ate four pomegranate seeds—that gave you four months with her. It's spring now—it's time for her to go home."

Hayes nods. The foul light slowly diminishes. Before he can change his mind I grab Carolyn by the wrist and hurry toward the door.

Mickey is standing there, blocking the way. I didn't even see him move; I would have sworn that he was still behind me. "No," he says. He's still smiling; it's all a game to him. "Let's have another Ice Age. The last one was such fun."

I let go of Carolyn and turn to look at Hayes. It's a mistake; Mickey shoves me toward the throne and tries to force me to the floor.

I sidestep him, sliding to one side and crouching down. He

is still lunging forward, and as he moves in front of me I punch him in the kidney.

He doubles over. Before he can get up I run for the door, taking Carolyn with me. The door opens easily.

We step outside. It's raining hard; we are drenched within seconds. I slam the door behind me and run down the street, taking Carolyn with me. As we reach the corner a taxi comes toward us. I hail it and we get inside.

I give the driver Dora Green's address and sit back. Carolyn stares through the wiper blades at the streets outside. There is a trace of sadness on her face, and—what seems worse to me—resignation. What does she think, having been delivered from the terrors of that warehouse? Has it happened before, as Mickey said? For how many years has she had to take this ride home?

A few minutes later we drive up to Ms. Green's house. I pay the driver and we walk up to the front door. I ring the bell.

The door opens. Dora Green steps outside and sees her daughter. She goes toward Carolyn and holds her close; they stand motionless for a long time. I cannot read the expression on her face.

The rain stops. A warm wind courses from somewhere, heavy with the scents of flowers and oranges. Tiny green leaves are budded on the branches of the trees; I hadn't noticed them before. They open as I watch.

After a long moment Dora releases her daughter and turns the full regard of her gaze to me. The air burns around her, bright as gold. She seems to read my entire life in an instant, both my past and what is to come. Her expression is perfectly balanced between joy and sorrow.

I want to fall to my knees before her. The goddess of earth, of fertility. "I thank you," Demeter says.

• • •

I am taking a leave of absence from my job, at least until the child is born and is old enough for daycare. Demeter has been more than generous in settling up her bill, and Hermes, the god of commerce, seems to have shrugged off the incident in the warehouse and has offered me a loan. He is also, as he was good enough to warn me, the god of thieves, but I've dealt with crooks before. I am very glad not to have to take money from my parents.

The doctor tells me the child will be a girl. I am going to call her Demetra.

THE BACKWARD LOOK

Isaac Asimov

"The Backward Look" was purchased by George Scithers, and appeared in the September 1979 issue of Asimov's, *with an interior illustration by Jack Gaughan.*

*A good case could be made for the proposition that the late Isaac Asimov was the most famous SF writer of the last half of the twentieth century. He was the author of almost five hundred books, including some of the best-known novels in the genre (*I, Robot *and the* Foundation *trilogy, for example); his last several novels kept him solidly on the nationwide bestseller lists throughout the '80s; he won two Nebulas and two Hugos, plus the prestigious Grandmaster Nebula; he wrote an enormous number of nonfiction books on a bewilderingly large range of topics, everything from the Bible to Shakespeare, and his many books on scientific matters made him perhaps the best-known scientific popularizer of our time; his nonfiction articles appeared everywhere from* Omni *to* TV Guide; *he was one of the most sought-after speakers in the country, and appeared on most of the late-night and afternoon talk shows of his day, and even did television commercials—and he was also the only SF writer famous enough to have had an SF*

magazine named after him, Asimov's Science Fiction
*magazine. A mere sampling of Asimov's other books,
even restricting ourselves to science fiction alone,
would include* The Stars Like Dust, The Currents of
Space, The Gods Themselves, Foundation's Edge,
The Robots of Dawn, Robots and Empire, Foundation's Earth, *and two expansions of famous Asimov
short stories into novel form,* The Ugly Little Boy
and Nightfall, *written in collaboration with Robert
Silverberg. His most recent fiction titles include the
novel* Forward the Foundation, *and the posthumous
collections* Gold *and* Fantasy.

*Asimov was almost as well-known in the mystery
field as he was in SF, for novels such as* Murder at
the ABA *as well as for the long-running series of
stories about that club of suave amateur investigators,* The Black Widowers. *He was also one of the
most successful practitioners of the art of blending
SF and mystery, with his series of stories about SF
armchair detective Wendell Urth, as well as what are
perhaps still the two most successful hybrid SF/mys-
tery novels ever written,* The Caves of Steel *and* The
Naked Sun, *featuring the robot detective R. Daneel
Olivaw.*

*Here he shows us once again the truth of that old
saying,* Don't look back—you don't know what may
be gaining on you . . .

If Emmanuel Rubin knew how not to be didactic, he never
exercised that knowledge.

"When you write a short story," he said, "you had better
know the ending first. The end of a story is only the end to
a reader. To a writer, it's the beginning. If you don't know
exactly where you're going every minute that you're writing,
you'll never get there—or anywhere."

Thomas Trumbull's young guest at this particular monthly
banquet of the Black Widowers seemed all eyes as he watched
Rubin's straggly gray beard quiver and his thick-lensed

glasses glint; and all ears as he listened to Rubin's firm, decibelic voice.

The guest himself was clearly in the early twenties, quite thin, with a somewhat bulging forehead and a rather diminutive chin. His clothing almost glistened in its freshness, as though he had broken out a brand-new costume for the great occasion. His name was Milton Peterborough.

He said, a small quiver in his voice, "Does that mean you have to write an outline, Mr. Rubin?"

"No," said Rubin, emphatically. "You can if you want to, but I never do. You don't have to know the exact road you're going to take. You have to know your destination, that's all. Once that's the case, any road will take you there. As you write you are continually looking backward from that known destination, and it's that backward look that guides you."

Mario Gonzalo, who was quickly and carefully drawing a caricature of the guest, making his eyes incredibly large and filling them with a childlike innocence, said, "Come on, Manny, that sort of tight plotting might fit your cockamamie mysteries, but a real writer deals with character, doesn't he? He creates *people*; and they behave in accordance with their characters; and that guides the story, probably to the surprise of the author."

Rubin turned slowly and said, "If you're talking about long, invertebrate novels, Mario—assuming you're talking about anything at all—it's possible for an experienced or gifted writer to meander along and produce something passable. But you can always tell the I-don't-know-where-I'm-going-but-I'm-going book. Even if you forgive it its amorphous character for the sake of its virtues, you have to *forgive* it, and that's a strain and a drawback. A tightly-plotted story with everything fitting together neatly is, on the other hand, the noblest work of literature. It may be bad, but it never need ask forgiveness. The backward look—"

At the other end of the room, Geoffrey Avalon glanced with resignation at Rubin and said, "I think it was a mistake, Tom, to tell Manny at the start that the young man was an aspiring writer. It brings out the worst in him, or—at any rate—the longest winded." He stirred the ice in his drink with his forefinger and brought his dark eyebrows together forbiddingly.

"Actually," said Thomas Trumbull, his lined face uncharacteristically placid, "the kid wanted to meet Manny. He admired his stories, God knows why. Well, he's the son of a friend of mine and a nice youngster and I thought I'd expose him to the seamy side of life by bringing him here."

Avalon said, "It won't hurt us to be exposed to youth now and then, either. But I hate being exposed to Rubin's theories of literature.—Henry."

The quiet and smoothly efficient waiter, who served at all the Black Widowers' banquets, was at his side at once without seeming to have moved in order to have achieved that. "Yes, sir?"

"Henry," said Avalon, "what are these strange manifestations?"

Henry said, "Tonight we will have a buffet dinner. The chef has prepared a variety of Indian and Pakistani dishes."

"With curry?"

"Rather heavy on the curry, sir. It was Mr. Trumbull's special request."

Trumbull flared under Avalon's accusing eye. "I wanted curry and I'm the host."

"And Manny won't eat it and will be unbearable."

Trumbull shrugged.

Rubin was not entirely unbearable but he was loud, and only Roger Halsted seemed unaffected by the Rubinian tirade against all things Indian. He said, "A buffet is a good idea," patted his lips with his napkin and went back for a third helping of everything, with a beatific smile on his face.

Trumbull said, "Roger, if you don't stop eating, we'll start the grilling session over your chewing."

"Go ahead," said Halsted, cheerfully. "I don't mind."

"You will later tonight," said Rubin, "when your stomach-wall burns through."

Trumbull said, "And you're going to start the grilling."

"If you don't mind my talking with my mouth full," said Halsted.

"Get started, then."

Halsted said thickly, "How do you justify your existence, Milton?"

"I can't," said Peterborough, a little breathlessly. "Maybe after I get my degrees."

"What's your school and major?"

"Columbia and chemistry."

"Chemistry?" said Halsted. "I would have thought it was English. Didn't I gather during the cocktail hour that you were an aspiring writer?"

"Anyone is allowed to be an aspiring writer," said Peterborough.

"Aspiring," said Rubin, darkly.

"And what do you want to write?" said Halsted.

Peterborough hesitated and said, with a trace of defensiveness in his voice, "Well, I've always been a science fiction fan. Since I was nine, anyway."

"Oh, God," muttered Rubin, his eyes rolling upward in mute appeal.

Gonzalo said instantly, "Science fiction? That's what your friend Isaac Asimov writes, isn't it, Manny?"

"He's not my friend," said Rubin. "He clings to me out of helpless admiration."

Trumbull raised his voice. "Will you two stop having a private conversation? Go on, Roger."

"Have you written any science fiction?"

"I've tried, but I haven't submitted anything. I'm going to, though. I have to."

"Why do you have to?"

"I made a bet."

"What kind?"

"Well," said Peterborough, helplessly. "It's rather complicated—and embarrassing."

"We don't mind the complications," said Halsted, "and we'll try not to be embarrassed."

"Well," said Peterborough, and there appeared on his face something that had not been seen at the Black Widowers banquets for years, a richly tinted blush, "there's this girl. I'm sort of cra—I like her, but I don't think she likes me, but I like her anyway. The trouble is she goes for a basketball player; a real idiot—six foot five to his eyebrows and nothing above."

Peterborough shook his head and continued, "I don't have much going for me. I can't impress her with chemistry; but she's an English Lit major, so I showed her some of my stories. She asked me if I had ever sold anything, and I said no. But then I said I intended to write something and sell it, and she laughed.

"That bothered me, and I thought of something. It seems that Lester del Rey—"

Rubin interposed. "Who?"

"Lester del Rey. He's a science fiction writer."

"Another one of those?" said Rubin. "Never heard of him."

"Well, he's no Asimov," admitted Peterborough, "but he's all right. Anyway, the way he got started was once when he read a science fiction story and thought it was terrible. He said to his girl, 'Hell, I can write something better than that,' and she said, 'I dare you,' and he did and sold it.

"So when this girl laughed, I said, 'I'll bet I write one and sell it,' and she said, 'I'll bet you don't,' and I said, 'I'll bet you a date against five dollars. If I sell the story, you go with me to a dinner and dance on a night of my choosing.' And she agreed.

"So I've just *got* to write the story now, because she said she'd go out with me if I wrote the story and she liked it, even if it didn't sell—which may mean she likes me more than I think."

James Drake, who had been listening thoughtfully, brushed his gray stub of a mustache with one finger and said, "Or that she's quite confident that you won't even write the story."

"I *will*," said Peterborough.

"Then go ahead," said Rubin.

"There's a catch. I can write the story, I know. I've got some good stuff. I even know the ending so I can give it that backward look you mentioned, Mr. Rubin. What I don't have is a motive."

"A motive?" said Rubin. "I thought you were writing a science fiction story."

"Yes, Mr. Rubin, but it's a science fiction mystery, and I need a motive. I have the modus operandi of the killing, and the way of killing but I don't know the *why* of the killing. I thought, though, if I came here, I could discuss it with you."

"You could *what?*" said Rubin, lifting his head.

"Especially you, Mr. Rubin. I've read your mystery stories—I don't read science fiction exclusively—and I think they're great. You're always so good with motivation. I thought you could help me out."

Rubin was breathing hard and gave every appearance of believing that that breath was flame. He had made his dinner very much out of rice and salad, plus, out of sheer famishing, two helpings of *coupe aux marrons*; and he was in no mood for even such sweet reason as he was, on occasion, observed to possess.

He said, "Let me get it straight, Joe College. You've made a bet. You're going to get a chance at a girl, or such chance as you can make of it, by writing a story she likes and maybe selling it—and now you want to win the bet and cheat the girl by having me write the story for you. Is that the way it is?"

"No, sir," said Peterborough, urgently, "that's *not* the way it is. I'll write it. I just want help with the motive."

"And except for that, you'll write it," said Rubin. "How about having me dictate the story to you. You can still *write* it. You can copy it out in your own handwriting."

"That's not the same at all."

"Yes, it is, young man; and you can stop right there. Either write the story yourself or tell the girl you can't."

Milton Peterborough looked about helplessly.

Trumbull said, "Damn it, Manny, why so much on the high horse? I've heard you say a million times that ideas are a dime a dozen; that it's the *writing* that's hard. Give him an idea, then; he'll still have the hard part to do."

"I won't," said Rubin, pushing himself away from the table and crossing his arms. "If the rest of you have an atrophied sense of ethics, go ahead and give him ideas—if you know how."

Trumbull said, "All right, I can settle this by fiat since I'm the host, but I'll throw it open to a vote. How many favor helping the kid if we can?"

He held up his hand, and so did Gonzalo and Drake.

Avalon cleared his throat a little uncertainly. "I'm afraid I've got to side with Manny. It would be cheating the girl," he said.

Halsted said, "As a teacher, I've got to disapprove of outside help on a test."

"Tie vote," said Rubin. "What are you going to do, Tom?"

Trumbull said, "We haven't all voted. Henry is a Black Widower and his vote will break the tie.—Henry?"

Henry paused a brief moment. "My honorary position, sir, scarcely gives me the right to—"

"You are not an honorary Black Widower, Henry. You are a Black Widower. Decide!"

Rubin said, "Remember, Henry, you are the epitome of honest men. Where do you stand on cheating a girl?"

"No electioneering," said Trumbull. "Go ahead, Henry."

Henry's face wrinkled into a rare frown. "I have never laid claim to extraordinary honesty, but if I did, I might treat this as a special case. Juliet told Romeo, 'At lovers' perjuries/They say Jove laughs.' Might we stretch a point?"

"I'm surprised, Henry," said Rubin.

Henry said, "I am perhaps swayed by the fact that I do not view this matter as lying between the young man and the young woman. Rather it lies between a bookish young man and an athlete. We are all bookish men; and, in our time, we may each have lost a young woman to an athlete. I am embarrassed to say that I have. Surely, then—"

Rubin said, "Well, I haven't. I've never lost a girl to—" He paused a moment in sudden thought, then said in an altered tone, "Well, it's irrelevant. All right, if I'm outvoted, I'm outvoted.—So what's the story, Peterborough?"

Peterborough's face was flushed and there was a trickle of perspiration at one temple. He said, "I won't tell you any of the story I've been planning except the barest essentials of the point I need help on. I don't want anything more than the minimum. I wouldn't want *that*, even, if this didn't mean— so much—" He ran down.

Rubin said, with surprising quietness, "Go on. Don't worry about it. We understand."

Peterborough said, "Thanks. I appreciate it. I've got two men, call them Murderer and Victim. I've worked out the way Murderer does it and how he gets caught and I won't say a word about that. Murderer and Victim are both eclipse buffs."

Avalon interrupted. "Are you an eclipse buff, Mr. Peterborough?"

"Yes, sir, I am. I have friends who go to every eclipse anywhere in the world even if it's only a five-percenter, but I can't afford that and don't have the time. I go to those I can reach. I've got a telescope and photographic equipment."

Avalon said, "Good! It helps, when one is going to talk about eclipses, if one knows something about them. Trying to write on a subject concerning which one is ignorant is a sure prescription for failure."

Gonzalo said, "Is the woman you're interested in an eclipse buff."

"No," said Peterborough. "I wish she were."

"You know," said Gonzalo, "if she doesn't share your interests, you might try finding someone who does."

Peterborough shook his head. "I don't think it works that way, Mr. Gonzalo."

"It sure doesn't," said Trumbull. "Shut up, Mario, and let him talk."

Peterborough said, "Murderer and Victim are both taking eclipse photographs; and, against all expectations, Victim, who is the underdog, the born loser, takes the better photograph; and Murderer, unable to endure this, decides to kill Victim. From there on, I have no trouble."

Rubin said, "Then you have your motive. What's your problem?"

"The trouble is—what *kind* of a better photograph? An eclipse photograph is an eclipse photograph. Some are better than others; but, assuming that both photographers are competent, not *that* much better. Not a murder's-worth better.''

Rubin shrugged. ''You can build the story in such a way as to make even a small difference murder-worthy—but I admit that would take an experienced hand. Drop the eclipse. Try something else.''

''I can't. The whole business of the murder, the weapon and the detection depends on photography and eclipses. So it has to stay.''

Drake said softly, ''What makes it a science fiction story, young man?''

''I haven't explained that, have I?—I'm trying to tell as little as possible about the story. For what I'm doing, I need advanced computers and science fictional photographic gimmickry. One of the two characters—I'm not sure which—takes a photograph of the eclipse from a stratospheric jet.''

''In that case, why not go whole hog?'' said Gonzalo. ''If it's going to go science-fictional . . . Look, let me tell you how I see it. Murderer and Victim are eclipse buffs and Murderer is the better man—so make it Murderer who's on that plane, and taking the best eclipse photograph ever seen, using some new photographic gimmick he's invented. Then have Victim, against all expectation, beat him out. Victim goes to the Moon and takes the eclipse photograph there. Murderer is furious at being beaten, goes blind with rage and there you are.''

Rubin said energetically, ''An eclipse photo on the *Moon?*''

''Why not?'' said Gonzalo, offended. ''We can get to the Moon right now so we can certainly do it in a science fiction story. And there's a vacuum on the Moon, right? There's no air. You don't have to be a scientist to know that. And you get a better picture without air. You get a sharper picture. Isn't that right, Milton?''

Peterborough said, ''Yes, but—''

Rubin overrode him. "Mario," he said, "listen carefully. An eclipse of the Sun takes place when the Moon gets exactly between the Sun and the Earth. Observers on Earth then see the Sun blacked out because the opaque body of the Moon is squarely in front of it. We on Earth are in the Moon's shadow. Now if you're *on* the Moon," his voice grew harsh, "how the Hell can you be in the Moon's shadow?"

Avalon said, "Not so fast, Manny; an eclipse is an eclipse is an eclipse. There is such a thing as a Lunar eclipse, when the Earth gets between the Sun and the Moon. The Moon is in the Earth's shadow in that case and the whole Moon gets dark.

"The way I see it, then, is that Murderer takes a beautiful photograph of an eclipse on Earth, with the Moon moving in front of the Sun. He has advanced equipment that he has invented himself so that no one can possibly take a better photo of the moon in front of the Sun. Victim, however, goes him one better by taking an even more impressive photograph of an eclipse on the Moon, where, as Mario says, there is no air, with the *Earth* moving in front of the Sun."

Peterborough mumbled, "Not the same thing."

"It sure isn't," said Halsted, who had pushed his coffee cup to one side and was doing some quick figuring. "As seen from Earth, the Moon and the Sun have the same apparent width, almost exactly. Pure coincidence, of course; no astronomical necessity at all. In fact, eons past, the Moon was closer and appeared larger, and eons future, the Moon will be—Well, never mind. The fact is that the Earth is larger than the Moon, and from the Moon you see the Earth at the same distance that you see the Moon when you're standing on Earth. The Earth in the Moon's sky is therefore as much larger than the Moon in appearance as it is in actuality. Do you get that?"

"No," said Gonzalo, flatly.

Halsted looked annoyed. "Well, then, don't get it. Take my word for it. The Earth in the Moon's sky is about 3⅔ as wide in appearance as the Moon is in Earth's sky. That means the Earth in the Moon's sky is also that much bigger than the Sun, because the Sun looks just the same from the Moon as from the Earth."

"So what's the difference?" said Gonzalo. "If the Earth is bigger, it gets in the way of the Sun that much better."

"No," said Halsted. "The whole point about the eclipse is that the Moon just fits over the Sun. It hides the bright circle of the gleaming Sun and allows its corona—that is, its upper atmosphere—to shine all about the hidden Sun. The corona gleams out in every direction with the light of the full Moon and does so in beautifully delicate curves and streamers.

"On the other hand, if you get a large body like the Earth in front of the Sun, it covers up the shining sphere and the corona as well. You don't see anything."

Avalon said, "That's assuming the Earth goes squarely in front of the Sun. When you see the eclipse before or after midpoint, at least part of the corona will stick beyond the Earth's sphere."

Peterborough said, "Part isn't the whole. It wouldn't be the same thing."

There was a short silence; and then Drake said, "I hope you don't mind if a fellow-chemist tries his hand at this, young man. I'm trying to picture the Earth in the sky, getting in the way of the Sun. And if we do that, then there's this to consider: the Earth has an atmosphere and the Moon has not.

"When the Moon moves in front of the Sun, as viewed from the Earth, the Moon's surface is sharp against the Sun. When the Earth moves in front of the Sun, as viewed from the Moon, the Earth's boundary is fuzzy and the Sun shines through Earth's atmosphere. Does that make a difference that you can use in the story?"

"Well," said Peterborough, "I've thought of that, actually. Even when the Sun is completely behind the Earth, its light is refracted through the Earth's atmosphere on every side, and a red-orange light penetrates it and reaches the Moon. It's as though the Moon can see a sunset all around the Earth. And that's not just theory. When there's a total eclipse of the Moon, you can usually see the Moon as a dull brick-red circle of light. It gleams in Earth's sunset atmosphere.

"As the eclipse, as viewed from the Moon, progresses, that side of the atmosphere that has just passed over the Sun is brighter, but grows gradually dimmer while the other side grows brighter. At eclipse mid-point, if you are viewing it from a part of the Moon which sees both Earth and Sun centered with respect to each other, the red-orange ring is evenly bright all the way around—assuming there isn't too much in the way of clouds in Earth's atmosphere at the time."

Drake said, "Well, for God's sake, isn't that a sufficiently spectacular sight for Victim to photograph? The Earth would be a black hole in the sky, with a thin orange rim all around. It would be—"

"No, sir," said Peterborough. "It isn't the same thing. It's too dull. It would be just a red-orange ring. Once the photograph is taken the first time, that would be it. It wouldn't be like the infinitely varying corona."

Trumbull said, "Let *me* try! You want the corona visible all around, is that it, Milton?"

"Yes, sir."

"Stop me if I'm wrong, but in my reading, I've been given to understand that the sky is blue because light is scattered by the atmosphere. On the Moon, where there is no atmosphere, the sky is black. The stars, which on Earth are washed out by the scattered light of our blue sky, would not be washed out in the Moon's airless sky. They would be visible."

"Yes, though I suspect the Sun's glare would make them hard to see."

Trumbull said, "That's not important. All you would have to do is cut an opaque circle of metal and hold it up in the air at the proper distance from your photographic equipment in order to just block out the Sun's blazing disc. You can't do that on Earth, because even if you blocked out the Sun, the scattered light of the sky obscures the corona. On the Moon, there's no scattered light in the sky and the corona would shine out."

Peterborough said, "In theory, that's possible. In fact, it can even be done on Earth on mountain tops, making use of a coronagraph. It still wouldn't be the real thing, though, for it's not just a matter of light scattered by the atmosphere. There's light scattered and reflected by the ground.

"The Lunar surface would be very brightly lit up and light would be coming in from every angle. The photographs you would take would not be good ones. You see, the reason the Moon does the good job it does here on Earth is that its shadow doesn't just fall on the telescope and camera. It falls on all the surrounding landscape. The shadow of the Moon can, under ideal conditions, be 160 miles wide and cover 21,000 square miles of the Earth's surface. Usually, it's considerably smaller than that; but generally it's enough to cover the immediate landscape—that is, if it happens to be a total eclipse."

Trumbull said, "A bigger opaque object, then—"

"It would have to be quite big and quite far away," said Peterborough, "to achieve the effect. That would be too cumbersome."

Halsted said, "Wait, I think I have it. You would need something big for the purpose, all right. Suppose there were spherical space settlements in the Moon's orbit. If Victim is in a spaceship and gets the space settlement between himself and the Sun, that would be exactly what he wants. He could arrange to be close enough to have the shadow—which, of course, is conical and narrows to a point if you get far enough away—to be just thick enough to enclose his entire ship. There would be no world-surface to reflect light, and there you are.''

Peterborough said, uneasily, "I hadn't thought of that. It's possible.''

Halsted grinned, and a flush of pleasure mounted to the hairline he had once had. "That's it, then.''

Peterborough said, "I don't want to be troublesome, but—but if we introduce the space motif, it's going to create some problems in the rest of the story. It's sort of important that everything stay on or near the Earth and yet that there be something so startling and unexpected that it would—''

He paused and Rubin completed the sentence for him, "So startling and unexpected that it would drive Murderer to rage and vengeance.''

"Yes.''

"Well,'' said Rubin, "since I'm the master of mystery here, I think I can work it out for you without leaving Earth very far behind, just as soon as I get some points straightened out.—You said that Murderer is taking the photographs from a plane. Why?''

"Oh. That's because the Moon's shadow, when it falls on Earth, moves quickly—up to 1440 miles an hour or about 0.4 miles a second. If you're standing in one place on Earth, the longest possible duration of a total eclipse is seven minutes and then the shadow has moved beyond you. That's when the Earth is as deep into the Moon's shadow as it ever gets. When the Earth isn't as deep in and is nearer the final point of the shadow, the total eclipse may last only a couple of minutes, or even only a few seconds. In fact, more than half the time, the Moon's shadow during an eclipse doesn't reach the

Earth's surface at all; and when the Moon is squarely in front of the Sun, the Sun overlaps it on all sides. That's an 'annular eclipse' and enough sunlight then slips past the Moon to wash out everything. An annular eclipse is no good at all.''

"But in the airplane?" prompted Rubin.

"In an airplane, you can race along with the shadow and make the total eclipse last for an hour or more even if it would only endure a very short time on one position on Earth. You have a great deal more time to take photographs and make scientific observations. That's not science-fictional; it's done right now."

"Can you take very good pictures from the plane?" asked Rubin. "Does it allow a steady enough basis for photography?"

"In my story," said Peterborough, "I've got a computer guiding the plane, allowing for wind movements, and keeping it perfectly steady. That's one of the places where the science fiction comes in."

"Still, the Moon's shadow eventually leaves the Earth's surface altogether, doesn't it?"

"Yes, the eclipse track covers a fixed portion of the Earth's surface, and it has an overall starting point and an overall ending point."

"Exactly," said Rubin. "Now Murderer is confident that his photographs taken from the stratosphere are going to include the best views of an eclipse ever seen, but he doesn't count on Victim's having a spaceship. Don't worry, there's no need to leave Earth very far. It's just that the spaceship follows the Moon's shadow *after* it leaves the Earth. Victim has a still longer chance to take photographs, a steadier base, and no atmospheric interference whatever. Murderer is hoist on his own petard for he sees that poor simp, Victim, do exactly what he does but go him one better. He snaps and becomes a killer."

Gonzalo waved both arms in the air in excitement. "Wait! Wait! We can do even better than that. Listen, what about that annular eclipse you mentioned a while ago? You said the shadow doesn't reach the Earth."

"It doesn't reach the surface. That's right."

"How high off the surface is it?"

"That depends. Under extreme conditions, the end point of the shadow could miss the Earth by hundreds of miles."

"Yes," said Gonzalo, "but could that end point miss Earth by, say, *ten* miles?"

"Oh, sure."

"Would it still be annular, and no good?"

"That's right," said Peterborough. "The Moon would come just barely short of covering the Sun. There would be just the thinnest sliver of Sun around the Moon, and that would give enough light to spoil things. If you took photographs, you'd miss the prominences, the flares, and the corona."

"But what if you went ten miles up into the atmosphere?" said Gonzalo. "Then you'd see it total, wouldn't you?"

"If you were in the right spot, yes."

"There it is, then. One of those annular eclipses comes along, and Murderer thinks he'll pull a fast one. He gets into his stratoplane, goes ten miles up to get into the point of the shadow or just over it, and follows it along. He's going to make a total eclipse out of an annular one—and Victim, the usual loser, does the same thing, except he uses a spaceship and follows it out into space and gets better pictures. What can get old Murderer more torn up than having him play his ace—and getting trumped."

Avalon nodded his head. "Good, Mario. That *is* an improvement."

Rubin looked as if he had unexpectedly bitten into a lemon. "I hate to say it, Mario—"

"You don't have to say it, Manny," said Gonzalo. "I see it all over you.—There you are, kid. Write the story."

Peterborough said, with a sigh, "Yes, I suppose that is the best that can be done."

"You don't sound overjoyed," said Gonzalo.

"I was hoping for something more—uh—outrageous, but I don't think it exists. If none of you could think up anything—"

"May I interrupt, sir?" said Henry.

"Huh? Oh—no, I don't want any more coffee, waiter," said Peterborough, absently.

"No, sir. I mean, concerning the eclipse."

Trumbull said, "Henry's a member of the club, Martin. He broke the tie on the matter of the discussion. Remember?"

Peterborough put a hand to his forehead. "Oh, sure. Ask away—uh—Henry."

"Actually, sir, would the photographs be that much better in a vacuum than in the thin air of the stratosphere? Would the difference in quality be enough to result in murder, unless Murderer was a close approach to a homicidal maniac?"

"That's the thing," said Peterborough, nodding. "That's what bothers me. That's why I keep saying I need a motive. These differences in quality of photos aren't big enough."

"Let us consider, then," said Henry, "Mr. Rubin's dictum that in telling a story one should look backward."

"I know the ending," said Peterborough. "I have the backward look."

"I mean it in another sense—that of deliberately looking in the other direction, the unaccustomed direction. In an eclipse, we always look at the Moon—just the Moon in a Lunar eclipse, and the Moon covering the Sun in a Solar eclipse—and that's what we take photographs of. What if we take a backward look at the Earth?"

"What's to see on Earth, Henry?" asked Gonzalo.

"When the Moon moves into the Earth's shadow, it is always in the full phase and it is usually completely darkened. What happens to the Earth when it moves into the Moon's shadow? It certainly doesn't darken completely."

"No," said Peterborough emphatically. "The Moon's shadow is thinner and shorter than the Earth's, and the Earth itself is larger than the Moon. Even when Earth passes as deeply as it can into the Moon's shadow, only a tiny bit of the Earth is darkened, a little dot of darkness that makes up, at most, about 1/600 of the Earth's circle of light."

"Could you see it from the Moon?" asked Henry.

"If you knew where to look and especially if you had a good pair of binoculars. You would see it start small, move west to east across the face of the Earth, getting bigger, then smaller, and then vanish. Interesting, but certainly not spectacular."

"Not from the Moon, sir," said Henry. "Now suppose we reverse the positions of the characters. It is Victim who has the airplane and who can get a photograph from the stratosphere. It is Murderer who intends to trump his opponent's ace by taking a better photograph from space—a marginally better photograph. Suppose, though, that Victim, against all expectations, from his airplane over-trumps Murderer in his spaceship."

Avalon said, "How can he do that, Henry?"

"Victim, in his plane, suddenly realizes he needn't look at the Moon. He looks backward at the ground and sees the Moon's shadow, racing toward him. The Moon's shadow is just a dark dot when seen from the Moon; it's just the coming of temporary night as seen from the Earth's surface—but from a plane in the stratosphere, it is a racing circle of darkness moving at 1440 miles an hour, swallowing up the land and sea—and clouds, for that matter—as it goes. The plane can move ahead of it, and it is no longer necessary to take single snapshots. A movie camera can produce the most dramatic film. In this way, Murderer, having fully expected to outdo Victim, finds that Victim has captured world attention even though he had only an airplane to Murderer's spaceship.''

Gonzalo broke into loud applause, and Trumbull said, ''Right on!'' Even Rubin smiled and nodded.

As for Peterborough, he fired up at once saying, ''Sure! And the approaching shadow would have a thin red rim, for at the moment the shadow overtakes you, the red prominences cast their light unmasked by the Sun's white light. That's it, Henry! The backward look does it!—If I write this one properly, I don't care even if it doesn't sell.—I won't care even'' (his voice shook) ''if—uh—*she* doesn't like it and doesn't go out with me. The story is more important!''

Henry smiled gently and said, ''I'm glad to hear that, sir. A writer should always have a proper sense of priorities.''

FAULT LINES

Nancy Kress

"Fault Lines" was purchased by Gardner Dozois, and appeared in the August 1995 issue of Asimov's, *with an illustration by Steve Cavallo. It was one of a long sequence of elegant and incisive stories by Kress that have appeared in* Asimov's *under four different editors over the last eighteen years, since her first* Asimov's *sale to George Scithers in 1979— stories that have made her one of the most popular of all the magazine's writers. Born in Buffalo, New York, Nancy Kress now lives in Silver Springs, Maryland, with her husband, SF author Charles Sheffield. Her books include the novels* The Prince Of Morning Bells, The Golden Grove, The White Pipes, An Alien Light, *and* Brain Rose, *the collection* Trinity And Other Stories. *She won both the Hugo and the Nebula Award in 1992 for her novella,* "Beggars in Spain," *an* Asimov's *story; the novel version,* Beggars in Spain, *appeared the following year, and was followed by a sequel,* Beggars and Choosers. *Her most recent books include a new collection,* The Aliens of Earth, *and a new novel,* Oaths & Miracles. *She has also won a Nebula Award for her story* "Out Of All Them Bright Stars."*

Here she offers us a compelling and fascinating story in which a retired New York cop must solve a series of brutal murders while at the same time unraveling an intricate and deadly biological mystery...

> *"If the truth shall kill them, let them die."*
> —Immanuel Kant

The first day of school, we had assault-with-intent in Ms. Kelly's room. I was in my room next door, 136, laying down the law to 7C math. The usual first-day bullshit: turn in homework every day, take your assigned seat as soon as you walk in, don't bring a weapon or an abusive attitude into my classroom or you'll wish you'd never been born. The kids would ignore the first, do the others—for me anyway. Apparently not for Jenny Kelly.

"Mr. Shaunessy! Mr. Shaunessy! Come quick, they throwing chairs next door! The new teacher crying!" A pretty, tiny girl I recognized from last year: Lateesha Jefferson. Her round face glowed with excitement and satisfaction. A riot! Already! On the very first day!

I looked over my class slowly, penetratingly, letting my gaze linger on each upturned face. I took my time about it. Most kids dropped their eyes. Next door, something heavy hit the wall. I lowered my voice, so everybody had to strain to hear me.

"Nobody move while I'm gone. You all got that?"

Some heads nodded. Some kids stared back, uncertain but cool. A few boys smirked and I brought my unsmiling gaze to their faces until they stopped. Shouts filtered through the wall.

"Okay, Lateesha, tell Ms. Kelly I'm coming." She took off like a shot, grinning, Paul Revere in purple leggings and silver shoes.

I limped to the door and turned for a last look. My students all sat quietly, watching me. I saw Pedro Valesquez and Steven Cheung surreptitiously scanning my jacket for the bulge of a service revolver that of course wasn't there. My reputation had become so inflated it rivaled the NYC budget. In the hall Lateesha screamed in a voice that could have deafened rock stars, ''Mr. Shaunessy coming! You ho's better stop!''

In 134, two eighth-grade girls grappled in the middle of the floor. For a wonder, neither seemed to be armed, not even with keys. One girl's nose streamed blood. The other's blouse was torn. Both screamed incoherently, nonstop, like stuck sirens. Kids raced around the room. A chair had apparently been hurled at the chalkboard, or at somebody once standing in front of the chalkboard; chair and board had cracked. Jenny Kelly yelled and waved her arms. Lateesha was wrong; Ms. Kelly wasn't crying. But neither was she helping things a hell of a lot. A few kids on the perimeter of the chaos saw me and fell silent, curious to see what came next.

And then I saw Jeff Connors, leaning against the window wall, arms folded across his chest, and his expression as he watched the fighting girls told me everything I needed to know.

I took a huge breath, letting it fill my lungs. I bellowed at top volume, and with no facial expression whatsoever, ''Freeze! Now!''

And everybody did.

The kids who didn't know me looked instantly for the gun and the back-up. The kids who did know me grinned, stifled it, and nodded slightly. The two girls stopped pounding each other to twist toward the noise—my bellow had shivered the hanging fluorescents—which was time enough for me to limp across the floor, grab the girl on top, and haul her to her feet. She twisted to swing on me, thought better of it, and stood there, panting.

The girl on the floor whooped, leaped up, and tensed to slug the girl I held. But then she stopped. She didn't know me, but the scene had alerted her: nobody yelling anymore, the other wildcat quiet in my grip, nobody racing around the room. She glanced around, puzzled.

Jeff still leaned against the wall.

They expected me to say something. I said nothing, just stood there, impassive. Seconds dragged by. Fifteen, thirty, forty-five. To adults, that's a long time. To kids, it's forever. The adrenaline ebbs away.

A girl in the back row sat down at her desk.

Another followed.

Pretty soon they were all sitting down, quiet, not exactly intimidated but interested. This was different, and different was cool. Only the two girls were left, and Jeff Connors leaning on the window, and a small Chinese kid whose chair was probably the one hurled at the chalkboard. I saw that the crack ran right through words printed neatly in green marker:

Ms. Kelly
English 8E

After a minute, the Chinese kid without a chair sat on his desk.

Still I said nothing. Another minute dragged past. The kids were uneasy now. Lateesha said helpfully, "Them girls supposed to go to the nurse, Mr. Shaunessy. Each one by they own self."

I kept my grip on the girl with the torn blouse. The other girl, her nose gushing blood, suddenly started to cry. She jammed her fist against her mouth and ran out of the room.

I looked at each face, one at a time.

Eventually I released my grip on the second girl and nodded at Lateesha. "You go with her to the nurse."

Lateesha jumped up eagerly, a girl with a mission, the only one I'd spoken to. "You come on, honey," she said, and led away the second girl, clucking at her under her breath.

Now they were all eager for the limelight. Rosaria said quickly, "They fighting over Jeff, Mr. Shaunessy."

"No they ain't," said a big, muscled boy in the second row. He was scowling. "They fighting cause Jonelle, she dissed Lisa."

"No, they—"

Everybody had a version. They all jumped in, intellectuals with theories, arguing with each other until they saw I wasn't saying anything, wasn't trying to sort through it, wasn't going to participate. One by one, they fell silent again, curious.

Finally Jeff himself spoke. He looked at me with his absolutely open, earnest, guileless expression and said, "It was them suicides, Mr. Shaunessy."

The rest of the class looked slightly confused, but willing to go along with this. They knew Jeff. But now Ms. Kelly, excluded for five full minutes from her own classroom, jumped in. She was angry. "*What* suicides? What are you talking about, uh . . ."

Jeff didn't deign to supply his name. She was supposed to know it. He spoke directly to me. "Them old people. The ones who killed theirselves in that hospital this morning. And last week. In the newspaper."

I didn't react. Just waited.

"You know, Mr. Shaunessy," Jeff went on, in that same open, confiding tone. "Them old people shooting and hanging and pushing theirselves out of windows. At their age. In their sixties and seventies and eighties." He shook his head regretfully.

The other kids were nodding now, although I'd bet my pension none of them ever read anything in any newspaper.

"It just ain't no example to us," Jeff said regretfully. "If even the people who are getting three good meals a day and got people waiting on them and don't have to work or struggle no more with the man—if *they* give up, how we supposed to think there's anything in this here life for us?"

He leaned back against the window and grinned at me:

triumphant, regretful, pleading, an inheritor of a world he hadn't made. His classmates glanced at each other sideways, glanced at me, and stopped grinning.

"A tragedy, that's what it is," Jeff said, shaking his head. "A tragedy. All them old people, deciding a whole life just don't make it worth it to stick to the rules. How *we* supposed to learn to behave?"

"You have to get control of Jeff Connors," I told Jenny Kelly at lunch in the faculty room. This was an exposed-pipes, flaking-plaster oasis in the basement of Benjamin Franklin Junior High. Teachers sat jammed together on folding metal chairs around brown formica tables, drinking coffee and eating out of paper bags. Ms. Kelly had plopped down next to me and practically demanded advice. "That's actually not as hard as it might look. Jeff's a hustler, an operator, and the others follow him. But he's not uncontrollable."

"Easy for you to say," she retorted, surprising me. "They look at you and see the macho ex-cop who weighs what? Two-thirty? Who took out three criminals before you got shot, and has strong juice at Juvenile Hall. They look at me and see a five-foot-three, one-hundred-twenty-pound nobody they can all push around. Including Jeff."

"So don't let him," I said, wondering how she'd heard all the stories about me so fast. She'd only moved into the district four days ago.

She took a healthy bite of her cheese sandwich. Although she'd spent the first half of the lunch period in the ladies' room, I didn't see any tear marks. Maybe she fixed her makeup to cover tear stains. Margie used to do that. Up close Jenny Kelly looked older than I'd thought at first: twenty-eight, maybe thirty. Her looks weren't going to make it any easier to control a roomful of thirteen-year-old boys. She pushed her short blond hair off her face and looked directly at me.

"Do you really carry a gun?"

"Of course not. Board of Education regs forbid any weapons by anybody on school property. You know that."

"The kids think you carry."

I shrugged.

"And you don't tell them otherwise."

I shrugged again.

"Okay, I can't do that either," she said. "But I'm not going to fail at this, Gene. I'm just not. You're a big success here, everybody says so. So tell me what I *can* do to keep enough control of my classes that I have a remote chance of actually teaching anybody anything."

I studied her, and revised my first opinion, which was that she'd be gone by the end of September. No tear stains, not fresh out of college, able to keep eating under stress. The verbal determination I discounted; I'd heard a lot of verbal determination from rookies when I was on the Force, and most of it melted away three months out of Police Academy. Even sooner in the City School District.

"You need to do two things," I said. "First, recognize that these kids can't do without connection to other human beings. Not for five minutes, not for one minute. They're starved for it. And to most of them, 'connection' means arguing, fighting, struggling, even abuse. It's what they're used to, and it's what they'll naturally create, because it feels better to them than existing alone in a social vacuum for even a minute. To compete with that, to get them to disengage from each other long enough to listen to you, you have to give them an equally strong connection to *you*. It doesn't have to be intimidation, or some bullshit fantasy about going up against the law. You can find your own way. But unless you're a strong presence—very strong, very distinctive—of one kind or another, they're going to ignore you and go back to connecting with each other.''

"Connection," she said, thinking about it. "What about connecting to the material? English literature has some pretty exciting stuff in it, you know."

"I'll take your word for it. But no books are exciting to most of these kids. Not initially. They can only connect to the material through a person. They're that starved."

She took another bite of sandwich. "And the second thing?"

"I already told you. Get control of Jeff Connors. Immediately."

"Who is he? And what was all that bullshit about old people killing themselves?"

I said, "Didn't you see it on the news?"

"Of course I did. The police are investigating, aren't they? But what did it have to do with my classroom?"

"Nothing. It was a diversionary tactic. A cover-up."

"Of what?"

"Could be a lot of things. Jeff will use whatever he hears to confuse and mislead, and he hears everything. He's bright, unmotivated, a natural leader, and—unbelievably—not a gang member. You saw him—no big gold, no beeper. His police record is clean. So far, anyway."

Jenny said, "You worked with him a little last year."

"No, I didn't work with him. I controlled him in class, was all." She'd been asking about me.

"So if *you* didn't really connect with him, how do I?"

"I can't tell you that," I said, and we ate in silence for a few minutes. It didn't feel strained. She looked thoughtful, turning over what I'd told her. I wondered suddenly whether she'd have made a good cop. Her ears were small, I noticed, and pink, with tiny gold earrings in the shape of little shells.

She caught me looking, and smiled, and glanced at my left hand.

So whoever she'd asked about me hadn't told her everything. I gulped my last bite of sandwich, nodded, and went back to my room before 7H came thundering up the stairs, their day almost over, one more crazy period where Mr. Shaunessy actually expected them to pay attention to some weird math instead of their natural, intense, contentious absorption in each other.

Two more elderly people committed suicide, at the Angels of Mercy Nursing Home on Amsterdam Avenue.

I caught it on the news, while correcting 7H's first-day quiz to find out how much math they remembered from last year. They didn't remember squat. My shattered knee was propped up on the hassock beside the bones and burial tray of a Hungry Man Extra-Crispy Fried Chicken.

". . . identified as Giacomo della Francesca, seventy-eight, and Lydia Smith, eighty. The two occupied rooms on the same floor, according to nursing home staff, and both had been in fairly good spirits. Mrs. Smith, a widow, threw herself from the roof of the eight-story building. Mr. della Francesca, who was found dead in his room, had apparently stabbed himself. The suicides follow very closely on similar deaths this morning at the Beth Israel Retirement Home on West End Avenue. However, Captain Michael Doyle, NYPD, warned against premature speculation about—"

I shifted my knee. This Captain Doyle must be getting nervous; this was the third pair of self-inflicted fatalities in nursing homes within ten days. Old people weren't usually susceptible to copy-cat suicides. Pretty soon the *Daily News* or the *Post* would decide that there was actually some nut running around Manhattan knocking off the elderly. Or that there was a medical conspiracy backed by Middle East terrorists and extraterrestrials. Whatever the tabloids chose, the NYPD would end up taking the blame.

Suddenly I knew, out of nowhere, that Margie was worse.

I get these flashes like that, out of nowhere, and I hate it. I never used to. I used to know things the way normal people know things, by seeing them or reading them or hearing them or reasoning them through. Ways that made sense. Now, for the last year, I get these flashes of knowing things some other way, thoughts just turning up in my mind, and the intuitions are mostly right. Mostly right, and nearly always bad.

This wasn't one of my nights to go to the hospital. But I flicked off the TV, limped to the trash to throw away my dinner tray, and picked up the cane I use when my leg has been under too much physical stress. The phone rang. I paused to listen to the answering machine, just in case it was Libby calling from Cornell to tell me about her first week of classes.

"Gene, this is Vince Romano." Pause. "Bucky." Pause. "I know it's been a long time."

I sat down slowly on the hassock.

"Listen, I was sorry to hear about Margie. I was going to . . . you were . . . it wasn't. . . ." Despite myself, I had to grin. People didn't change. Bucky Romano never could locate a complete verb.

He finished floundering. ". . . to say how sorry I am. But that's not why I'm calling." Long pause. "I need to talk to you. It's important. Very important." Pause. "It's not about Father Healey again, or any of that old . . . something else entirely." Pause. "Very important, Gene. I can't . . . it isn't . . . you won't . . ." Pause. Then his voice changed, became stronger. "I can't do this alone, Gene."

Bucky had never been able to do anything alone. Not when we were six, not when we were eleven, not when we were seventeen, not when he was twenty-three and it wasn't any longer me but Father Healey who decided what he did. Not when he was twenty-seven and it was me again deciding for him, more unhappy about that than I'd ever been about anything in my life until Margie's accident.

Bucky recited his phone number, but he didn't hang up. I could hear him breathing. Suddenly I could almost see him, somewhere out there, sitting with the receiver pressed so close to his mouth that it would look like he was trying to swallow it. Hoping against hope that I might pick up the phone after all. Worrying the depths of his skinny frantic soul for what words he could say to make me do this.

"Gene . . . it's about . . . I shouldn't say this, but after all you're a . . . were a . . . it's about those elderly deaths." Pause. "I work at Kelvin Pharmaceutical now." And then the click.

What the hell could anybody make of any of that?

I limped to the elevator and caught a cab to St. Clare's Hospital.

Margie *was* worse, although the only way I could tell was that there was one more tube hooked to her than there'd been last night. She lay in bed in the same position she'd lain in for eighteen months and seven days: curled head to knees, splinter-thin arms bent at the elbows. She weighed ninety-nine pounds. Gastrostomy and catheter tubes ran into her, and now an IV drip on a pole as well. Her beautiful brown hair, worn away a bit at the back of her head from constant contact with the pillow, was dull. Its sheen, like her life, had faded deep inside its brittle shafts, unrecoverable.

"Hello, Margie. I'm back."

I eased myself into the chair, leg straight out in front of me.

"Libby hasn't called yet. First week of classes, schedule to straighten out, old friends to see—you know how it is." Margie always had. I could see her and Libby shopping the week before Libby's freshman year, laughing over the Gap bags, quarreling over the price of something I'd buy either of them now, no matter what it cost. Anything.

"It's pretty cool out for September, sweetheart. But the leaves haven't changed yet. I walked across the Park just yesterday—all still green. Composing myself for today. Which wasn't too bad. It's going to be a good school year, I think."

Have a great year! Margie always said to me on the first day of school, as if the whole year would be compressed in that first six hours and twenty minutes. For three years she'd said it, the three years since I'd been retired from the Force and limped into a career as a junior-high teacher. I remembered her standing at the door, half-dressed for her secretarial job at Time-Warner, her silk blouse stretched across those generous breasts, the slip showing underneath. *Have a great day! Have a great five minutes!*

"Last-period 7H looks like a zoo, Margie. But when doesn't last period look like a zoo? They're revved up like Ferraris by then. But both algebra classes look good, and there's a girl in 7A whose transcript is incredible. I mean, we're talking future Westinghouse Talent winner here."

Talk to her, the doctor had said. *We don't know what coma patients can and cannot hear.* That had been a year and a half ago. Nobody ever said it to me now. But I couldn't stop.

"There's a new sacrificial lamb in the room next to mine, eighth-grade English. She had a cat fight in there today. But I don't know, she might have more grit than she looks. And guess who called. Bucky Romano. After all this time. Thirteen years. He wants me to give him a call. I'm not sure yet."

Her teeth gapped and stuck out. The anti-seizure medication in her gastrostomy bag made the gum tissue grow too much. It displaced her teeth.

"I finally bought curtains for the kitchen. Like Libby

nagged me to. Although they'll probably have to wait until she comes home at Thanksgiving to get hung. Yellow. You'd like them.''

Margie had never seen this kitchen. I could see her in the dining room of the house I'd sold, up on a chair hanging drapes, rubbing at a dirty spot on the window. . . .

''Gene?''

''Hi, Susan.'' The shift nurse looked as tired as I'd ever seen her. ''What's this new tube in Margie?''

''Antibiotics. She was having a little trouble breathing, and an X-ray showed a slight pneumonia. It'll clear right up on medication. Gene, you have a phone call.''

Something clutched in my chest. *Libby*. Ever since that '93 Lincoln had torn through a light on Lexington while Margie crossed with a bag of groceries, any phone call in an unexpected place does that to me. I limped to the nurses' station.

''Gene? This is Vince. Romano. Bucky.''

''Bucky.''

''I'm sorry to bother you at . . . I was so sorry to hear about Margie, I left a message on your machine but maybe you haven't been home to . . . listen, I need to see you, Gene. It's important. Please.''

''It's late, Bucky. I have to teach tomorrow. I teach now, at—''

''*Please*. You'll know why when I see you. I have to see you.''

I closed my eyes. ''Look, I'm pretty tired. Maybe another time.''

''*Please*, Gene. Just for a few minutes. I can be at your place in fifteen minutes!''

Bucky had never minded begging. I remembered that, now. Suddenly I didn't want him to see where I lived, how I lived, without Margie. What I really wanted was to tell him ''no.''

But I couldn't. I never had, not our whole lives, and I couldn't now—why not? I didn't know.

"All right, Bucky. A few minutes. I'll meet you in the lobby here at St. Clare's."

"Fifteen minutes. God, thanks, Gene. Thanks so much, I really appreciate it, I need to—"

"Okay."

"See you soon."

He didn't mind begging, and he made people help him. Even Father Healey had found out that. Coming in to Bucky's life, and going out.

The lobby of St. Clare's never changed. Same scuffed green floor, slashed gray vinyl couches mended with wide tape, information-desk attendant who looked like he could have been a bouncer at Madison Square Garden. Maybe he had. Tired people yelled and whispered in Spanish, Greek, Korean, Chinese. Statues of the Madonna and St. Clare and the crucified Christ beamed a serenity as alien here as money.

Bucky and I grew up in next-door apartments in a neighborhood like this one, a few blocks from Our Lady of Perpetual Sorrows. That's how we defined our location: "two doors down from the crying Broad." We made our First Communion together, and our Confirmation, and Bucky was best man when I married Marge. But by that time he'd entered the seminary, and any irreverence about Our Lady had disappeared, along with all other traces of humor, humility, or humanity. Or so I thought then. Maybe I wasn't wrong. Even though he always made straight A's in class, Bucky-as-priest-in-training was the same as Bucky-as-shortstop or Bucky-as-third-clarinet or Bucky-as-altar-boy: intense, committed, short-sightedly wrong.

He'd catch a high pop and drop it. He'd know "Claire de Lune" perfectly, and be half a beat behind. Teeth sticking out, skinny face furrowed in concentration, he'd bend over the altar rail and become so enraptured by whatever he saw there that he'd forget to make the response. We boys would nudge each other and grin, and later howl at him in the parking lot.

But his decision to leave the priesthood wasn't a howler. It wasn't even a real decision. He vacillated for months, growing thinner and more stuttery, and finally he'd taken a bottle of pills and a half pint of vodka. Father Healey and I found him, and had his stomach pumped, and Father Healey tried to talk him back into the seminary and the saving grace of God. From his hospital bed Bucky had called me, stuttering in his panic, to come get him and take him home. He was terrified. Not of the hospital—of Father Healey.

And I had, coming straight from duty, secure in my shield and gun and Margie's love and my beautiful young daughter and my contempt for the weakling who needed a lapsed-Catholic cop to help him face an old priest in a worn-out religion. God, I'd been smug.

"Gene?" Bucky said. "Gene Shaunessy?"

I looked up at the faded lobby of St. Clare's.

"Hello, Bucky."

"God, you look . . . I can't . . . you haven't changed a bit!"

Then he started to cry.

I got him to a Greek place around the corner on Ninth. The dinner trade was mostly over and we sat at a table in the shadows, next to a dirty side window with a view of a brick alley, Bucky with his back to the door. Not that he cared if anybody saw him crying. I cared. I ordered two beers.

"Okay, what is it?"

He blew his nose and nodded gratefully. "Same old Gene. You always just . . . never any . . ."

"Bucky. What the fuck is wrong?"

He said, unexpectedly, ''You hate this.''

Over his shoulder, I eyed the door. Starting eighteen months ago, I'd had enough tears and drama to last me the rest of my life, although I wasn't going to tell Bucky that. If he didn't get it over with. . . .

''I work at Kelvin Pharmaceuticals,'' Bucky said, suddenly calmer. ''After I left the seminary, after Father Healey . . . you remember . . .''

''Go on,'' I said, more harshly than I'd intended. Father Healey and I had screamed at each other outside Bucky's door at St. Vincent's, while Bucky's stomach was being pumped. I'd said things I didn't want to remember.

''I went back to school. Took a B.S. in chemistry. Then a Ph.D. You and I, about that time of . . . I wanted to call you after you were shot but . . . I could have tried harder to find you earlier, I know . . . anyway. I went to work for Kelvin, in the research department. Liked it. I met Tommy. We live together.''

He'd never said. But, then, he'd never had to. And there hadn't been very much saying anyway, not back then, and certainly not at Our Lady of Perpetual Sorrows.

''I liked the work at Kelvin. Like it. Liked it.'' He took a deep breath. ''I worked on Camineur. You take it, don't you, Gene?''

I almost jumped out of my skin. ''How'd you know that?''

He grinned. ''Not by any medical record hacking. Calm down, it isn't . . . people can't tell. I just guessed, from the profile.''

He meant *my* profile. Camineur is something called a neurotransmitter uptake-regulator. Unlike Prozac and the other antidepressants that were its ancestors, it fiddles not just with serotonin levels but also with norepinephrine and dopamine and a half dozen other brain chemicals. It was prescribed for me after Marge's accident. Non-addictive, no bad side effects, no dulling of the mind. Without it, I couldn't sleep, couldn't eat, couldn't concentrate. Couldn't stop wanting to kill somebody every time I walked into St. Clare's.

I had found myself in a gun shop on Avenue D, trigger-testing a nine-millimeter, which felt so light in my hand it floated. When I looked at the thoughts in my head, I went to see Margie's doctor.

Bucky said, quietly for once, "Camineur was designed to prevent violent ideation in people with strong but normally controlled violent impulses, whose control has broken down under severe life stress. It's often prescribed for cops. Also military careerists and doctors. Types with compensated paranoia restrained by strong moral strictures. Nobody told you that the Camineur generation of mood inhibitors was that specific?"

If they did, I hadn't been listening. I hadn't been listening to much in those months. But I heard Bucky now. His hesitations disappeared when he talked about his work.

"It's a good drug, Gene. You don't have to feel . . . there isn't anything shameful about taking it. It just restores the brain chemistry to whatever it was before the trauma."

I scowled, and gestured for two more beers.

"All right. I didn't mean to . . . There's been several generations of neural pharmaceuticals since then. And that's why I'm talking to you."

I sipped my second beer, and watched Bucky drain his.

"Three years ago we . . . there was a breakthrough in neuropharm research, really startling stuff, I won't go into the . . . we started a whole new line of development. I was on the team. Am. On the team."

I waited. Sudden raindrops, large and sparse, struck the dirty window.

"Since Camineur, we've narrowed down the effects of neuropharms spectacularly. I don't know how much you know about this, but the big neurological discovery in the last five years is that repeated intense emotion doesn't just alter the synaptic pathways in the brain. It actually changes your brain structure from the cellular level up. With any intense experience, new structures start to be built, and if the experience is repeated, they get reinforced. The physical changes can make you, say, more open to risk-taking, or calmer in the face of stress. Or the physical structures that get built can make it hard or even impossible to function normally, even if you're trying with all your will. In other words, your life literally makes you crazy.''

He smiled. I said nothing.

''What we've learned is how to affect only those pathways created by depression, only those created by fear, only those created by narcissistic rage . . . we don't touch your memories. They're there. You can see them, in your mind, like billboards. But now you drive past them, not through them. In an emotional sense.''

Bucky peered at me. I said, not gently, ''So what pills do *you* take to drive past your memories?''

He laughed. ''I don't.'' I stayed impassive but he said hastily anyway, ''Not that people who do are . . . it isn't a sign of weakness to take neuropharms, Gene. Or a sign of strength not to. I just . . . it isn't . . . I was waiting, was all. I was waiting.''

''For what? Your prince to come?'' I was still angry.

He said simply, ''Yes.''

Slowly I lowered my beer. But Bucky returned to his background intelligence.

''This drug my team is working on now . . . the next step was to go beyond just closing down negative pathways. Take, as just one example, serotonin. Some researcher said . . . there's one theory that serotonin, especially, is like cops. Having enough of it in your cerebral chemistry keeps riots and looting and assault in the brain from getting out of control. But just holding down crime doesn't, all by itself, create prosperity or happiness. Or joy. For that, you need a new class of neuropharms that create positive pathways. Or at least strengthen those that are already there.''

"Cocaine," I said. "Speed. Gin and tonic."

"No, no. Not a rush of power. Not a temporary high. Not temporary at all, and not isolating. The neural pathways that make people feel . . . the ones that let you . . .'' He leaned toward me, elbows on the table. "Weren't there moments, Gene, when you felt so close to Margie it was like you crawled inside her skin for a minute? Like you *were* Margie?''

I looked at the window. Raindrops slid slowly down the dirty glass, streaking it dirtier. In the alley, a homeless prowled the garbage cans. "What's this got to do with the elderly suicides? If you have a point to make, make it.''

"They weren't suicides. They were murders.''

"Murders? Some psycho knocking off old people? What makes you think so?''

"Not some psycho. And I don't think so. I *know*.''

"How?''

"All eight elderlies were taking J-24. That's the Kelvin code name for the neuropharm that ends situational isolation. It was a clinical trial.''

I studied Bucky, whose eyes burned with Bucky light: intense, pleading, determined, inept. And something else, something that hadn't been there in the old days. "Bucky, that makes no sense. The NYPD isn't perfect, God knows, but they can tell the difference between suicide and murder. And anyway, the suicide rate rises naturally among old people, they get depressed—'' I stopped. He had to already know this.

"That's just it!'' Bucky cried, and an old Greek couple at a table halfway across the room turned to stare at him. He lowered his voice. "The elderly in the clinical trial *weren't* depressed. They were very carefully screened for it. No psychological, chemical, or social markers for depression. These were the . . . when you see old people in travel ads, doing things, full of life and health, playing tennis and dancing by candlelight . . . the team psychologists looked for our clinical subjects very carefully. *None* of them was depressed!"

"So maybe your pill made them depressed. Enough to kill themselves."

"No! No! J-24 couldn't . . . there wasn't any . . . it didn't make them depressed. I saw it." He hesitated. "And besides . . ."

"Besides what?"

He looked out at the alley. A waiter pushed a trolley of dirty dishes past our table. When Bucky spoke again, his voice sounded odd.

"I gave five intense years to J-24 and the research that led to it, Gene. Days, evenings, weekends—eighty hours a week in the lab. Every minute until I met Tommy, and maybe too much time even after that. I know everything that the Kelvin team leaders know, everything that *can* be known about that drug's projected interaction with existing neurotransmitters. J-24 was my life."

As the Church had once been. Bucky couldn't do anything by halves. I wondered just what his position on "the team" had actually been.

He said, "We designed J-24 to combat the isolation that even normal, healthy people feel with age. You get old. Your friends die. Your mate dies. Your children live in another state, with lives of their own. All the connections you built up over decades are gone, and in healthy people, those connections created very thick, specific, strong neural structures. Any new friends you make in a nursing home or retirement community—there just aren't the years left to duplicate the

strength of those neural pathways. Even when outgoing, un-
depressed, risk-taking elderlies try.''

I didn't say anything.

''J-24 was specific to the neurochemistry of connection.
You took it in the presence of someone else, and it opened
the two of you up to each other, made it possible to genuinely—*genuinely*, at the permanent chemical level—imprint
on each other.''

''You created an *aphrodisiac for geezers?*''

''No,'' he said, irritated. ''Sex had nothing to do with it.
Those impulses originate in the limbic system. This was ...
emotional bonding. Of the most intense, long-term type. Don't
tell me all you ever felt for Margie was sex!''

After a minute he said, ''I'm sorry.''

''Finish your story.''

''It *is* finished. We gave the drug to four sets of volunteers,
all people who had long-term terminal diseases but weren't
depressed, people who were willing to take risks in order to
enhance the quality of their own perceptions in the time left.
I was there observing when they took it. They bonded like
baby ducks imprinting on the first moving objects they see.
No, not like that. More like ... like ...'' He looked over my
shoulder, at the wall, and his eyes filled with water. I glanced
around to make sure nobody noticed.

''Giacomo della Francesca and Lydia Smith took J-24 together almost a month ago. They were transformed by this
incredible joy in each other. In knowing each other. Not each
other's memories, but each other's ... souls. They talked, and
held hands, and you could just feel that they were completely
open to each other, without all the psychological defenses we
use to keep ourselves walled off. They knew each other. They
almost *were* each other.''

I was embarrassed by the look on his face. ''But they didn't
know each other like that, Bucky. It was just an illusion.''

"No. It wasn't. Look, what happens when you connect with someone, share something intense with them?"

I didn't want to have this conversation. But Bucky didn't really need me to answer; he rolled on all by himself, unstoppable.

"What happens when you connect is that you exhibit greater risk taking, with fewer inhibitions. You exhibit greater empathy, greater attention, greater receptivity to what is being said, greater pleasure. And *all* of those responses are neurochemical, which in turn create, reinforce, or diminish physical structures in the brain. J-24 just reverses the process. Instead of the experience causing the neurochemical response, J-24 supplies the physical changes that create the experience. And that's not all. The drug boosts the *rate* of structural change, so that every touch, every word exchanged, every emotional response, reinforces neural pathways one or two hundred times as much as a normal life encounter."

I wasn't sure how much of this I believed. "And so you say you gave it to four old couples . . . does it only work on men and women?"

A strange look passed swiftly over his face: secretive, almost pained. I remembered Tommy. "That's all who have tried it so far. Can you . . . have you ever thought about what it would be like to be really merged, to know him, to be him—think of it, Gene! I could—"

"I don't want to hear about that," I said harshly. Libby would hate that answer. My liberal, tolerant daughter. But I'd been a cop. Lingering homophobia went with the territory, even if I wasn't exactly proud of it. Whatever Bucky's fantasies were about him and Tommy, I didn't want to know.

Bucky didn't look offended. "All right. But just imagine— an end to the terrible isolation that we live in our whole tiny lives. . . ." He looked at the raindrops sliding down the window.

"And you think somebody murdered those elderly for that? Who? Why?"

"I don't know."

"Bucky. Think. This doesn't make any sense. A drug company creates a . . . what did you call it? A neuropharm. They get it into clinical trials, under FDA supervision—"

"No," Bucky said.

I stared at him.

"It would have taken years. Maybe decades. It's too radical a departure. So Kelvin—"

"You knew there was no approval."

"Yes. But I thought . . . I never thought . . ." He looked at me, and suddenly I had another one of those unlogical flashes, and I saw there was more wrong here even than Bucky was telling me. He believed that he'd participated, in whatever small way, in creating a drug that led someone to murder eight old people. Never mind if it was true—Bucky believed it. He believed this same company was covering its collective ass by calling the deaths depressive suicides, when they could not have been suicides. And yet Bucky sat in front of me without chewing his nails to the knuckles, or pulling out his hair, or hating himself. Bucky, to whom guilt was the staff of life.

I'd seen him try to kill himself over leaving the Church. I'd watched him go through agonies of guilt over ignoring answering-machine messages from Father Healey. Hell, I'd watched him shake and cry because at ten years old we'd stolen three apples from a market on Columbus Avenue. Yet there he sat, disturbed but coherent. For Bucky, even serene. Believing he'd contributed to murder.

I said, "What neuropharms do you take, Bucky?"

"I told you. None."

"None at all?"

"No." His brown eyes were completely honest. "Gene, I

want you to find out how these clinical subjects really died.
You have access to NYPD records—''

''Not anymore.''

''But you *know* people. And cases get buried there all the
time, you used to tell me that yourself, with enough money
you can buy yourself an investigation unless somebody high
up in the city is really out to get you. Kelvin Pharmaceuticals
doesn't have those kinds of enemies. They're not the Mob.
They're just . . .''

''Committing murder to cover up an illegal drug trial? I
don't buy it, Bucky.''

''Then find out what *really* happened.''

I shot back, ''What do *you* think happened?''

''I don't know! But I do know this drug is a good thing!
Don't you understand, it holds out the possibility of a perfect,
totally open connection with the person you love most in the
world. . . . Find out what happened, Gene. It wasn't suicide.
J-24 doesn't cause depression. I *know* it. And for this drug to
be denied people would be . . . it would be a sin.''

He said it so simply, so naturally, that I was thrown all
over again. This wasn't Bucky, as I had known him. Or
maybe it was. He was still driven by sin and love.

I stood and put money on the table. ''I don't want to
get involved in this, Bucky. I really don't. But—one thing
more—''

''Yeah?''

''Camineur. Can it . . . does it account for . . .'' Jesus, I
sounded like him. ''I get these flashes of intuition about things
I've been thinking about. Sometimes it's stuff I didn't know.''

He nodded. ''You knew the stuff before. You just didn't
know you knew. Camineur strengthens intuitive right-brain
pathways. As an effect of releasing the stranglehold of violent
thoughts. You're more distanced from compulsive thoughts of
destruction, but also more likely to make connections among

various non-violent perceptions. You're just more intuitive, Gene, now that you're less driven.''

And I'm less Gene, my unwelcome intuition said. I gazed down at Bucky, sitting there with his skinny fingers splayed on the table, an unBucky-like serenity weirdly mixed with his manic manner and his belief that he worked for a corporation that had murdered eight people. Who the hell was *he?*

"I don't want to get involved in this," I repeated.

"But you will," Bucky said, and in his words I heard utter, unshakable faith.

Jenny Kelly said, "I set up a conference with Jeff Connors and he never showed." It was Friday afternoon. She had deep circles around her eyes. Raccoon eyes, we called them. They were the badge of teachers who were new, dedicated, or crazy. Who sat up until 1:00 A.M. in a frenzy of lesson planning and paper correcting, and then arrived at school at 6:30 A.M. to supervise track or meet with students or correct more papers.

"Set up another conference," I suggested. "Sometimes by the third or fourth missed appointment, guilt drives them to show up."

She nodded. "Okay. Meanwhile, Jeff has my class all worked up over something called the Neighborhood Safety Information Network, where they're supposed to inform on their friends' brothers' drug activity, or something. It's somehow connected to getting their Social Services checks. It's got the kids all in an uproar . . . I sent seventeen kids to the principal in three days."

"You might want to ease up on that, Jenny. It gives everybody—kids and administration—the idea that you can't control your own classroom."

"I can't," she said, so promptly and honestly that I had to smile. "But I *will*."

"Well, good luck."

"Listen, Gene, I'm picking the brains of everybody I can get to talk to me about this. Want to go have a cup of coffee someplace?"

"Sorry."

"Okay." She didn't look rebuffed, which was a relief. Today her earrings matched the color of her sweater. A soft blue, with lace at the neck. "Maybe another time."

"Maybe." It was easier than an outright no.

Crossing the parking lot to my car, I saw Jeff Connors. He slapped me a high-five. "Ms. Kelly's looking for you, Jeff."

"She is? Oh, yeah. Well, I can't today. Busy."

"So I hear. There isn't any such thing as the Neighborhood Safety Information Network, is there?"

He eyed me carefully. "Sure there is, Mr. S."

"Really? Well, I'm going to be at Midtown South station house this afternoon. I'll ask about it."

"It's, like, kinda new. They maybe don't know nothing about it yet."

"Ah. Well, I'll ask anyway. See you around, Jeff."

"Hang loose."

He watched my car all the way down the block, until I turned the corner.

The arrest room at Midtown South was full of cops filling out forms: fingerprint cards, On-line Booking System Arrest Worksheets, complaint reports, property invoices, requests for laboratory examinations of evidence, Arrest Documentation Checklists. The cops, most of whom had changed out of uniform, scribbled and muttered and sharpened pencils. In the holding pen alleged criminals cursed and slept and muttered and sang. It looked like fourth-period study hall in the junior-high cafeteria.

I said, "Lieutenant Fermato?"

A scribbling cop in a Looney Tunes sweatshirt waved me toward an office without even looking up.

"Oh my God. Gene Shaunessy. Risen from the fuckin' dead."

"Hello, Johnny."

"Come *in*. God, you look like a politician. Teaching must be the soft life."

"Better to put on a few pounds than look like a starved rat."

We stood there clasping hands, looking at each other, not saying the things that didn't need saying anyway, even if we'd had the words, which we didn't. Johnny and I had been partners for seven years. We'd gone together through foot pursuits and high-speed chases and lost files and violent domestics and bungled traps by Internal Affairs and robberies-in-progress and the grueling boredom of the street. Johnny's divorce. My retirement. Johnny had gone into Narcotics a year before I took the hit that shattered my knee. If he'd been my partner, it might not have happened. He'd made lieutenant only a few months ago. I hadn't seen him in a year and a half.

Suddenly I knew—or the Camineur knew—why I'd come to Midtown South to help Bucky after all. I'd already lost too many pieces of my life. Not the life I had now—the life I'd had once. My real one.

"Gene—about Marge . . ."

I held up my hand. "Don't. I'm here about something else. Professional."

His voice changed. "You in trouble?"

"No. A friend is." Johnny didn't know Bucky; they'd been separate pieces of my old life. I couldn't picture them in the same room together for more than five minutes. "It's about the suicides at the Angels of Mercy Nursing Home. Giacomo della Francesca and Lydia Smith."

Johnny nodded. "What about it?"

"I'd like to see a copy of the initial crime-scene report."

Johnny looked at me steadily. But all he said was, "Not my jurisdiction, Gene."

I looked back. If Johnny didn't want to get me the report, he wouldn't. But either way, he *could*. Johnny'd been the best undercover cop in Manhattan, mostly because he was so good at putting together his net of criminal informers, inside favors, noncriminal spies, and unseen procedures. I didn't believe he'd dismantled any of it just because he'd come in off the street. Not Johnny.

"Is it important?"

I said, "It's important."

"All right," he said, and that was all that had to be said. I asked him instead about the Neighborhood Safety Information Network.

"We heard about that one," Johnny said. "Pure lies, but somebody's using it to stir up a lot of anti-cop crap as a set-up for something or other. We're watching it."

"Watches run down," I said, because it was an old joke between us, and Johnny laughed. Then we talked about old times, and Libby, and his two boys, and when I left, the same cops were filling out the same forms and the same perps were still sleeping or cursing or singing, nobody looking at each other in the whole damn place.

By the next week, the elderly suicides had disappeared from the papers, which had moved on to another batch of mayhem and alleged brutality in the three-oh. Jenny Kelly had two more fights in her classroom. One I heard through the wall and broke up myself. The other Lateesha told me about in the parking lot. "That boy, Mr. Shaunessy, that Richie Tang, he call Ms. Kelly an ugly bitch! He say she be sorry for messing with *him!*"

"And then what?" I said, reluctantly.

Lateesha smiled. "Ms. Kelly, she yell back that Richie

might act like a lost cause but he ain't lost to *her*, and she be damned if anybody gonna talk to her that way. But Richie just smile and walk out. Ms. Kelly, she be gone by Thanksgiving."

"Not necessarily," I said. "Sometimes people surprise you."

"Not me, they don't."

"Maybe even you, Lateesha."

Jenny Kelly's eyes wore permanent rings: sleeplessness, anger, smudged mascara. In the faculty room she sat hunched over her coffee, scribbling furiously with red pen on student compositions. I found myself choosing a different table.

"Hi, Gene," Bucky's voice said on my answering machine. "Please call if you . . . I wondered whether you found out any . . . give me a call. Please. I have a different phone number, I'll give it to you." Pause. "I've moved."

I didn't call him back. Something in the "I've moved" hinted at more pain, more complications, another chapter in Bucky's messy internal drama. I decided to call him only if I heard something from Johnny Fermato.

Who phoned me the following Tuesday, eight days after my visit to Midtown South. "Gene. John Fermato."

"Hey, Johnny."

"I'm calling to follow through on our conversation last week. I'm afraid the information you requested is unavailable."

I stood in my minuscule kitchen, listening to the traffic three stories below, listening to Johnny's cold formality. "Unavailable?"

"Yes. I'm sorry."

"You mean the file has disappeared? Been replaced by a later version? Somebody's sitting on it?"

"I'm sorry, the information you requested isn't available."

"Right," I said, without expression.

"Catch you soon."

"Bye, Lieutenant."

After he hung up I stood there holding the receiver, surprised at how much it hurt. It was a full five minutes before the anger came. And then it was distant, muffled. Filtered through the Camineur, so that it wouldn't get out of hand.

Safe.

Jeff Connors showed up at school after a three-day absence, wearing a beeper, and a necklace of thick gold links.

"Jeff, he big now," Lateesha told me, and turned away, lips pursed like the disapproving mother she would someday be.

I was patrolling the hall before the first bell when Jenny Kelly strode past me and stopped at the door to the boys' room, which wasn't really a door but a turning that hid the urinals and stalls from obvious view. The door itself had been removed after the fifth wastebasket fire in two days. Jeff came around the corner, saw Ms. Kelly, and stopped. I could see he was thinking about retreating again, but her voice didn't let him. "I want to see you, Jeff. In my free period." Her voice said he would be there.

"Okay," Jeff said, with no hustle, and slouched off, beeper riding on his hip.

I said to her, "He knows when your free period is."

She looked at me coolly. "Yes."

"So you've gotten him to talk to you."

"A little." Still cool. "His mother disappeared for three days. She uses. She's back now, but Jeff doesn't trust her to take care of his little brother. Did you even know he had a little brother, Gene?"

I shook my head.

"Why not?" She looked like Lateesha. Disapproving mother. The raccoon eyes were etched deeper. "This boy is in trouble, and he's one we don't have to lose. We can still save him. *You* could have, last year. He admires you. But you never gave him the time of day, beyond making sure he wasn't any trouble to *you*."

"I don't think you have the right to judge whether—"

"Don't I? Maybe not. I'm sorry. But don't you see, Jeff only wanted from you—"

"That's the bell. Good luck today, Ms. Kelly."

She stared at me, then gave me a little laugh. "Right. And where were *you* when the glaciers melted? Never mind." She walked into her classroom, which diminished in noise only a fraction of a decibel.

Her earrings were little silver hoops, and her silky blouse was red.

After school I drove to the Angels of Mercy Nursing Home and pretended I was interested in finding a place for my aging mother. A woman named Karen Gennaro showed me a dining hall, bedrooms, activity rooms, a little garden deep in marigolds and asters, nursing facilities. Old people peacefully played cards, watched TV, sat by sunshiny windows. There was no sign that eighty-year-old Lydia Smith had thrown herself from the roof, or that her J-24-bonded boyfriend Giacomo della Francesca had stabbed himself to death.

"I'd like to walk around a little by myself now," I told Ms. Gennaro. "Just sort of get the feel of the place. My mother is . . . particular."

She hesitated. "We don't usually allow—"

"Mom didn't like Green Meadows because too many corridors were painted pale blue and she hates pale blue. She rejected Saint Anne's because the other women didn't care enough about their hairdos and so the atmosphere wasn't self-respecting. She wouldn't visit Havenview because there was no piano in the dining room. This is the tenth place I've reported on."

She laughed. "No wonder you sound so weary. All right, just check out with me before you leave."

I inspected the day room again, chatting idly with a man watching the weather channel. Then I wandered to the sixth floor, where Lydia Smith and Giacomo della Francesca had lived. I chatted with an elderly man in a wheelchair, and a sixteen-year-old Catholic Youth volunteer, and a Mrs. Locurzio, who had the room on the other side of Lydia Smith's. Nothing.

A janitor came by mopping floors, a heavy young man with watery blue eyes and a sweet, puzzled face like a bearded child.

"Excuse me—have you worked here long?"

"Four years." He leaned on his mop, friendly and shy.

"Then you must come to know the patients pretty well."

"Pretty well." He smiled. "They're nice to me."

I listened to his careful, spaced speech, a little thick on each initial consonant. "Are all of them nice to you?"

"Some are mean. Because they're sick and they hurt."

"Mrs. Smith was always nice to you."

"Oh, yes. A nice lady. She talked to me every day." His doughy face became more puzzled. "She died."

"Yes. She was unhappy with her life."

He frowned. "Mrs. Smith was unhappy? But she . . . no. She was happy." He looked at me in appeal. "She was *always* happy. Aren't you her friend?"

"Yes," I said. "I just made a mistake about her being unhappy."

"She was *always* happy. With Mr. Frank. They laughed and laughed and read books."

"Mr. della Francesca."

"He said I could call him Mr. Frank."

I said, "What's your name?"

"Pete," he said, as if I should know it.

"Oh, you're Pete! Yes, Mrs. Smith spoke to me about you. Just before she died. She said you were nice, too."

He beamed. "She was my friend."

"You were sad when she died, Pete."

"I was sad when she died."

I said, "What exactly happened?"

His face changed. He picked up the mop, thrust it into the rolling bucket. "Nothing."

"Nothing? But Mrs. Smith is dead."

"I gotta go now." He started to roll the bucket across the half-mopped floor, but I placed a firm hand on his arm. There's a cop intuition that has nothing to do with neuropharms.

I said, "Some bad people killed Mrs. Smith."

He looked at me, and something shifted behind his pale blue gaze.

"They didn't tell you that, I know. They said Mrs. Smith killed herself. But you know she was very happy and didn't do that, don't you? What did you see, Pete?"

He was scared now. Once, a long time ago, I hated myself for doing this to people like Pete. Then I got so I didn't think about it. It didn't bother me now, either.

"Mrs. Gennaro killed Mrs. Smith," I said.

Shock wiped out fear. "No, she didn't! She's a nice lady!"

"I say Mrs. Gennaro and the doctor killed Mrs. Smith."

"You're crazy! You're an asshole! Take it back!"

"Mrs. Gennaro and the doctor—"

"Mrs. Smith and Mr. Frank was all alone together when they went up to that roof!"

I said swiftly, "How do you know?"

But he was panicked now, genuinely terrified. Not of me—of what he'd said. He opened his mouth to scream. I said,

"Don't worry, Pete. I'm a cop. I work with the cops you talked to before. They just sent me to double check your story. I work with the same cops you told before."

"With Officer Camp?"

"That's right," I said. "With Officer Camp."

"Oh." He still looked scared. "I told them already! I told them I unlocked the roof door for Mrs. Smith and Mr. Frank like they asked me to!"

"Pete—"

"I gotta go!"

"Go ahead, Pete. You did good."

He scurried off. I left the building before he could find Karen Gennaro.

A call to an old friend at Records turned up an Officer Joseph Camphausen at Midtown South, a Ralph Campogiani in the Queens Robbery Squad, a Bruce Campinella at the two-four, and a detective second grade Joyce Campolieto in Intelligence. I guessed Campinella, but it didn't matter which one Pete had talked to, or that I wouldn't get another chance inside Angels of Mercy. I headed for West End Avenue.

The sun was setting. Manhattan was filled with river light. I drove up the West Side Highway with the window down, and remembered how much Margie had liked to do that, even in the winter. *Real air, Gene. Chilled like good beer.*

Nobody at the Beth Israel Retirement Home would talk to me about the two old people who died there, Samuel Fetterolf and Rose Kaplan. Nor would they let me wander around loose after my carefully guided tour. I went to the Chinese restaurant across the street and waited.

From every street-side window in Beth Israel I'd seen them head in here: well-dressed men and women visiting their parents and aunts and grandmothers after work. They'd stay an hour, and then they'd be too hungry to go home and cook, or maybe too demoralized to go home without a drink, a steady stream of overscheduled people dutifully keeping up connections with their old. I chose a table in the bar section, ordered, and ate slowly. It took a huge plate of moo goo gai pan and three club sodas before I heard it.

"How can you *say* that? She's not senile, Brad! She knows whether her friends are suicidal or not!"

"I didn't say she—"

"Yes, you did! You said we can't trust her perceptions! She's only old, not stupid!" Fierce thrust of chopsticks into her sweet and sour. She was about thirty, slim and tanned, her dark hair cut short. Preppy shirt and sweater. He wasn't holding up as well, the paunch and bald spot well underway, the beleaguered husband look not yet turned resentful.

"Joanne, I only said—"

"You said we should just discount what Grams said and leave her there, *even though* she's so scared. You always discount what she says!"

"I don't. I just—"

"Like about that thing at Passover. What Grams wanted was completely reasonable, and you just—"

"Excuse me," I said, before they drifted any more. The thing at Passover wouldn't do me any good. "I'm sorry, but I couldn't help but overhear. I have a grandmother in Beth Israel, too, and I'm a little worried about her, otherwise I wouldn't interrupt, it's just that . . . my grandmother is scared to stay there, too."

They inspected me unsmilingly, saying nothing.

"I don't know what to do," I said desperately. "She's never been like this."

"I'm sorry," Brad said stiffly, "we can't help."

"Oh, I understand. Strangers. I just thought . . . you said something about your grandmother being frightened . . . I'm sorry." I got up to leave, projecting embarrassment.

"Wait a minute," Joanne said. "What did you say your name was?"

"Aaron Sanderson."

"Joanne, I don't think—"

"Brad, if he has the same problem as—Mr. Sanderson, what is your grandmother afraid of? Is she usually nervous?"

"No, that's just it," I said, moving closer to their table. Brad frowned at me. "She's never nervous or jittery, and never depressed. She's fantastic, actually. But ever since those two residents died . . ."

"Well, that's just *it*," Joanne said. Brad sighed and shifted his weight. "Grams was friendly with Mrs. Kaplan, and she told me that Mrs. Kaplan would never in a million years commit suicide. She just *wouldn't*."

"Same thing my grandmother said. But I'm sure there couldn't be actual danger in Beth Israel," I said. Dismiss what the witness said and wait for the contradiction.

"Why not?" Joanne said. "They could be testing some new medication . . . in fact, Grams said Mrs. Kaplan had volunteered for some clinical trial. She had cancer."

Brad said, "And so naturally she was depressed. Or maybe depression was a side effect of the drug. You read about that shit all the time. The drug company will be faced with a huge lawsuit, they'll settle, they'll stop giving the pills, and everybody's grandmother is safe. That simple."

"No, smartie." Joanne glared at him. "It's not that simple. Grams said she spent the afternoon with Mrs. Kaplan a week or so *after* she started the drug. Mrs. Kaplan was anything but depressed. She was really up, and she'd fallen in love with Mr. Fetterolf who was also in the trial, and his daughter-in-law Dottie was telling me—"

"Joanne, let's go," Brad said. "I don't really feel like arguing here."

I said, "My grandmother knew Mr. Fetterolf slightly. And she's worried about his suicide—"

"So am *I*," Joanne said. "I keep telling and telling Brad—"

"Joanne, I'm going. You do what the hell you want."

"You can't just—all right, all right! Everything has to be your way!" She flounced up, threw me an apologetic look, and followed her husband out.

There were four Fetterolfs in the Manhattan phone directory. Two were single initials, which meant they were probably women living alone. I chose Herman Fetterolf on West Eighty-sixth.

The apartment building was nice, with a carpeted lobby and deep comfortable sofas. I said to the doorman, "Please tell Mrs. Dottie Fetterolf that there's a private investigator to talk to her about her father-in-law's death. My name is Joe Carter. Ask her if she'll come down to the lobby to talk to me."

He gave me a startled look and conveyed the message. When Mrs. Fetterolf came down, I could see she was ready to be furious at somebody, anybody. Long skirt swishing, long vest flapping, she steamed across the lobby. "You the private investigator? Who are you working for?"

"I'm not at liberty to say, Mrs. Fetterolf. But it's someone who, like you, has lost an elderly relative to suicide."

"Suicide! Ha! It wasn't any suicide! It was murder!"

"Murder?"

"They killed him! And no one will admit it!"

"What makes you think so?"

"Think? *Think?* I don't have to think, I *know!* One week he's fine, he's friends with this Mrs. Kaplan, they play Scrabble, they read books together, he's happy as a clam. Maybe even a little something gets going between them, who am I to say, more power to them. And then on the same night— the *same* night—he hangs himself and she walks in front of a bus! Coincidence? I don't think so! . . . Besides, there would be a note.''

''I beg your—''

''My father-in-law would have left a note. He was thoughtful that way. You know what I'm saying? He wrote everybody in the whole family all the time, nobody could even keep up with reading it all. He would have left a note for sure.''

''Did he—''

''He was lonely after his wife died. Sarah. A saint. They met fifty-six years ago—''

In the end, she gave me her father-in-law's entire history. Also Rose Kaplan's. I wrote it all down.

When I called Johnny Fermato, I was told by a wary desk sergeant that Lieutenant Fermato would get back to me.

In my dreams.

''Somebody's being screwed over, Margie,'' I said. ''And it's probably costing somebody else pay-off money.''

She lay there in the fetal position, her hands like claws. The IV was gone, but she was still connected by tubes to the humidified air supply, the catheter bag, the feeding pump. The pump made soft noises: *ronk, ronk.* I laid my briefcase on the bottom of her bed, which Susan would probably object to.

''It wasn't depression,'' I said to Margie. ''Della Francesca and Mrs. Smith went up to that roof together. Alone together. Samuel Fetterolf and Rose Kaplan were in love.'' J-24 chemically induced love.

The bag in Margie's IV slowly emptied. The catheter bag slowly filled. Her ears were hidden under the dry, brittle, lifeless hair.

''Johnny Fermato knows something. Maybe only that the word's been passed down to keep the case closed. I did get the coroners' reports. They say 'self-inflicted fatal wounds.' All eight reports.''

Somewhere in the hospital corridors, a woman screamed. Then stopped.

"Margie," I heard myself saying, "I don't want to come here anymore."

The next second, I was up and limping around the room. I put my forehead against the wall and ground it in. How could I say that to her? Margie, the only woman I'd ever loved, the person in the world I was closest to. . . . On our wedding night, which was also her nineteenth birthday, she'd told me she felt like she could die from happiness. And I'd known what she meant.

And on that other night eight years later, when Bucky had done his pills-and-vodka routine, Margie had been with me when the phone rang. *Gene . . . Gene . . . I did it. . . .*

Did what? Jesus, Bucky, it's after midnight—

But I don't . . . Father Healey . . .

Bucky, I gotta start my shift at eight tomorrow morning. Goodnight.

Gene, who's calling at this hour?

. . . say . . . good-bye. . . .

Of all the inconsiderate . . . the phone woke Libby!

Tell Father Healey I never would have made . . . good priests don't doubt like . . . I can't touch God anymore. . . .

And then I'd known. I was out of the apartment in fifteen seconds. Shoes, pants, gun. In my pajama top I drove to the seminary, leaned on the bell. Bucky wasn't there, but Father Healey was. I searched the rooms, the chapel, the little meditation garden, all the while traffic noises drowning out the thumping in my chest. Father Healey shouting questions at me. I wouldn't let him in my car. Get away from me you bastard you killed him, you and your insistence on pushing God on a mind never tightly wrapped in the first place . . . Bucky wasn't at his mother's house. Now I had two people screaming at me.

I found him at Our Lady of Perpetual Sorrows. Where I should have looked first. He'd broken a stained glass window, just smashed it with a board, no subtlety. He was in front of the altar, breathing shallow, already unconscious. EMS seemed to take forever to get there. The on-duty cops were faster; the stained-glass was alarm-wired.

But when it was over, Bucky's stomach pumped, sleeping it off at St. Vincent's, I had crawled back in bed next to Margie. Libby asleep in her little bedroom. I'd put my arms around my wife, and I'd vowed that after Bucky got out of the hospital, I'd never see him and his messy stupid dramas of faith again.

"I didn't mean that," I said to Margie, inert in her trach collar. "Sweetheart, I didn't mean it. Of course I want to be here. I'll be here as long as you're breathing!"

She didn't move. IV bag emptying, catheter bag filling.

Susan came in, her nurse's uniform rumpled. "Hi, Gene."

"Hello, Susan."

"We're about the same tonight."

I could see that. And then the Camineur kicked in and I could see something else, in one of those unbidden flashes of knowledge that Bucky called heightened connective cognition. Bucky hadn't phoned me because he didn't really want to know what had happened to those old people. He already had enough belief to satisfy himself. He just wanted J-24 cleared publicly, and he wanted me to start the stink that would do it. He was handing the responsibility for Rose Kaplan and Samuel Fetterolf and Lydia Smith and Giacomo della Francesca to me. Just the way he'd handed me the responsibility for his break with Father Healey the night of his attempted suicide. I'd been used.

"Fuck that!"

Susan turned, startled, from changing Margie's catheter bag. "I beg your pardon?"

Margie, of course, said nothing.

I limped out of the hospital room, ignoring the look on Susan's face. I was angrier than I had been in eighteen months. Anger pushed against the inside of my chest and shot like bullets through my veins.

Until the Camineur did its thing.

A dozen boys crowded the basketball hoop after school, even though it was drizzling. I limped toward my car. Just as I reached it, a red Mercedes pulled up beside me and Jeff Connors got out from the passenger side.

He wore a blue bandana on his head, and it bulged on the left side above the ear. Heavy bandaging underneath; somebody had worked on him. He also wore a necklace of heavy gold links, a beeper, and jacket of supple brown leather. He didn't even try to keep the leather out of the rain.

His eyes met mine, and something flickered behind them. The Mercedes drove off. Jeff started toward the kids at the hoops, who'd all stopped playing to watch the car. There was the usual high-fiving and competitive dissing, but I heard its guarded quality, and I saw something was about to go down.

Nothing to do with me. I unlocked my car door.

Jenny Kelly came hurrying across the court, through the drizzle. Her eyes flashed. "Jeff! Jeff!"

She didn't even know enough not to confront him in front of his customers. He stared at her, impassive, no sign of his usual likable hustle. To him, she might as well have been a cop.

"Jeff, could I see you for a minute?"

Not a facial twitch. But something moved behind his eyes.

"Please? It's about your little brother."

She was giving him an out: family emergency. He didn't take it.

"I'm busy."

Ms. Kelly nodded. "Okay. Tomorrow, then?"

"I'm busy."

"Then I'll catch you later." She'd learned not to argue. But I saw her face after she turned from the boys sniggering behind her. She wasn't giving up, either. Not on Jeff.

Me, she never glanced at.

I got into my car and drove off, knowing better than Jenny Kelly what was happening on the basketball court behind me, not even trying to interfere. If it didn't happen on school property, it would happen off it. What was the difference, really? You couldn't stop it. No matter what idealistic fools like Jenny Kelly thought.

Her earrings were little pearls, and her shirt, damp from the rain, clung to her body.

The whole next week, I left the phone off the hook. I dropped Libby a note saying to write me instead of calling because NYNEX was having trouble with the line into my building. I didn't go to the hospital. I taught my math classes, corrected papers in my own classroom, and left right after eighth period. I only glimpsed Jenny Kelly once, at a bus stop a few blocks from the school building. She was holding the hand of a small black kid, three or four, dressed in a Knicks sweatshirt. They were waiting for a bus. I drove on by.

But you can't really escape.

I spotted the guy when I came out of the metroteller late Friday afternoon. I'd noticed him earlier, when I dropped off a suit at the drycleaner's. This wasn't the kind of thing I dealt with anymore—but it happens. Somebody you collared eight years ago gets out and decides to get even. Or somebody spots you by accident and suddenly remembers some old score on behalf of his cousin, or your partner, or some damn thing you yourself don't even recall. It happens.

I couldn't move fast, not with my knee. I strolled into Mulcahy's, which has a long aisle running between the bar and the tables, with another door to the alley that's usually left open if the weather's any good. The men's and ladies' rooms are off an alcove just before the alley, along with a pay phone and cigarette machine. I nodded at Brian Mulcahy behind the bar, limped through, and went into the ladies'. It was empty. I kept the door cracked. My tail checked the alley, then strode toward the men's room. When his back was to the ladies' and his hand on the heavy door, I grabbed him.

He wasn't as tall or heavy as I was—average build, brown hair, nondescript looks. He twisted in my grasp, and I felt the bulge of the gun under his jacket. "Stop it, Shaunessy! NYPD!"

I let him go. He fished out his shield, looking at me hard. Then he said, "Not here. This is an informant hangout—didn't you *know?* Meet me at 248 West Seventieth, apartment 8. Christ, why don't you fix your goddamn *phone?*" Then he was gone.

I had a beer at the bar while I thought it over. Then I went home. When the buzzer rang an hour and a half later, I didn't answer. Whoever stood downstairs buzzed for ten minutes straight before giving up.

That night I dreamed someone was trying to kill Margie, stalking her through the Times Square sleaze and firing tiny chemically poisoned darts. I couldn't be sure, dreams being what they are, but I think the stalker was me.

The Saturday mail came around three-thirty. It brought a flat manilla package, no return address, no note. It was a copy of the crime-scene report on the deaths of Lydia Smith and Giacomo della Francesca.

Seven years as partners doesn't just wash away. No matter what the official line has to be.

There were three eight-by-ten color crime scene photos: an

empty rooftop; Mrs. Smith's body smashed on the pavement below; della Francesca's body lying on the floor beside a neatly made bed. His face was in partial shadow but his skinny spotted hands were clear, both clutching the hilt of the knife buried in his chest. There wasn't much blood. That doesn't happen until somebody pulls the knife out.

The written reports didn't say anything that wasn't in the photos.

I resealed the package and locked it in my file cabinet. Johnny had come through; Bucky had screwed me. The deaths were suicides, just like Kelvin Pharmaceuticals said, just like the Department said. Bucky's superconnective pill was the downer to end all downers, and he knew it, and he was hoping against hope it wasn't so.

Because he and Tommy had taken it together.

I've moved, Bucky had said in his one message since he told me about J-24. I'd assumed he meant that he'd changed apartments, or lovers, or lives, as he'd once changed from fanatic seminarian to fanatic chemist. But that's not what he meant. He meant he'd made his move with J-24, because he wanted the effect for himself and Tommy, and he refused to believe the risk applied to him. Just like all the dumb crack users I spent sixteen years arresting.

I dialed his number. After four rings, the answering machine picked up. I hung up, walked from the living room to the bedroom, pounded my fists on the wall a couple times, walked back and dialed again. When the machine picked up I said, "Bucky. This is Gene. Call me *now*. I mean it—I have to know you're all right."

I hesitated . . . he hadn't contacted me in weeks. What could I use as leverage?

"If you don't call me tonight, Saturday, by nine, I'll . . ." What? Not go look for him. Not again, not like thirteen years ago, rushing out in pants and pajama top, Margie calling after me *Gene! Gene! For God's sake . . .*

I couldn't do it again.

"If you don't phone by nine o'clock, I'll call the feds with what I've found about J-24, without checking it out with you first. So *call me,* Bucky."

Usually on Saturday afternoon I went to the hospital to see Margie. Not today. I sat at my kitchen table with algebra tests from 7B spread over the tiny surface, and it took me an hour to get through three papers. I kept staring at the undecorated wall, seeing Bucky there. Seeing the photos of Lydia Smith and Giacomo della Francesca. Seeing that night thirteen years ago when Bucky had his stomach pumped. Then I'd wrench myself back to the test papers and correct another problem. *If train A leaves point X traveling at a steady fifty miles per hour at six* A.M. . . .

If a bullet leaves a gun traveling at 1500 feet per second, it can tear off a human head. Nobody realizes that but people who have seen it. Soldiers. Doctors. Cops.

After a while, I realized I was staring at the wall again, and picked up another paper. *If 3X equals 2Y . . .* Some of the names on the papers I didn't even recognize. Who was James Dillard? Was he the tall quiet kid in the last row, or the short one in shoes held together with tape, who fell asleep most mornings? They were just names.

On the wall, I saw Jenny Kelly holding the hand of Jeff Connors's little brother.

At seven-thirty I shoved the papers into my briefcase and grabbed my jacket. Before I left, I tried Bucky's number once more. No answer. I turned off the living room light and limped along the hall to the door. Before I opened it, my foot struck something. Without even thinking about it, I flattened against the wall and reached behind me for the foyer light.

It was only another package. A padded mailer, nine by

twelve, the cheap kind that leaks oily black stuffing all over you if you open it wrong. The stuffing was already coming out a little tear in one corner. There were no stamps, no address; it had been shoved under the door. Whoever had left it had gotten into the building—not hard to do on a Saturday, with people coming and going, just wait until someone else has unlocked the door and smile at them as you go in, any set of keys visible in your hand. In the upper left corner of the envelope was an NYPD evidence sticker.

I picked up the package just as the phone rang.

"Bucky! Where are—"

"Gene, this is Jenny Kelly. Listen, I need your help. Please! I just got a call from Jeff Connors, he didn't know who else to call . . . the police have got him barricaded in a drug house, they're yelling at him to come out and he's got Darryl with him, that's his little brother, and he's terrified—Jeff is—that they'll knock down the door and go in shooting . . . God, Gene, please go! It's only four blocks from you, that's why I called, and you know how these things work . . . please!"

She had to pause for breath. I said tonelessly, "What's the address?"

She told me. I slammed the receiver down in the midst of her thank-you's. If she'd been in the room with me, I think I could have hit her.

I limped the four blocks north, forcing my damaged knee, and three blocks were gone before I realized I still had the padded envelope in my hand. I folded it in half and shoved it in my jacket pocket.

The address wasn't hard to find. Two cars blocked the street, lights whirling, and I could hear more sirens in the distance. The scene was all fucked up. A woman of twenty-one or twenty-two was screaming hysterically and jumping up and down: "He's got my baby! He's got a gun up there! He's going to kill my son!" while a uniform who looked about nineteen was trying ineptly to calm her down. Her clothes were torn and bloody. She smacked the rookie across the arm and his partner moved in to restrain her, while another cop with a bullhorn shouted up at the building. Neighbors poured out onto the street. The one uniform left was trying to do crowd control, funneling them away from the building, and nobody was going. He looked no older than the guy holding the woman, as if he'd had about six hours total time on the street.

I had my dummy shield. We'd all had our shields duplicated, one thirty-second of an inch smaller than the real shield, so we could leave the real one home and not risk a fine and all the paperwork if it got lost. When I retired, I turned in my shield but kept the dummy. I flashed it now at the rookie struggling with the hysterical girl. That might cost me a lot of trouble later, but I'd worry about that when the time came.

The street thinking comes back so fast.

"This doesn't look right," I shouted at the rookie over the shrieking woman. She was still flailing in his hold, screaming, "He's got my baby! He's got a gun! For Chrissake, get my baby before he kills him!" The guy with the bullhorn stopped shouting and came over to us.

"Who are you?"

"He's from Hostage and Barricade," the rookie gasped, although I hadn't said so. I didn't contradict him. He was trying so hard to be gentle with the screaming woman that she was twisting like a dervish while he struggled to cuff her.

"Look," I said, "she's not the mother of that child up there. He's the perp's little brother, and she sure the hell doesn't look old enough to be the older kid's mother!"

"How do you—" the uniform began, but the girl let out a shriek that could have leveled buildings, jerked one hand free and clawed at my face.

I ducked fast enough that she missed my eyes, but her nails

tore a long jagged line down my cheek. The rookie stopped
being gentle and cuffed her so hard she staggered. The sleeve
of her sweater rode up when he jerked her arms behind her
back, and I saw the needle tracks.

Shit, shit, shit.

Two back-up cars screamed up. An older cop in plain
clothes got out, and I slipped my dummy shield back in my
pocket.

"Listen, officer, I *know* that kid up there, the one with the
baby. I'm his teacher. He's in the eighth grade. His name is
Jeff Connors, the child with him is his little brother Darryl,
and this woman is *not* their mother. Something's going down
here, but it's not what she says."

He looked at me hard. "How'd you get that wound?"

"She clawed him," the rookie said. "He's from—"

"He phoned me," I said urgently, holding him with my
eyes. "He's scared stiff. He'll come out with no problems if
you let him, and leave Darryl there."

"You're his teacher? That why he called you? You got
ID?"

I showed him my United Federation of Teachers card,
driver's license, Benjamin Franklin Junior High pass. The uni-
forms had all been pressed into crowd control by a sergeant
who looked like he knew what he was doing.

"Where'd he get the gun? He belong to a gang?"

I said, "I don't know. But he might."

"How do you know there's nobody else up there with
him?"

"He didn't say so on the phone. But I don't know for
sure."

"What's the phone number up there?"

"I don't know. He didn't give it to me."

"Is he on anything?"

"I don't know. I would guess no."

He stood there, weighing it a moment. Then he picked up the bullhorn, motioned to his men to get into position. His voice was suddenly calm, even gentle. "Connors! Look, we know you're with your little brother, and we don't want either of you to get hurt. Leave Darryl there and come down by yourself. Leave the gun and just come on down. You do that and everything'll be fine."

"He's going to kill my—" the woman shrieked, before someone shoved her into a car and slammed the door.

"Come on, Jeff, we can do this nice and easy, no problems for anybody."

I put my hand to my cheek. It came away bloody.

The negotiator's voice grew even calmer, even more reasonable.

"I know Darryl's probably scared, but he doesn't have to be, just come on down and we can get him home where he belongs. Then you and I can talk about what's best for your little brother. . . ."

Jeff came out. He slipped out of the building, hands on his head, going, "Don't shoot me, please don't shoot me, don't shoot me," and he wasn't the hustler of the eighth grade who knew all the moves, wasn't the dealer in big gold on the basketball court. He was a terrified thirteen-year-old in a dirty blue bandana, who'd been set up.

Cops in body armor rushed forward and grabbed him. More cops started into the building. A taxi pulled up and Jenny Kelly jumped out, dressed in a low-cut black satin blouse and black velvet skirt.

"Jeff! Are you all right?"

Jeff looked at her, and I think if they'd been alone, he might have started to cry. "Darryl's up there alone. . . ."

"They'll bring Darryl down safe," I said.

"I'll take Darryl to your aunt's again," Jenny promised. A man climbed out of the taxi behind her and paid the driver.

He was scowling. The rookie glanced down the front of Jenny's blouse.

Jeff was cuffed and put into a car. Jenny turned to me. "Oh, your face, you're hurt! Where will they take Jeff, Gene? Will you go, too? Please?"

"I'll have to. I told them it was me that Jeff phoned."

She smiled. I'd never seen her smile like that before, at least not at me. I kept my eyes raised to her face, and my own face blank. "Who set him up, Jenny?"

"Set him up?"

"That woman was yelling she's Darryl's mother and Jeff was going to kill her baby. Somebody wanted the cops to go storming in there and start shooting. If Jeff got killed, the NYPD would be used as executioners. If he didn't, he'd still be so scared they'll own him. Who is it, Jenny? The same one who circulated that inflammatory crap about a Neighborhood Safety Information Network?"

She frowned. "I don't know. But Jeff has been . . . there were some connections that . . ." She trailed off, frowned again. Her date came up to us, still scowling. "Gene, this is Paul Snyder. Paul, Gene Shaunessy. . . . Paul, I'm sorry, I have to go with Gene to wherever they're taking Jeff. I'm the one he really called. And I said I'd take Darryl to his aunt."

"Jenny, for Chrissake . . . we have tickets for the Met!"

She just looked at him, and I saw that Paul Snyder wasn't going to be seeing any more of Jenny Kelly's cleavage.

"I'll drive you to the precinct, Jenny," I said. "Only I have to be the first one interviewed, I have to be as quick as I can because there's something else urgent tonight. . . ." Bucky. Dear God.

Jenny said quickly, "Your wife? Is she worse?"

"She'll never be worse. Or better," I said before I knew I was going to say anything, and immediately regretted it.

"Gene . . ." Jenny began, but I didn't let her finish. She

was standing too close to me. I could smell her perfume. A fold of her black velvet skirt blew against my leg.

I said harshly, "You won't last at school another six months if you take it all this hard. You'll burn out. You'll leave."

Her gaze didn't waver. "Oh no, I won't. And don't talk to me in that tone of voice."

"Six months," I said, and turned away. A cop came out of the building carrying a wailing Darryl. And the lieutenant came over to me, wanting to know whatever it was I thought I knew about Jeff Connors's connections.

It was midnight before I got home. After the precinct house there'd been a clinic, with the claw marks on my face disinfected and a tetanus shot and a blood test and photographs for the assault charges. After that, I looked for Bucky.

He wasn't at his apartment, or at his mother's apartment. The weekend security guard at Kelvin Pharmaceuticals said he'd been on duty since four P.M. and Dr. Romano hadn't signed in to his lab. That was the entire list of places I knew to look. Bucky's current life was unknown to me. I didn't even know Tommy's last name.

I dragged myself through my apartment, pulling off my jacket. The light on the answering machine blinked.

My mind—or the Camineur—made some connections. Even before I pressed the MESSAGE button, I think I knew.

"Gene, this is Tom Fletcher. You don't know me . . . we've never met. . . ." A deeper voice than I'd expected but ragged, spiky. "I got your message on Vince Romano's machine. About the J-24. Vince . . ." The voice caught, went on. "Vince is in the hospital. I'm calling from there. St. Clare's, it's on Ninth at Fifty-first. Third floor. Just before he . . . said to tell you . . ."

I couldn't make out the words in the rest of the message.

I sat there in the dark for a few minutes. Then I pulled my jacket back on and caught a cab to St. Clare's. I didn't think I could drive.

The desk attendant waved me through. He thought I was just visiting Margie, even at this hour. It had happened before. But not lately.

Bucky lay on the bed, a sheet pulled up to his chin but not yet over his face. His eyes were open. Suddenly I didn't want to know what the sheet was covering—how he'd done it, what route he'd chosen, how long it had taken. All the dreary algebra of death. *If train A leaves the station at a steady fifty miles per hour. . . .* There were no marks on Bucky's face. He was smiling.

And then I saw he was still breathing. Bucky, the ever inept, had failed a second time.

Tommy stood in a corner, as if he couldn't get it together enough to sit down. Tall and handsome, he had dark well-cut hair and the kind of fresh complexion that comes with youth and exercise. He looked about fifteen years younger than Bucky. When had they taken the J-24 together? Lydia Smith and Giacomo della Francesca had killed themselves within hours of each other. So had Rose Kaplan and Samuel Fetterolf. How much did Tommy know?

He held out his hand. His voice was husky. "You're Gene."

"I'm Gene."

"Tom Fletcher. Vince and I are—"

"I know," I said, and stared down at Bucky's smiling face, and wondered how I was going to tell this boy that he, too, was about to try to kill himself for chemically induced love.

I flashed on Bucky and me sitting beside the rainstreaked alley window of the Greek diner. *What are you waiting for, Bucky, your prince to come?*

Yes. And, *Have you ever thought what it would be like to be really merged—to know him, to be him?*

"Tom," I said. "There's something we have to discuss."

"Discuss?" His voice had grown even huskier.

"About Bucky. Vince. You and Vince."

"What?"

I looked down at Bucky's smiling face.

"Not here. Come with me to the waiting room."

It was deserted at that hour, a forlorn alcove of scratched furniture, discarded magazines, too-harsh fluorescent lights. We sat facing each other on red plastic chairs.

I said abruptly, "Do you know what J-24 is?"

His eyes grew wary. "Yes."

"What is it?" I couldn't find the right tone. I was grilling him as if he were under arrest and I were still a cop.

"It's a drug that Vince's company was working on. To make people bond to each other, merge together in perfect union." His voice was bitter.

"What else did he tell you?"

"Not much. What should he have told me?"

You never see enough, not even in the streets, to really prepare you. Each time you see genuine cruelty, it's like the first time. Damn you, Bucky. Damn you to hell for emotional greed.

I said, "He didn't tell you that the clinical subjects who took J-24 ... the people who bonded ... he didn't tell you they were all elderly?"

"No," Tom said.

"The same elderly who have been committing suicide all over the city? The ones in the papers?"

"Oh, my God."

He got up and walked the length of the waiting room, maybe four good steps. Then back. His handsome face was gray as ash. "They killed themselves after taking J-24? Because of J-24?"

I nodded. Tom didn't move. A long minute passed, and then he said softly, "My poor Vince."

"Poor *Vince*? How the hell can you . . . don't you get it, Tommy boy? You're next! You took the bonding drug with poor suffering Vince, and your three weeks or whatever of joy are up and you're dead, kid! The chemicals will do their thing in your brain, super withdrawal, and you'll kill yourself just like Bucky! Only you'll probably be better at it and actually succeed!"

He stared at me. And then he said, "Vince didn't try to kill himself."

I couldn't speak.

"He didn't attempt suicide. Is that what you thought? No, he's in a catatonic state. And *I* never took J-24 with him."

"Then who . . ."

"God," Tom said, and the full force of bitterness was back. "He took it with God. At some church, Our Lady of Everlasting Something. Alone in front of the altar, fasting and praying. He told me when he moved out."

When he moved out. Because it wasn't Tommy that Bucky really wanted, it was God. It had always been God, for thirteen solid years. *Tell Father Healey I can't touch God anymore. . . . Have you ever thought what it would be like to be really merged, to know him to be him? . . .* No. To know Him. To be Him. *What are you waiting for, your Prince?*

Yes.

Tom said, "After he took the damned drug, he lost all interest in me. In everything. He didn't go to work, just sat in the corner smiling and laughing and crying. He was like . . . high on something, but not really. I don't know what he was. It wasn't like anything I ever saw before."

Nor anybody else. Merged with God. *They knew each*

other, they almost were each other. Think, Gene! To have an end to the terrible isolation in which we live our whole tiny lives. . . .

"I got so *angry* with him," Tom said, "and it did no good at all. I just didn't count anymore. So I told him to get out, and he did, and then I spent three days looking for him but I couldn't find him anywhere, and I was frantic. Finally he called me, this afternoon. He was crying. But again it was like I wasn't even really there, not me, Tom. He sure the hell wasn't crying over *me*."

Tom walked to the one small window, which was barred. Back turned to me, he spoke over his shoulder. Carefully, trying to get it word-perfect.

"Vince said I should call you. He said, 'Tell Gene—it wears off. And then the grief and loss and anger . . . *especially* the anger that it's over. But I can beat it. It's different for me. They couldn't.' Then he hung up. Not a word to me."

I said, "I'm sorry."

He turned. "Yeah, well, that was Vince, wasn't it? *He* always came first with himself."

No, I could have said. God came first. And that's how Bucky beat the J-24 withdrawal. Human bonds, whether forged by living or chemicals got torn down as much as built up. But you don't have to live in a three-room apartment with God, fight about money with God, listen to God snore and fart and say things so stupid you can't believe they're coming out of the mouth of your beloved, watch God be selfish or petty or cruel. God was *bigger* than all that, at least in Bucky's mind, was so big that He filled everything. And this time when God retreated from him, when the J-24 wore off and Bucky could feel the bonding slipping away, Bucky slipped along after it. Deeper into his own mind, where all love exists anyway.

"The doctor said he might never come out of the catatonia,'' Tom said. He was starting to get angry now, the anger of self-preservation. ''Or he might. Either way, I don't think I'll be waiting around for him. He's treated me too badly.''

Not a long-term kind of guy, Tommy. I said, ''But you never took J-24 yourself.''

''No,'' Tom said. ''I'm not *stupid*. I think I'll go home now. Thanks for coming, Gene. Good to meet you.''

''You, too,'' I said, knowing neither of us meant it.

''Oh, and Vince said one more thing. He said to tell you it was, too, murder. Does that make sense?''

''Yes,'' I said. But not, I hoped, to him.

After Tom left, I sat in the waiting room and pulled from my jacket the second package. The NYPD evidence sticker had torn when I'd jammed the padded mailer in my pocket.

It was the original crime scene report for Lydia Smith and Giacomo della Francesca, the one Johnny Fermato must have known about when he sent me the phony one. This report was signed Bruce Campinella. I didn't know him, but I could probably pick him out of a line-up from the brief tussle in Mulcahy's: average height, brown hair, undistinguished looks, furious underneath. Your basic competent honest cop, still outraged at what the system had for sale. And for sale at a probably not very high price. Not in New York.

There were only two photos this time. One I'd already seen: Mrs. Smith's smashed body on the pavement below the nursing home roof. The other was new. Della Francesca's body lying on the roof, not in his room, before the cover-up team moved him and took the second set of pictures. The old man lay face up, the knife still in his chest. It was a good photo; the facial expression was very clear. The pain was there, of course, but you could see the fury, too. The incredible rage. *And then the grief and loss and anger . . . especially the anger that it's over.*

Had della Francesca pushed Lydia Smith first, after that shattering quarrel that came from losing their special, unearthly union, and then killed himself? Or had she found the strength in her disappointment and outrage to drive the knife in, and then she jumped? Ordinarily, the loss of love doesn't mean hate. Just how unbearable was it to have had a true, perfect, unhuman end to human isolation—and then *lose* it? How much rage did that primordial loss release?

Or maybe Bucky was wrong, and it had been suicide after all. Not the anger uppermost, but the grief. Maybe the rage on della Francesca's dead face wasn't at his lost perfect love, but at his own emptiness once it was gone. He'd felt something so wonderful, so sublime, that everything *else* afterward fell unbearably short, and life itself wasn't worth the effort. No matter what he did, he'd never ever have its like again.

I thought of Samuel Fetterolf before he took J-24, writing everyone in his family all the time, trying to stay connected. Of Pete, straining every cell of his damaged brain to protect the memories of the old people who'd been kind to him. Of Jeff Connors, hanging onto Darryl even while he moved into the world of red Mercedes and big deals. Of Jenny Kelly, sacrificing her dates and her sleep and her private life in her frantic effort to connect to the students, who she undoubtedly thought of as "her kids." Of Bucky.

The elevator to the fifth floor was out of order. I took the stairs. The shift nurse barely nodded at me. It wasn't Susan. In Margie's room the lights had been dimmed and she lay in the gloom like a curved dry husk, covered with a light sheet. I pulled the chair closer to her bed and stared at her.

And for maybe the first time since her accident, I remembered.

Roll the window down, Gene.

It's fifteen degrees out there, Margie!

It's real air. Chilled like good beer. It smells like a god-damn factory in this car.

Don't start again. I'm warning you.

Are you so afraid the job won't kill you that you want the cigarettes to do it?

Stop trying to control me.

Maybe you should do better at controlling yourself.

The night I'd found Bucky at Our Lady of Perpetual Sorrows, I'd been in control. It was Bucky who hadn't. I'd crawled back in bed and put my arms around Margie and vowed never to see Bucky and his messy stupid dramas of faith ever again. Margie hadn't been asleep. She'd been crying. I'd had enough hysteria for one night; I didn't want to hear it. I wouldn't even let her speak. I stalked out of the bedroom and spent the night on the sofa. It was three days before I'd even talk to her so we could work it out and make it good between us again.

Have a great year! she'd said my first September at Benjamin Franklin. But it hadn't been a great year. I was trying to learn how to be a teacher, and trying to forget how to be a cop, and I didn't have much time left over for her. We'd fought about that, and then I'd stayed away from home more and more to get away from the fighting, and by the time I returned *she* was staying away from home a lot. Over time it got better again, but I don't know where she was going the night she crossed Lexington with a bag of groceries in front of that '93 Lincoln. I don't know who the groceries were for. She never bought porterhouse and champagne for *me*.

Maybe we would have worked that out, too. Somehow.

Weren't there moments, Gene, Bucky had said, *when you felt so close to Margie it was like you crawled inside her skin for a minute? Like you were Margie?* No. I was never Margie. We were close, but not that close. What we'd had was good, but not *that* good. Not a perfect merging of souls.

Which was the reason I could survive its loss.

I stood up slowly, favoring my knee. On the way out of the room, I took the plastic bottle of Camineur out of my pocket and tossed it in the waste basket. Then I left, without looking back.

Outside, on Ninth Avenue, a patrol car suddenly switched on its lights and took off. Some kids who should have been at home swaggered past, heading downtown. I looked for a pay phone. By now, Jenny Kelly would be done delivering Darryl to his aunt, and Jeff Connors was going to need better than the usual overworked public defender. I knew a guy at Legal Aid, a hotshot, who still owed me a long-overdue favor.

I found the phone, and the connection went through.

ASIMOV'S SCIENCE FICTION

__ROBOT DREAMS   0-441-73154-6/$5.99
This collection of stories, spanning the body of Asimov's
fiction from the 1940s to the 1980s, are all classic
Asimovian themes. They include a scientific puzzle, an
extraterrestrial thriller, and a psychological discourse.

*Enter into a searing examination of Asimov's
Three Laws of Robotics, a challenge welcomed
and sanctioned by Isaac Asimov, and written
with his cooperation by Roger MacBride Allen.*

__UTOPIA   0-441-00245-5/$13.00 *(Trade Paperback)*

__INFERNO   0-441-00023-1/$12.00 *(Trade Paperback)*

The Second Law of Robotics states: A robot must obey
the orders given it by human beings except where such
orders would conflict with the First Law. When a key
politician is murdered, Caliban is suspected. Plus, he is
challenging long held ideas of a robot's place in
society. Will Caliban lead his New Law robots in a
rebellion that threatens all humanity?

A Byron Preiss Visual Publications, Inc. Book
VISIT PENGUIN PUTNAM ON THE INTERNET:
http://www.penguinputnam.com